RENEWALS 458-4574

WITHDRAWN
UTSA LIBRARIES

Scenes of Sympathy

Scenes of Sympathy

Identity and Representation in Victorian Fiction

Audrey Jaffe

Cornell University Press

Ithaca and London

Library
University of Texas
at San Antonio

Copyright © 2000 by Cornell University

All rights reserved. Except for brief quotations in a review, this book, or parts
thereof, must not be reproduced in any form without permission in writing
from the publisher. For information, address Cornell University Press,
Sage House, 512 East State Street, Ithaca, New York 14850.

First published 2000 by Cornell University Press

Printed in the United States of America

LIBRARY OF CONGRESS CATALOGING-IN-PUBLICATION DATA

Jaffe, Audrey.
   Scenes of sympathy : identity and representation in Victorian fiction / Audrey Jaffe.
      p. cm.
   Includes bibliographical references and index.
   ISBN 0-8014-3712-1 (cloth)
      1. English fiction—19th century—History and criticism.   2. Capitalism and
literature—Great Britain—History—19th century.   3. Literature and society—Great
Britain—History—19th century.   4. Group identity in literature.   5. Sympathy in literature
6. Mimesis in literature   I. Title.

PR878.C25 J34 2000
823'.809—dc21   99-047449

Cornell University Press strives to use environmentally responsible suppliers and materials
to the fullest extent possible in the publishing of its books. Such materials include
vegetable-based, low-VOC inks and acid-free papers that are recycled, totally chlorine-
free, or partly composed of nonwood fibers. Books that bear the logo of the FSC (Forest
Stewardship Council) use paper taken from forests that have been inspected and certified as
meeting the highest standards for environmental and social responsibility. For further
information, visit our website at www.cornellpress.cornell.edu.

Cloth printing   10 9 8 7 6 5 4 3 2 1

Library
University of Texas
at San Antonio

Contents

Acknowledgments

I have benefited from the wisdom of the following friends and colleagues, who read and commented on various parts of the manuscript at various times: Deborah Dyson, Catherine Gallagher, Jean Gregorek, Nicholas Howe, Beth Ina, Jill Matus, Mary Ann O'Farrell, Linda Raphael, David Riede, Peter Schwartz, Julie Solomon, David Suchoff, Herbert Tucker, and Susan Williams. I am also grateful to audiences at the Dickens Project in Santa Cruz, the University of Virginia, Texas A&M, and Ohio State for their responses. Portions of the book have appeared, in somewhat different forms, in the following publications: Chapter 1 as "Spectacular Sympathy: Visuality and Ideology in Dickens's *A Christmas Carol*," *PMLA* 109 (1994): 254–65; Chapter 2 as "Detecting the Beggar: Arthur Conan Doyle, Henry Mayhew, and 'The Man with the Twisted Lip,'" *Representations* 31 (1990): 96–117, © 1990 by the Regents of the University of California; and Chapter 3 as "Under Cover of Sympathy: *Ressentiment* in Gaskell's *Ruth*," *Victorian Literature and Culture* 21 (1993): 51–65. I am grateful for permission to reprint.

Many of the ideas that inform this book emerged in discussions with Peter Schwartz, not the least of whose contributions was to suggest that I read a Sherlock Holmes story called "The Man with the Twisted Lip." And it is a pleasure, once again, to acknowledge the undeconstructable sympathy and intellectual energy of Mary Ann O'Farrell.

For Eli Jaffe Schwartz, a message: Mom has written a book, and pretty soon, if you want to, you can read it.

Introduction

The following two passages, illustrations offered in support of theoretical arguments, frame the period and the issues under discussion in this book. The first is a late-twentieth-century, confessional reflection on a California street scene; the second, an eighteenth-century philosophical fiction. Together they define a continuum: a recurrent narrative about sympathy, spectatorship, and the spirit of capitalism.[1]

Several times a week I must negotiate my way past the crowds of homeless people on Telegraph Avenue in Berkeley. Every time I do so, I am overcome with irrational panic.... Then, one day, I realized that I always studiously avoided looking at the homeless people, whom, with ruthless arbitrariness, I either help or don't help. And I began to understand that my panic on these occasions is not just economic but specular. What I feel myself being asked to do, and what I resist with every fiber of my being, is to locate myself within bodies which would, quite simply, be ruinous of my middle-class self—within bodies that are calloused from sleeping on the pavement, chapped from their exposure to sun and rain,

---

[1] I use this phrase—obviously appropriated from Max Weber's *The Protestant Ethic and the Spirit of Capitalism* (1930)—to describe the way in which, under capitalism, economic relations structure social relations. Weber's formulation is especially relevant to the kind of street scene discussed here, in which people encounter one another primarily as economic subjects.

I

and grimy from weeks without access to a shower, and which can conse-
quently make no claim to what, within our culture, passes for "ideality."[2]

As we have no immediate experience of what other men feel, we can
form no idea of the manner in which they are affected, but by conceiv-
ing what we ourselves should feel in the like situation. Though our
brother is upon the rack, as long as we ourselves are at our ease, our senses
will never inform us of what he suffers. They never did, and never can,
carry us beyond our own person, and it is by the imagination only that we
can form any conception of what are his sensations. . . . It is the impression
of our own senses only, not those of his, which our imaginations copy.[3]

These passages—the first from Kaja Silverman's *The Threshold of the
Visible World* (1995), the second from Adam Smith's *The Theory of Moral
Sentiments* (1759 / 1790)—link sympathy and spectacle in a way that, I will
argue in this book, takes paradigmatic form in Victorian fiction. In each,
a confrontation between a spectator "at ease" and a sufferer raises issues
about their mutual constitution; in each, the sufferer is effectively replaced
by the spectator's image of him or herself. As instances of what I wish to
call "scenes of sympathy," these two passages, along with other scenes and
texts discussed in the chapters that follow, document modern sympathy's

---

[2] Kaja Silverman, *The Threshold of the Visible World* (New York: Routledge, 1995), 26.
"Ideality" is Silverman's name for the "ego-ideal" or idealized self expressed in, and indeed
indistinguishable from, "an idealized image of the body" (70). "There is perhaps no more
fundamental manifestation of these kinds of 'difference' [gender, race, class, sex]," Silverman writes,

> than the customary reluctance on the part of the sexually, racially, or economically priv-
> ileged subject to identify outside of the bodily coordinates which confer that status upon
> him or her, to form imaginary alignments which would threaten the coherence and ide-
> ality of his or her corporeal ego. Typically, this subject either refuses "alien" identifications
> altogether, or forms them only on the basis of an idiopathic or assimilative model; he or
> she imaginatively occupies the position of the other, but only in the guise of the self or
> bodily ego. This kind of identification is familiar to all of us through that formula with
> which we extend sympathy to someone less fortunate than ourselves without in any way
> jeopardizing our *moi:* "I can imagine myself in his (or her) place." (25)

Silverman in fact defines the conventional formula—the self in the other's place—as a
refusal to identify, on the grounds that doing so would endanger the corporeal ego.
[3] Adam Smith, *The Theory of Moral Sentiments,* ed. D. D. Raphael and A. L. Macfie
(Indianapolis: Liberty Classics, 1976), 9.

inseparability from representation: both from the fact of representation, in a text's swerve toward the visual when the topic is sympathy, and from issues that surround representation, such as the relation between identity and its visible signs. The Victorian subject, as numerous studies have pointed out, was figured crucially and with increasing emphasis as a spectator; as such, moreover, that subject was frequently called upon to watch—and to participate in—a continual drama of rising and falling fortunes. In such a context, these scenes illustrate, economic status signifies visibly and spectatorship is inseparable from self-reflection. Society becomes a field of visual cues and its members alternative selves: imaginary possibilities in a field of circulating social images, confounded and interdependent projections of identity.[4]

[4] There is an immense body of literature about modernity and spectatorship. I am especially indebted to Richard Sennett, *The Fall of Public Man* (New York: Vintage, 1978). Elaine Hadley describes a late-eighteenth-century shift from secure, paternalistic social relations to a specular market culture, in which "the vast array of customary rights and obligations, for so long central to rural society, gives way to enclosure and leaseholds. In short, kinship rights and responsibilities are replaced by contractual obligations among discrete and contending economic parties.... The ranks became increasingly like strangers to one another, both literally and figuratively." *Melodramatic Tactics: Theatricalized Dissent in the English Marketplace, 1880–1885* (Stanford: Stanford University Press, 1995), 18–19. For a fundamental discussion of the idea of theatricality in this connection, see Jean-Christophe Agnew, *Worlds Apart: The Market and the Theater in Anglo-American Thought, 1550–1750* (Cambridge: Cambridge University Press, 1986). Guy Debord articulates the connection between capitalism and spectatorship as follows: "In societies where modern conditions of production prevail, all of life presents itself as an immense accumulation of spectacles. Everything that was directly lived has moved away into a representation." Debord, *Society of the Spectacle* (Detroit: Black and Red, 1983). In *Discipline and Punish* (New York: Pantheon, 1976), Michel Foucault locates the origins of modernity in the Panopticon's construction of a subject of imagined visibility: a disciplinary subject who imagines him or herself as always under surveillance. Foucault's model resembles Smith's idea of the imagined "impartial spectator" who regulates individual behavior in ethical society; in each case, as in my argument about sympathy, the construction that explains social behavior takes shape as an imaginary scene. As I argue in more detail in Chapter 1, the capitalist subject is also a self-scrutinizing one, and the spectator—the individual who, as in Debord's remark, sees life as representation—the prototypical consumer. For further discussions of spectatorship and modernity, see Anne Friedberg, *Window Shopping: Cinema and the Postmodern* (Berkeley: University of California Press, 1993); Deborah Nord, *Walking the Victorian Streets* (Ithaca: Cornell University Press, 1995); Dana Brand, *The Spectator and the City in Nineteenth-Century American Literature* (Cambridge: Cambridge University Press, 1991); Rachel Bowlby, *Just Looking: Consumer Culture in Dreiser,*

Smith depicts sympathy not as a direct response to a sufferer but rather as a response to a sufferer's representation in a spectator's mind. As Peter de Bolla points out, for Smith, "sympathetic sentiment is, in the last analysis, 'imaginary.'"[5] Each participant in what has come to be called, not incidentally, "the sympathetic exchange," envisions himself (and both participants are, for Smith, implicitly male) as the other must see him. The result is the transformation of sympathy with the other into sympathy with the self—a self already figured as representation. "As they are constantly considering what they themselves would feel, if they actually were the sufferers, so he is as constantly led to imagine in what manner he would be affected if he was only one of the spectators of his own situation" (22). In Smith's formulation, when sympathetic spectator and sufferer occupy different places in the social hierarchy (the problem with imagining the other's position is, after all, that "we ourselves are at our ease"), what circulates in the spectator's mind are positive and negative cultural fantasies: images of social degradation and, simultaneously, of what Silverman calls "ideality." The scene of sympathy in effect effaces both its participants, substituting for them images, or fantasies, of social and cultural identity. And it is because of the interdependence of and continual oscillation between images of cultural ideality and degradation in the scenes I discuss

---

Gissing, and Zola (New York: Methuen, 1985); Jonathan Crary, *Techniques of the Observer: Vision and Modernity in the Nineteenth Century* (Cambridge: MIT Press, 1990). For a recent discussion of the role of race in similar scenes, and of the way the image of the spectator replaces that of the object in narratives of slavery, see Saidiya V. Hartman, *Scenes of Subjection: Terror, Slavery, and Self-Making in Nineteenth-Century America* (New York: Oxford University Press, 1997), chap. 1.

Between Smith and Victorian fiction comes, for the purposes of this narrative, Wordsworth, in whose work sympathy appears as a similarly specular relation between observer and observed, and who, in ways too complex to be enumerated here, repeatedly displaces the social into the poetic. Wordsworth often constitutes poetic authority in narratives of social difference that give way to assertions of likeness, as a character—the solitary reaper or leech gatherer, for instance—becomes an occasion for the poet's reflections on his own authority and creativity. For my purposes, the most relevant recent commentary on such displacements and their role in constructing the liberal subject is Celeste Langan, *Romantic Vagrancy: Wordsworth and the Simulation of Freedom* (Cambridge: Cambridge University Press, 1995). See also David G. Riede, *Oracles and Hierophants: Constructions of Romantic Authority* (Ithaca: Cornell University Press, 1991).

[5] Peter DeBolla, "The Visibility of Visuality," in *Vision in Context,* ed. Teresa Brennan and Martin Jay (New York: Routledge, 1996), 75.

here—products of the imagination of a spectator positioned, phantasmati-cally, between them—that I consider Smith's scene of sympathy to stand both as a primal scene in the history of sympathetic representation and as a visual emblem of the structure of middle-class identity.[6]

Kaja Silverman offers the passage cited above to illustrate a thesis about the bodily determination of self-image. Though not explicitly about sym-pathy, her narrative renders manifest, even as it raises questions about, the implicit threat the homeless sufferer poses to a middle-class observer's identity. What, for instance, in this narrative, accounts for the "ruthless ar-bitrariness" that bestows money on some beggars but not on others? What logic links "economic" and "specular" panic? And when Silverman feels she is being "asked" to inhabit a body other than her own, who or what is doing the asking? The act of looking, in her account, fills the spec-tator with the anxiety of bodily contagion, the fear of inhabiting the beg-gar's place. That anxiety is warded off by imagining a self victimized by the mere sight of a person without a home: the middle-class self on dis-play here is a self assaulted by the visual, one with no apparent defense against the draining of funds, feeling, and identity to which that sight is felt to lead. Desiring her money, the foundation of her ideality, the beggar threatens *her* place, and in the bourgeois imagination there are never enough places to go around. Given the close relationship between identification and violent appropriation—what Diana Fuss has called "killing off the other in fantasy in order to usurp the other's place, the place where the subject desires to be"—one has to wonder, in Silverman's account, who is killing whom? Imagining that the other wants her iden-tity, her "ideality," the spectator wards off the threat as only a spectator can, "killing off" the other by refusing to look.[7]

---

[6] My idea of the scene of sympathy is indebted to Mary Ann Doane's discussion of the term "scenario": "Spectatorship in the cinema has been theorized through recourse to the 'scenario' as a particularly vivid representation of the organization of psychical processes. The scenario—with its visual, auditory, and narrative dimensions—seems particularly ap-propriate in the context of film theory. . . . Freudian and Lacanian texts appear to be priv-ileged at least partially for their ability to generate convincing scenarios which act as con-densations of several larger psychical structures or as evocations of a particularly crucial 'turning point' or movement." *The Desire to Desire: The Woman's Film of the 1940's* (Bloomington: Indiana University Press, 1987), 13–14.

[7] Diana Fuss, *Identification Papers* (New York: Routledge, 1995), 9.

The specular panic Silverman describes here is, she recognizes, an effect of capitalist economics. The passage reveals the same anxiety about "fellow feeling" Smith does when he writes that "persons of delicate fibres and a weak constitution of body complain, that in looking on the sores and ulcers which are exposed by beggars in the streets, they are apt to feel an itching or uneasy sensation in the correspondent part of their own bodies."[8] In both accounts the sight of a sufferer, associated with requests for money, is imagined as physically invasive or contagious, a metaphorical assault on the observer's person and a threat to the integrity of his or her identity. Were she to inhabit one of the "calloused" and "grimy" bodies she sees, Silverman feels, she would no longer "precisely" be "herself"(26), and the self she would no longer be is not only a clean and well-rested one, but the perceived object of appeal: the subject constituted as a culturally valued identity. Indeed, in Silverman's narrative, no actual request is made: the mere presence of the homeless person is imagined as constituting such a request. The scene suggests a negative version of the Althusserian scenario of interpellation, in which response to an appeal on the street—in that case, a policeman's "hailing"—is said to transform the individual into a subject.[9] Here, the homeless person's presence constitutes the appeal that forms the subject. But despite its idealizing effect, the other's gaze, rendering the spectator its object, poses a threat: a threat to which not looking constitutes a response. Not looking, Silverman denies the social self's constitution in relation to other social selves; not looking, she avoids the literal gaze that, as she imagines it, at once defines her as ideal and asks, she fears, for that ideality (not just for her money, that is, but for her life, with "life" defined as cultural life: the ability to participate in what Silverman elsewhere calls the culture's dominant fiction).[10] Silverman's claim that, "if homeless, I would precisely no longer be 'myself' " (26) defends against her obvious ability to make the identification: it defends against, even as it invokes, her implication in the narrative of decline, the image of the self in the other's place. Sympathy in this scene, as in

---

[8] Smith, *Theory of Moral Sentiments*, 10.

[9] Louis Althusser, "Ideology and Ideological State Apparatuses: Notes toward an Investigation," in *Lenin and Philosophy* (New York: Monthly Review, 1971), 127–86.

[10] See Silverman's discussion of this term in *Male Subjectivity at the Margins* (New York: Routledge, 1992), 42–51.

Smith's, is the name for a self engaged in an act of self-definition and self-identification, and the middle-class self is the self that is repeatedly and paradigmatically called upon to perform this act: the self that, looking anxiously both high and low, circulates between positions in the sympathetic exchange, and never comes to rest in either one. Indeed, the fact that the sight of a homeless person suggests to Silverman the possibility of switched identities registers, as Celeste Langan writes, "the pervasiveness with which [in a capitalist society] the model of exchange governs all social relations."[11] The threat encoded in the sympathetic exchange is that on which a capitalist economy relies: the possibility that the spectator "at ease" and the beggar might indeed, someday, change places.

Both passages collapse the difference between looking and not looking; in both, the act of looking at a sympathetic object provokes a narrative in which that object is by definition—the term "object" says it all—displaced into representation. The tendency to ward off actual bodies in the sympathetic encounter, replacing them with cultural fictions and self-projections, complicates Catherine Gallagher's argument that fiction, in doing away with actual bodies, does away with the barrier that constitutes an obstacle to sympathy.[12] For not looking, literally or figuratively, accomplishes the same thing. Indeed, in Smith's scenario, the sufferer has no nonfictional existence: sympathy by definition produces its object. Thus the distinction between sympathy for fictional characters and sympathy for actual people dissolves into—or rather, may be reformulated as—the difference between the pleasurable sympathetic feelings fiction invites and the potential threat of an encounter with an actual person. Pleasure, here, coincides with an absence of reciprocity: a fictional character cannot look back. But in both accounts sympathy is fictional, in the sense that it is fundamentally involved with representation; in both, sympathetic representation takes place

---

[11] Langan, *Romantic Vagrancy,* 223.

[12] Catherine Gallagher, *Nobody's Story: The Vanishing Acts of Women Writers in the Marketplace, 1670–1820* (Berkeley: University of California Press, 1995), 171. Gallagher's argument, which focuses here on Hume, is concerned with the relationship between sympathy, fiction, and property, the last term forming the "invisible link" between the first two. Her account emphasizes the difference between sympathy with actual people and sympathy with fictional characters, or "nobodies." I argue that fiction draws much of its power from the way readers have already imaginatively converted other persons into their own—in Gallagher's and Hume's term—"impressions."

within and constitutes a cultural narrative about the identities of sympathetic object and subject. The dynamic of projection, displacement, and
imagined exchange that appears in Smith, Silverman, and elsewhere in this
book is the cultural narrative that shapes the sympathetic scene.

What I call "scenes of sympathy" illustrate in exemplary fashion the way
sympathy in Victorian fiction takes shape in, and as, a series of visualized
narratives—narratives that render visible otherwise invisible determinations of social identity. By "render visible," however, I do not mean to suggest the presence of some purifiable sympathetic essence underlying these
scenes. Rather, I argue that sympathy in Victorian fiction is inseparable
from issues of visuality and representation because it is inextricable from
the middle-class subject's status as spectator and from the social figures to
whose visible presence the Victorian middle classes felt it necessary to formulate a response. Victorian representations of sympathy are, as sympathy
was for Smith, specular, crucially involving the way capitalist social relations transform subjects into spectators of and objects for one another;
they are also spectacular, their representational dimension reinforced by
the spectatorial character of Victorian culture. Not an attempt to define
sympathy per se, then, this book rather exposes and explores the recurrent
connection between sympathy, representation, and constructions of social
identity in a series of Victorian texts. And my object, it follows, is not the
analysis of authors but rather that of texts and images, some of which (such
as Dickens's "A Christmas Carol") have come to represent Victorian sympathy for twentieth-century readers and audiences. Indeed, the fact that
certain scenes tend to signify Victorian sympathy in the contemporary
popular imagination speaks directly to my purpose, since this phenome-
non suggests the inseparability of Victorian sympathy from its particular
representations and from representation itself.

———————

The scene that, for my purposes, gives shape to and renders visible the
meanings of Victorian sympathy involves a spectator's (dread) fantasy of
occupying another's social place. Though its content varies, what remains
consistent is its reliance on a phantasmatic opposition between images of
cultural ideality and degradation. This opposition, also imagined as an attenuation of the spectator's identity, raises crucial questions about the
structure and interdependence of Victorian social identities; so too does

the economic metaphor that frequently informs it, in which sympathy is represented as an investment in or exchange with others. What circulates in Victorian representations of sympathy—what these representations both circulate and reveal as constituted in that circulation—are social identities; in particular, scenes of sympathy in Victorian fiction mediate and construct middle-class identities.

Occupying the metaphorical space between "high" and "low" in Victorian culture, the Victorian middle classes simultaneously aspired to an aristocratic ideal and were haunted by the specter of economic and social failure. But incessant attention to their progress and distance from the lower classes suggests the anxious disavowal of what was perceived as a continuum of identity—the dependence, as Miriam Bailin puts it, of "who one was" on "who one wasn't, and, perhaps more important, who one no longer was."[13] The "objects" of Victorian sympathy are inseparable from Victorian middle-class self-representation precisely because they embody, to a middle-class spectator, his or her own potential narrative of social decline: they capture the fragility of respectable identities psychically positioned between high and low, defined within the parameters of a narrative of rising and falling. Having, in effect, already been "seen" by the middle-class subject, they need not—as in Silverman's narrative—be seen at all; they function for that subject as embodiments of cultural possibility, images of what he or she might become. Indeed, the imagining of the self in the other's place on which Christian charity and Victorian sympathetic ideology typically rely—"there but for the grace of God go I" (significantly a refusal of Smith's formulation, simultaneously evoking and denying what the observer in the sympathetic scene cannot help but imagine: the self in the other's place)—designates "place" as identity's primary component: the difference between self and other appears, if only momentarily, as nothing more than the difference between here and there.

The emphasis in the following readings on visuality, framing, and representation calls attention to the powerful interplay between the specular quality of Victorian sympathy and the spectatorial character of Victorian culture. As I argue in particular for "A Christmas Carol," cultural forms such as novels and films exist in a circular relationship with other struc-

---

[13] Miriam Bailin, *The Sickroom in Victorian Fiction: The Art of Being Ill* (Cambridge: Cambridge University Press, 1994), 83.

tures of spectatorship, not creating but rather giving material form to the value with which particular objects and persons are invested. Similarly, cultural incitements to sympathy both depend on and reinforce the status of the sympathetic object as representation.[14] The texts discussed in this book repeatedly stage sympathy as representation, as if the attempt to feel for another across a social divide is necessarily mediated by the image of the self *as* image: the self perceived as an effect of social determinants. The scene of sympathy opens up a space between self and representation which gives way to a perception of the self as representation; imagining the self occupying another's place is only a step away from imagining the self as merely occupying its own. What "place" signifies, then, is cultural possibility: a negative or, conversely, idealized image of identity. Sympathy in Victorian culture, I argue, is sympathy both for and against images of cultural identity.

Smith's scenario bears on this argument in a number of ways; most significant is his recourse to a social, specular dynamic in order to explain how sympathy works. For Smith, sympathy requires a scene—both within his own argument and in the mind of his hypothetical spectator. The other's experience, Smith argues, may be apprehended only through the mediation of the spectator's self-image, and the sympathetic object is, in effect, a projection or fantasy of the spectator's identity. Smith's sympathy is a circulation of representations, and his account of sympathy is—it follows—encapsulated in a series of scenes illustrating the effect of images of suffering on a spectator. "When we see a stroke aimed and just ready to fall upon the leg and arm of another person," Smith writes, "we naturally shrink and draw back our own leg or our own arm, and when it does fall, we feel it in some measure, and are hurt by it as well as the sufferer."[15] De Bolla notes that "such sympathetic reactions are primarily governed by what we *see*. . . . the visual is crucial in determining the entire system."[16] But

---

[14] For further discussion of the relationship between sympathy and representation, especially theatricality, see David Marshall, *The Figure of Theater: Shaftesbury, Defoe, Adam Smith, and George Eliot* (New York: Columbia University Press, 1986), and *The Surprising Effects of Sympathy: Marivaux, Diderot, Rousseau, and Mary Shelley* (Chicago: University of Chicago Press, 1988).

[15] Smith, *Theory of Moral Sentiments*, 10.

[16] De Bolla, "Visibility of Visuality," 75.

the purpose of the visual here is to produce secondary experience in a spectator, an image or copy of pain whose significance—better, interest (for there is no small degree of scientific detachment here)—lies not in its effect on the sufferer but rather in its representational potential: in the power of its ripple effect, its capacity to reverberate in the spectator's mind and body, literally moving the latter. (Paradoxically and yet characteristically, the sign of the spectator's liberality in this illustration—of his, or, in Smith's language, "our," expansive sensibility—is a "shrinking" away. Marking sympathy itself as pain, the scene dramatizes the ambivalence inscribed in sympathetic spectatorship: the way it represents, simultaneously, both an expansion and a potential diminishment of the spectator's identity.)

With the image of the Panopticon, Michel Foucault drew the form of modern subjectivity and theorized the modern subject as a self-scrutinizing one. Smith's scene of sympathy sketches a class-inflected image of this monitoring, an image of the construction of subjectivity in a hierarchical but increasingly mobile society in which the middle-class self exists in a perpetually vexed relationship with the figures of social difference that surround it. Smith, imagining sympathy as a scene, tells us that self-construction is social: sympathy is always embodied. But in his illustrations, sympathy "does away" with bodies in order to produce representations, replacing persons with mental pictures, generalized images of ease and of suffering. Sympathy in these scenes takes shape as a constellation of images in which a threat to individual identity is both imagined and, theoretically, overcome, with the spectator's identity emerging as an effect of the sympathetic encounter itself.[17]

Victorian scenes of sympathy, too, match culturally valued identities against identities that, in the period's pervasive economic metaphor, represent respectability's social and psychic cost. In a social system for which

[17] "What we find in liberalism is not itself a plan of political and social action that *responds* to perceived conditions of distress or inequity, but rather the represented conjunction of surplus and distress, the 'moving spectacle' contained in the image, for example, of a man bent double by a pack of merchandise. The 'revolution in manners,' which Burke proclaimed as the most profound of revolutions witnessed in 1789, is the supplanting of an ethic of 'liberal, plenteous hospitality' ... by a liberal *attitude*—in common parlance, a social conscience. Where 'The Old Cumberland Beggar' envisions 'liberality' as voluntary charity, 'The Ruined Cottage' celebrates its spiritualization into voluntary *sympathy*" (Langan, *Romantic Vagrancy*, 229–30).

vampirism is an apt metaphor—in the psychic as well as financial economy of capitalism, one person's rise is tied to another's fall—the subject
who seeks confirmation of his or her desired image in the external world
(as Scrooge does in Dickens's "A Christmas Carol") encounters a less-
than-pleasing likeness, a figure nevertheless recognized as one of that subject's structuring identifications.[18] Rather than encountering an idealized
image of the self (in Lacan's useful terms, the image identified with the
mirror's reflection and affirmed by the dominant culture's gaze), the
middle-class or respectable subject encounters his or her social shadow, the
negative image that respectability necessarily implies—an image that simultaneously invites identification (since a plea for sympathy is itself a
claim for identification, a claim for a common humanity) and requires
disidentification.[19] Victorian objects of sympathy thus signify both cultural value and its absence. For the subject desiring to align him or herself
with such value, they represent an insurmountable distance from it—a distance that manifests itself, in the texts I discuss here, in a fantasy of the subject's death. This scenario imagines the possibility, so vividly illustrated in
"A Christmas Carol," of being "left out" of the dominant culture and
therefore, as seems to follow, of life itself. Sympathy with particular social
figures takes shape in these texts as sympathy for or against—for *and*
against—images of cultural identity, and the texts themselves project alternative identities for their central characters in distinct representations—
scenes or pictures (such as those witnessed by Dickens's Scrooge, Wood's
Isabel Vane, and Eliot's Daniel Deronda)—with which these characters
identify and in relation to which their identities become attenuated. These
representations display the valued or devalued identities produced by
specific cultural narratives.

Indeed, the novels I discuss here frequently emphasize what might be
called an alternative scene of sympathy: characters situated not in a dread

[18] Elaine Scarry describes the relation between worker and capitalist as a confrontation
between embodied and disembodied figures and suggests that, vampiristically, the capitalist's absence depends upon the worker's physicality. See my discussion in Chapter 2. Scarry,
The Body in Pain (New York: Oxford University Press, 1985), 276.

[19] This formulation draws both on Lacan, "The Mirror Stage," and on the Althusserian idea
of interpellation, in which the subject is formed at the moment he responds to a policeman's
"hailing": "Hey, you there!" Jacques Lacan, "The Mirror Stage," in *Ecrits*, trans. Alan Sheridan
(New York: Norton, 1977), 1–7; Althusser, "Ideology and Ideological State Apparatuses."

relation to a degraded image but in a desiring relation to an idealized one. (Hence the importance of Smith's expansion of the term "sympathy" to include observations on sympathizing with pleasure: "When we consider the condition of the great, in those delusive colours in which the imagination is apt to paint it, it seems to be almost the abstract idea of a perfect and happy state. It is the very state which, in all our waking dreams and idle reveries, we had sketched to ourselves as the final object of all our desires. We feel, therefore, a peculiar sympathy with the satisfaction of those who are in it.")[20] These novels tell the story of a subject's attempt to embody the cultural truth of a particular idealized identity, often as an alternative to a degraded image with which that subject is also identified (as in the examples of Ruth, Daniel Deronda, and Dorian Gray). And the nature of that idealization sometimes lies in the subject's capacity for sympathy: in *Daniel Deronda,* for instance, the idealized character is a liberal subject whose capaciousness and mobile sensibility obscures his culture's investment in identities defined in more specific terms. In its apparently infinite capaciousness, its aura of all-inclusiveness, and its apparent vacancy and availability for projection, what appears finally as sympathetic identity per se, in these texts, itself becomes an object of desire.

To the extent, then, that objects of sympathy are embedded in (are, indeed, the products of) cultural narratives—indeed, to the extent that sympathy *is* a cultural narrative (Silverman's "studious avoidance" of looking, for instance, remains a well-known stance the middle-class subject prepares to take when sighting the beggar up ahead)—it is not so much the absence of actual bodies in novels that produces sympathy as it is sympathy or its expectation that produces an effect of fictionality—a scene— with its concomitant displacements into narrative and representation (for instance, the narrative of whether the beggar is deserving or not deserving; the question of how much, if anything, to give; the imagining of the self in the other's place). The cultural narratives that constitute sympathy themselves do away with the body; indeed, many of the texts I discuss here literally do away with bodies, replacing them with pictures or narratives, thereby implicitly defining identity as cultural image and fantasy. Silverman's scenario is relevant, then, less for its conclusion than for the familiarity of its tropes: for the way in which, even as it puts flesh on Smith's

---

[20] Smith, *Theory of Moral Sentiments,* 51–52.

theoretical skeleton ("our brother on the rack"), it remains firmly within the boundaries he describes. Indeed, read together, Smith and Silverman suggest that what Smith and other theorists of sympathy typically represent as an inability to imagine the self in the other's place may in fact be a resistance to doing so: a response, in the context of a capitalist economics of identity, to the seemingly endless demand posed by the spectacle of those worse off than oneself.[21]

————

Victorian fiction assisted its readers in what Richard Sennett has described as "the constant attempt [of the nineteenth-century 'personality'] to formulate what it is one feels."[22] In this capacity, Victorian novels also helped formulate the ideological meanings borne by emotional response, chief among which were the social images and relations that accumulated around the term "sympathy." Indeed, the regular recurrence of the adjective "Dickensian" in twentieth-century descriptions of urban poverty suggests that Victorian novels more than any other form (and Dickens more than any other Victorian novelist) continue to provide the terms and images of contemporary sympathetic representation.

In a modern dispensation structured in part by the Victorian novel's own structuring and valuing of interiority, ideologies of feeling draw their power from feeling's presumed self-evidence: feeling, ostensibly emerging from the deepest interiority, seems by definition beyond the reach of social regulation, and its cultural value depends on that inaccessibility. And yet feeling's usefulness as a conduit for ideological meaning derives from the relation to the visible sign such presumed inaccessibility defines. For feeling, of course, depends upon representation: in order to be known, it must appear; insofar as it is known, it is constituted by representation. And though the ideological power of feeling relies on the idea of an essence or truth to which language and representation are said to remain inadequate, the specific nature of that power becomes visible in the terms of its rep-

---

[21] Hence the relevance of Silverman's identification with the supposed rationality of a government agency, when she feels called upon to find some principle on the basis of which to distribute money: "I fantasized that my crisis would be solved if I could only find an intelligent formula for determining whom I should help" (*Threshold of the Visible World*, 26).

[22] Sennett, *Fall of Public Man*, 152.

resentation. Feeling is inseparable from the scenes that may seem merely to provoke it and the signs by means of which it becomes known.[23]

In Victorian fiction and the work of its critics, the term "sympathy" has commonly been used to describe an individualistic, affective solution to the problem of class alienation: the attempt to ameliorate social differences with assurances of mutual feeling and universal humanity. Such assurances take the form of attempts to resolve class differences through direct knowledge of a sufferer's experience, as in Louisa Gradgrind's visit to Stephen Blackpool in Dickens's *Hard Times* or the reconciliation between John Barton and Mr. Carson at the end of Gaskell's *Mary Barton*. In each of these examples, the perception of the other as a participant in a common humanity replaces the stock appraisal of him or her as a worker or employer; as Gaskell writes, "The mourner before him was no longer an employer, a being of another race . . . no longer the enemy, the oppressor, but a very poor, and desolate old man."[24] With its ostensible effacement of differences and asserted dissolution of individuals into a common humanity, sympathy thus formulated seeks to efface the social and political problems for which it is offered as a resolution. Attempting to transcend the socioeconomic or bodily markers that signify difference, it defines as human what is least subject to the contingencies of politics. Victorian identity, so bound to markers of class and place, is thus said to yield—in sympathy—to an ideal that redefines its most crucial features as merely contingent.

Sympathy thus conceived grounds the self in the dissolution of the social, doing away with representation in order to reach a common ground

---

[23] Visuality in this study may thus be understood as a metaphor for representation and knowledge: what can be known at any given time is what can be seen. For more on this idea, see John Rajchman, "Foucault's Art of Seeing," *October* 44 (1988): 88–117.

[24] Elizabeth Gaskell, *Mary Barton* (Harmondsworth, England: Penguin, 1970), 435. Such sympathy, and the relevance of *Hard Times* in this context, have been discussed recently by Martha Nussbaum in *Poetic Justice: The Literary Imagination and Public Life* (Boston: Beacon, 1995). For a discussion of the way the novel of the 1840s became the novel of social reform, see Kathleen Tillotson, *Novels of the Eighteen Forties* (New York: Oxford University Press, 1954), 124: "But in the late eighteen forties, people read novels more than ever; for the novel was now ready and able to absorb and minister to their 'speculations on reform.' No longer does it belong to the world of indolent languid men on sofas, of Aesthetic Tea. . . . It belongs to the no-man's-land on the frontier between the two nations."

of feeling—as if the only escape from social difference were in a common humanity attained in dissolution and death. But representations of sympathy in Victorian fiction repeatedly return to the social differences such scenes discount; in them, sympathy is frequently the metaphorical currency by means of which identity is constituted and undone. For instance: insofar as sympathy's "truth" is made manifest in circulation, sympathy threatens the foundation of feeling on which individual identity is supposedly based. If, as I have suggested, emotion is subject to interpretation only insofar as it manifests itself visibly, sympathy has a special relation to representation for the Victorians in that it frequently becomes visible in another form of representation: money. Victorian charity, with its alignment of feeling and funds and its emphasis on individual judgment, figures both sympathy and coin in an economy of self-regulation in which middle-class subjects must evaluate the truth or falseness of non-middle-class ones, and an error in judgment—such as the investment of "true" feeling in "false" identity—threatens the integrity of the self doing the giving. Sympathy and charity situate the self in a hydraulic relation with other selves, in which a flow of funds in one direction represents a drain unless balanced by some—usually moral—return. The offer of sympathy for narrative, as in Andrew Halliday's encounter with the beggar in my discussion of Mayhew (Chapter 2), recapitulates the capitalist myth that an exchange of funds draws on, and constitutes evidence for, the existence of transcendent value, and it locates that value in human feeling and human identity. But narratives meant to express and embody sympathy's value display a circular logic whereby the truth of an appeal for sympathy can only be validated by further narrative. Exchanged for narrative, sympathy resembles the fluid, multiply signifying nature of money itself. And the tendency to regard appeals for sympathy as, potentially, nothing more than representation reflects the sympathizer's vulnerability to the same charge: the need to verify the identity of the sympathetic object suggests that the spectator's identity is itself fallen and in need of verification, lapsed from an idealized and naturalized aristocratic past. Concern with the truth or fraudulence of a beggar's appeal for sympathy thus registers concern about the legibility of social identity per se, and in particular about the construction of middle-class identity as a tenuous balance between degraded and idealized cultural images.

The preceding account applies, perhaps too specifically, to the man on the street. And yet for the contemporary subject who is the perceived object of charitable appeal, as in Silverman's narrative, class may figure more prominently than gender as an identity-defining issue. But in Victorian discussions and, frequently, in contemporary critical analyses, sympathy tends to appear explicitly as a woman's issue.[25] According to Ruskin, for instance, women's position within the family renders them better at feeling than men. As the centers of Victorian domestic life, women were expected to defer their own desires and work toward the fulfillment of others', and the name given that generalized identification was frequently sympathy. And that sympathy, in turn, suggested a more generalized capacity to identify with others, as in this Ruskinian account of imaginative identification:"She is to exercise herself in imagining what would be the effects upon her mind and conduct, if she were daily brought into the presence of the suffering which is not the less real because shut from her sight."[26] In a discussion of nationalism, Samuel Smiles links sympathy learned in childhood to the adult exercises of charity and philanthropy: "The nation comes from the nursery. Public opinion is for the most part the outgrowth of the home, and the best philanthropy comes from the fireside. . . . From this little central spot, the human sympathies may extend in an ever widening circle, until the world is embraced for though true philanthropy, like charity, begins at home, assuredly it does not end there."[27]

The association of women with feeling informs the representation of female characters in what I call scenes of sympathy. But sympathy is not uniquely a women's issue; rather, Victorian representations offer competing and complimentary structures variously associated with sympathy. For both male and female characters, sympathy provokes confusion in the signs of class identity (disguise, disfigurement); for both, sympathy is associated

[25] Separate spheres ideology is, of course, grounded in the representation that women are more emotionally adept than men. As Amanda Anderson writes, "Part of the way the wider cultural discourse redressed the negative moral implications of self-interestedness was to allocate a redemptive sympathy to the sphere of private domesticity and to the character of femininity." *Tainted Souls and Painted Faces: The Rhetoric of Fallenness in Victorian Culture* (Ithaca: Cornell University Press, 1993), 41. For a reading of the politics of this construction of the Victorian domestic woman, see Nancy Armstrong, *Desire and Domestic Fiction: A Political History of the Novel* (New York: Oxford University Press, 1987).

[26] John Ruskin, *Sesame and Lilies* (New York: Wiley and Sons, 1885), 106.

[27] Samuel Smiles, *Self-Help* (London, 1859), 394.

with a fear of falling (the woman fears the sexual fall, the man the economic one). These scenes repeatedly project an image of sympathetic identification as a loss of identity, a dissolution or evacuation of an essential self that is often identified with, and represented as leading to, a loss of life. But the dispensation of charity, like the handling of money, is imagined chiefly as a masculine function: the masculine subject, who "makes" money, tends in these texts to be conflated with the invisible circulation of money itself, while women, frequently imagined as sympathy's objects, tend to become indistinguishable from the dominant culture's projections of them.

My last two chapters suggest another way of contextualizing the relationship between sympathy and gender. Both Daniel Deronda and Dorian Gray are aestheticized types; their availability for sympathetic identification is figured as a beauty defined by an absence of physical particularity. This absence—a blank receptivity that invites a spectator's projections—is defined in other discussions of these novels either as femininity or as an effect of the challenge that same-sex desire poses to normative constructions of heterosexuality.[28] Despite the power of many of these arguments, however, their insistence on the priority of gender labeling masks the question of femininity's or masculinity's cultural meaning—in this case, the way femininity is coded as sympathetic receptivity. Daniel Deronda and Dorian Gray may appear to be feminized, that is, precisely because of the way their representative status makes them available for sympathy. In these novels, as in their cultural contexts, sympathy's face is a conventionally feminine one: blank, receptive, and available for fantasy.

═══

The figures Victorian society defined as objects of sympathy were, of course, its outcasts; situated outside respectable identity, they were essential to its definition. Such characters as beggars and fallen women cir-

---

[28] For an example of such a reading of *Daniel Deronda,* see Jacob Press, "Same-Sex Unions in Modern Europe: *Daniel Deronda, Altneuland,* and the Homoerotics of Jewish Nationalism," in *Novel Gazing: Queer Readings in Fiction,* ed. Eve Kosofsky Sedgwick (Durham: Duke University Press, 1997), 299–329; on Wilde see Kathy Alexis Psomiades, *Beauty's Body: Femininity and Representation in British Aestheticism* (Stanford: Stanford University Press, 1997), 181–89.

culate in these texts as projections of a fear of falling embedded within the structure of Victorian middle-class identity; they expose the way in which middle-class identity was experienced as a fall from a natural condition of aristocratic identity into the representation and dissimulation that the realm of the social seemed, by contrast, to require. Identification with such figures, accompanied by incessant concern about the authenticity of their identities, registers an identification with fallenness and guilt that threatens the desired stability and presumed naturalness of middle-class identity. The encounter between "who one was" and "who one wasn't" challenges the complacency of the stable self, theoretically ready to offer sympathy and coin; Bailin's use of the past tense captures the temporal disjunction experienced by a middle-class observer suddenly perceiving in the sympathetic object a figure for identity's contingent, social nature—suddenly perceiving identity as narrative, as fallen. Each sympathetic encounter thus has the effect of an identity with sympathy itself: it is a fall into representation.[29] Victorian representations of sympathy capture the tension between an emphasis on sympathy and charity as humanitarian values, on the one hand, and an uneasy identification with sympathy's visible objects, on the other. Closely tied to a sense of economic well-being, sympathy follows a capitalist logic: like money it must be meted out with care lest it—and the identity it represents—dissipate entirely. For the Victorian middle classes, then, the attempt to imagine the self in the other's place was less an enjoyable theatrical exercise than a reminder of identity's contingency. In such efforts, what Diana Fuss calls "the detour through the

---

[29] For a similar view of middle-class identity, see Marjorie Levinson, *Keats's Life of Allegory: The Origins of a Style* (Oxford: Blackwell, 1988). Somewhat contradictorily as well, however, the cultural narratives surrounding the beggar in such encounters also figure as intrusions of the real on the activities of representation and speculation; the beggar's appeal, which demands the kind of "active interchange" (Sennett, *Fall of Public Man,* 27) no longer typical of urban life, seems momentarily to disrupt the Victorian urban spectator's detached appropriation of everything he sees. A request for change requires exchange, and in so doing confronts the man on the street with the misrecognitions and denials involved in the construction of the respectable self.

Balzac describes the flaneur as able to enjoy a "gastronomy of the eye" in which "one is open to everything, one rejects nothing a priori from one's purview, provided one needn't become a participant, enmeshed in a scene" (See Sennett, *Fall of Public Man,* 27; Brand, *Spectator and the City,* 42). The beggar's appeal "enmeshes" the spectator in a scene, taking away the privilege of spectatorship.

other that defines a self"—the swerve along a linear route to identity—threatens to become the place in which identity gets stuck.[30]

The readings that follow locate in Victorian representations of sympathy a conceptual fluidity that both was (and remains today) ideologically useful. Rather than fixing a definition of the term, they seek to elucidate its mechanisms and gestures, scenarios and identifications. Tying specularity to economics, and to the perception and articulation of identity, sympathy emerges in these readings and in the Victorian middle-class imaginary as a vehicle for the circulation of effects and identities between classes. It expresses resentment and desire; it prompts the exchange of objects such as gifts, disease, or coin; it sets in motion or reinforces a belief in its own transcendent value as emotional currency; it produces narrative. Indeed, rather than producing truths of identity, Victorian representations of sympathy define identity as sympathetic currency—currency that circulates in avowedly fictional form (as in *Ruth*) as well as in the form of ostensibly "true" selves (as in "A Christmas Carol" and *Daniel Deronda*). In the scenes discussed here, sympathy's requisite attenuation of self provokes narratives about the truth or falsity of self-representation; these scenes establish links between sympathy, disguise, and deception that call ostensibly

---

[30] Fuss, *Identification Papers*, 2. Sympathy's importance as a middle-class realm of feeling perhaps accounts for the tendency, from Wordsworth to Nussbaum, to align literary representations of suffering with imaginative identification itself. In Nussbaum's argument, for instance, what awakens the "literary imagination" is the reader's perception that "it might have been otherwise" for the sufferer. "When we read *Hard Times* as sympathetic participants, our attention has a special focus. Since the sufferings and anxieties of the characters are among the central bonds between reader and work, our attention is drawn in particular to those characters who suffer and fear. Characters who are not facing any adversity simply do not hook us in as readers; there is no drama in a life in which things are going smoothly." But anxiety for the character is heightened by the feeling that "it might have been otherwise" for the reader as well. "One way in which the situation of the poor or oppressed is especially bad is that it might have been otherwise. We see this especially clearly when we see their situation side by side with the rich and prosperous. In this way our thought will naturally turn in the direction of making the lot of the worst off more similar to the lot of the rich and powerful; since we ourselves might be, or become, either of these two people, we want to raise the floor" (Nussbaum, *Poetic Justice*, 91). This analysis suggests that the apprehension of suffering may be especially keen in the literary imagination precisely *because* of the bourgeois sensibility (in Nussbaum's universalizing language, "our" sensibility) which finds it "natural" that "drama" should inhere in the reflexivity, the potential reversibility, between the "worse off" and the "rich and powerful."

secure identities into question. Breaking down and confusing social boundaries and identities, they render disguise a figure for sympathy and its projections.

Some of the texts discussed here—"A Christmas Carol," *Ruth, East Lynne,* and *Daniel Deronda*—issue paradigmatic appeals for sympathy. Working the borders between sympathy and transgression, they attempt to redeem figures defined as marginal or deviant and in the process complicate the social categories and identities they seek to stabilize. In a scenario reminiscent of René Girard's accounts of victim sacrifice, figures positioned outside mainstream Victorian society—defined, as I suggest above, as that society's negative image—are transformed into exemplars of cultural value, embodying ideals of universality and inviting the harmonious resolution of social conflict. The sympathy and adulation lavished on a few deserving "victims," in this scenario, displaces attention from the destructive consequences of industrialization and the rise to power of the middle class. But knowledge of those consequences is not, in fact, erased; rather, sympathy emerges as a circulation of representations, as these figures dissolve into the conflicting images they suggest to the middle-class imagination. Gaskell's Ruth, for instance, embodies the cultural anxieties evoked by the very possibility Gaskell wished to dramatize: that of sympathy for the fallen woman.[31]

The first part of the book establishes a number of connections between capitalism and spectatorship in Victorian representations of sympathy. Both "A Christmas Carol" and Arthur Conan Doyle's "The Man with the Twisted Lip" align sympathetic representation with the circulation of social images. In both texts, the sympathetic exchange—Halliday's encounter with the beggar, Scrooge's identification with his own image—illustrates a more general problematic of exchange, in which the identities of beggar and capitalist collapse into each other. Part II traces the representation and circulation of feminine identity and feminine sympathy in *Ruth* and *East Lynne,* exploring the way anxiety about the fallenness of middle-class identity is projected onto each text's sympathetic object. Here, exchanged identity appears as illegitimacy, and, as in Conan Doyle, as disguise: identity disengaged from any naturalizing origin.

---

[31] René Girard, *Violence and the Sacred* (Baltimore: Johns Hopkins University Press, 1972).

In these first two parts of the book, emphasis on economic determinations of identity suggests similarities between Victorian representations of sympathy and contemporary ones. In Part III, the topic of Victorian sympathy intersects with, and suggests a lineage for, a different set of contemporary identity issues. My chapters outline a narrative in which the self-undoing visuality of Victorian cross-class sympathy gives way, in the latter part of the century, to explicit images of similitude: assertions of mysterious affinities between like-minded individuals.[32] This is not to argue that the nineteenth century saw a fundamental change in the representation of sympathy, or that vertical sympathy—the sympathy of the middle- and upper-classes for the poor—disappears from literary representation. My intention is rather to characterize the ideological discourses of group identity that emerge in the latter half of the nineteenth century (such as nationalism) as scenes of sympathy because of their evocation of and reliance on generalized and opposing images of cultural identity, and to suggest that this characterization reveals some of the limitations of, and contradictions within, liberal claims to universal sympathy. In particular, what has come to be known as identity politics, which conceives of identity as a form of group identification, reveals the tension between the liberal ideal of universal sympathy and the specificity of particular identifications.

The investments of *Daniel Deronda* and *The Picture of Dorian Gray* in ideals of sympathetic affinity, I argue, suggest a genealogy of contemporary identity politics, refocusing that politics as a narrative of sympathy in which identity is organized, on the model of nationalism, as the need to construct, desire, and consent to a particular kind of self. Sympathy in these novels enables the formation of cultural bonds and solidarities on the basis of a conjoined similarity and desire: these texts describe an ineffable and inexplicable attraction between individuals, so that a sympathy that might challenge identity gives way to (is exchanged for) a sympathy that seems unequivocally to affirm it, and sympathy with the other gives way, explicitly, to what in one way or another it has always been: sympathy with the self—the subject's attempt to identify with his or her idealized image. Yet what might appear at this stage of the argument as a revelation or exposure is in fact merely another perspective on Adam Smith's

---

[32] I owe the formulation "self-undoing visuality" to an anonymous reader for Cornell University Press.

originary scene: one according to which a spectator's generalized imaginative possibilities—including the possibility of sympathizing with "our brother on the rack"—are undercut by the very particularities of group identity that delimit the bourgeois subject in the first place (defining that subject as, for instance, a national one). The image of the self as a member of a group thus turns out to be the flip side—the political unconscious—of the scene of sympathetic exchange.

In these late-nineteenth-century novels, the mid-Victorian focus on class shifts to a cultivation of like-mindedness that presumes to transcend all social boundaries, but in fact only transcends some (such as those of class) in order to enable the establishment of others (such as those of nationality), and the crucial category is no longer class but the even more diffuse "sensibility." Differences ascribed to taste, ostensibly grounded in personal identity and choice rather than in accidents of birth, enable the assimilation of individuals into larger, corporate bodies such as nations, or categories of group identity based, for instance, on sexuality. What produces affinities between individuals in these novels, then, is less a spirit of humanitarianism than an ineffable and exclusionary determination of like-mindedness. These late-nineteenth-century scenes of sympathy, I wish to suggest, both participate in and reveal the boundary-drawing implicit in earlier ones: sympathy in Victorian fiction is always about the construction of social and cultural identities, about the individual subject's relation to the group. But because late-nineteenth-century ideologies construct individual identity as a function of group identity, the pain sympathy manifestly relieves, in these later formulations, is not that of physical suffering or class alienation but rather that of a potential separation from identity itself. In these novels, as in the lives of many of their late-twentieth-century readers, identity has become a matter of national and sexual allegiances which must be discovered, declared, and consented to.

PART I

Sympathy and the Spirit
of Capitalism

I

Sympathy and Spectacle in Dickens's "A Christmas Carol"

In a well-known essay, Sergei Eisenstein describes literature in general and Dickens in particular as cinema's predecessors because of their evocation of visual effects. Literature, Eisenstein writes, provides cinema with "parents and [a] pedigree, . . . a past"; it is "the art of viewing."[1] What Eisenstein construes as aesthetic development may be regarded, however, as evidence for what Christian Metz calls a persistent "regime of perception" in Western culture—one in which appeals to the eye play a significant role in the production and circulation of ideology.[2] An emphasis on visuality, whether literary or cinematic, promotes spectatorship as a dominant cultural activity. But such an emphasis also reinforces, and thereby naturalizes, forms of spectatorship already inscribed in the social structures within which particular cultural representations are produced. The idea of a continuity between literature and film may thus be significant less for what it reveals about the genealogy of cinema than for

---

[1] Sergei Eisenstein, "Dickens, Griffith, and the Film Today," in *Film Forum* (New York: Harcourt, 1949), 33.

[2] According to Metz, the "regime of perception" perpetuated by cinema is one for which the spectator has been " 'prepared' by the older arts of representation (the novel, representational painting, etc.) and by the Aristotelian tradition of Western art in general." *The Imaginary Signifier* (Bloomington: Indiana University Press, 1977), 118–19.

what it tells about the role of visuality and its literary evocations in defining, reinforcing, and disseminating some of Western culture's dominant values.

"A Christmas Carol" (1843) is arguably Dickens's most visually evocative text. In its detailed attention to and elaboration of surfaces, its reliance on contrasts between darkness and light, its construction as a series of scenes (a structure reproduced in the images the spirits exhibit to Scrooge), and particularly its engagement with a dynamic of spectatorial desire, the story is an artifact of, and an exemplary text for understanding, the commodity culture Guy Debord terms a "society of the spectacle"; the mechanism of Scrooge's conversion is, after all, spectatorship.[3] Projecting Scrooge's identity into past and future, associating spectatorial and consumer desire with images of an idealized self, "A Christmas Carol" elaborates what I wish to argue is the circular relation that obtains between, on the one hand, spectacular forms of cultural representation, and, on the other, persons, objects, or scenes invested with ideological value and thus already, within their cultural contexts, spectacular. Moreover, an understanding of the story's representational effects helps explain the peculiar power of spectacle as a vehicle for ideology. For while "A Christmas Carol" anatomizes the relationship between an individual subject and spectacular culture, it also unfolds as an allegory of the subject's relation to culture in general, defined, by Clifford Geertz, as "an imaginative universe within which...acts are signs."[4]

A recent revision of "A Christmas Carol" reproduces the story's circularity. At the end of the film "Scrooged" (1988), the character played by Bill Murray, involved in making a television version of Dickens's story, steps out of television space and into cinematic space to address the viewer "directly." The point of this shift is, of course, to frame television space as fictional by seeming to move into a more "real" space, and the point of his address is to direct spectators to do the same: to become engaged with the world beyond television. Telling viewers not to watch television, Murray's

---

[3] Dickens's story has long been recognized as an exemplary commodity text for its unabashed celebration of excess and consumption, its commercial rendering of the "Christmas spirit," and the seemingly infinite adaptability and marketability attested to by its annual reappearance as literary text, public reading, theatrical performance, and film.

[4] Clifford Geertz, *The Interpretation of Cultures* (New York: Basic Books, 1973), 13.

character reinforces, however, the idea that some medium is needed to send them that message. Implicit in the directive to leave fiction behind and move into the world, in both this film and the text on which it is based, is the claim that the way to the world lies through representation.

Presenting Scrooge with images of his past, present, and future lives, Dickens's spectacular text seeks to awaken that character's sympathy and direct it to the world beyond representation. As a model of socialization through spectatorship, the narrative posits the visual as a means toward recapturing one's lost or alienated self—and becoming one's best self. If it fails to explain how the process occurs—how sympathy emerges from identification, and identification from spectatorship—it nevertheless asks its readers' assent to this series of effects. And if, as I argue, Scrooge's sympathetic self emerges from his relation to representation, such is also the implied effect of the reader's relation to the scenes of "A Christmas Carol," given the text's explicit analogy between Scrooge's activity and the reader's (the narrator notes, for example, that Scrooge is as close to the Spirit of Christmas Past as the narrator is to the reader: "and I am standing in the spirit at your elbow").[5]

Making visual representation necessary for the production of individual sympathy and thus, ultimately, to social harmony, Dickens's text both participates in and reinforces the perceptual regime to which Metz refers. For at stake in the story's appeal to visuality is not just the assertion of a connection between spectatorship and sympathy but a definition of spectatorship as a means of access to cultural life. Paul Davis has used the term "culture-text" to describe the way the "Carol" has been rewritten to reflect particular cultural and historical circumstances.[6] I wish to argue that the story deserves this name, however, because it identifies itself with culture: it projects images of, has come to stand for, and constitutes an exemplary narrative of enculturation into the dominant values of its time.

"A Christmas Carol" tells the story of a Victorian businessman's interpellation as the subject of a phantasmatic commodity culture in which

[5] Charles Dickens, "A Christmas Carol," in *The Christmas Books,* vol. 1, ed. Michael Slater (Harmondsworth, England: Penguin, 1971), 68. Subsequent references included in text.

[6] Paul Davis, *The Lives and Times of Ebenezer Scrooge* (New Haven: Yale University Press, 1990).

laissez-faire economics is happily wedded to natural benevolence. And, in a manner that would be appropriate for a general definition of culture but is especially suited to a spectacular society, the story articulates the relation between the subject and culture as a relation between the subject and representation. Scrooge gains access to his former, feeling self and to a community with which that self is in harmony—and, not incidentally, he saves his own life—by learning to negotiate the text's field of visual representations. Cultural "frames" embedded in the story's images invite the spectator's identification, collapsing sympathy into an identification with representation itself. Making participation in its scenes dependent on such identification, the story constitutes both its idealized charitable self and the ideal subject of commodity culture. "A Christmas Carol" reconciles Christmases Past and Christmases Yet to Come, that is, by conjuring up an illusion of presence.

———

The story's ideological project—its attempt to link sympathy and business by incorporating a charitable impulse into its readers' self-conceptions—underlies its association of charitable feeling with participation in cultural life.[7] A narrative whose ostensible purpose is the production of social sympathy, "A Christmas Carol" both recalls and revises those scenes in eighteenth-century fiction that, depicting encounters between charity givers and receivers, model sympathy for readers positioned as witnesses.[8] Although such scenes have an instructional function and were meant to

[7] Despite the importance of feminine subjectivity to Victorian ideologies of feeling, "A Christmas Carol" links charity to a masculine-identified form of power: to the proper functioning of the economy. Relevant here is Kaja Silverman's discussion of the way in which "our dominant fiction calls upon the male subject to see himself, and the female subject to recognize and desire him, only through the mediation of images of an unimpaired masculinity." *Male Subjectivity at the Margins* (New York: Routledge, 1992), 42. Scrooge's miserliness is by implication a corollary of his rejection of female companionship and the family; the story presents Scrooge with images of his own impaired masculinity and permits him to restore himself, through gift giving, as a symbolic father to the Cratchit family ("to Tiny Tim, who did NOT die, he was a second father" [133–34]).

[8] I refer to such novels as Henry Mackenzie's *The Man of Feeling* and Laurence Sterne's *A Sentimental Journey.* These scenes are themselves "culture-texts," in that they stage confrontations between characters situated in different social contexts and demonstrate emotion's inseparability from social configurations.

direct readers from the text to the world beyond it, they also posit the existence of strictly "literary" feeling; intended to "inculcate...humanity
and benevolence," they nevertheless provided "a course in the development of emotional response, whose beginning and end are literary."[9]
What I have described as a certain circularity in representations of sympathy is thus not new in the nineteenth century. But from the eighteenth-
century novel's scenes of sympathy to the spectacles observed by Scrooge,
the sympathetic text has both widened its scope and tightened its grasp on
the reader; from a display of virtue meant to incite imitation and teach
judgment to a relatively select audience, it has moved to a profound manipulation of the reader's visual sense in the form of—and by means of—
the mass marketing of sympathetic representations. In the "Carol," the
subject is not the man of feeling but the man who has forgotten how to
feel; in Victorian England, the potential charity giver no less than the beggar requires socialization. Not simply a representation of an act of benevolence or an exhortation about the pleasures of sympathy, Dickens's text
situates its readers in the position of the man without feeling in a narrative whose function is to teach him how to feel, and it constructs them as
sympathetic subjects no less than as spectacular ones by manipulating "visual" effects in a manner that mirrors Scrooge's own interpellation
through spectacle.

The story opens on a world shrouded in fog that gradually dissolves to
reveal Scrooge working in his counting house (47). Here, as in numerous
other scenes that evoke contrasts between darkness and light or in other
ways emphasize the visual, the story draws attention to its own surface and
its control over visual techniques (what Metz calls "mechanisms of desire")—its power to let readers, positioned as spectators, see or not see.[10]

---

[9] Janet Todd, *Sensibility: An Introduction* (New York: Methuen, 1986), 91–93. See also John
Mullan, *Sentiment and Sociability: The Language of Feeling in the Eighteenth Century* (Cambridge: Cambridge University Press, 1988).

[10] See Metz, *Imaginary Signifier*, 77, for an account of techniques that emphasize the camera's control over the spectator's vision. In evoking "the boundary that bars the look," Metz
suggests, the camera eroticizes seeing, in a "veiling-unveiling procedure" that excites the
viewer's desire. This kind of procedure characterizes Dickens's writing in passages such as
the following: "Meanwhile the fog and darkness thickened so, that people ran about with
flaring links, proffering their services to go before horses in carriages, and conduct them
on their way. The ancient tower of a church...became invisible.... In the main street, at

In doing so, it seems to create spectacle out of a grab bag of projective or framing devices that it implicitly describes as the property of literary texts. But while suggesting that literature can transform any reality into spectacle, the story focuses chiefly on objects, persons, and scenes that are already spectacular in Victorian culture: already invested with cultural value and desire. As the story seems to spectacularize the real, that is, it in fact reinforces the desirability of a series of culturally valorized images and contributes to a sense that nothing exists—at least, nothing worth looking at—outside those images.

Spectacle depends on a distinction between vision and participation, a distance that produces desire in a spectator. The early parts of Dickens's story dramatize the elder Scrooge's identification with images of his youth and associate the effect of those images with that of literary texts. The scenes of Scrooge's youth possess an immediacy that the Spirit of Christmas Past underscores by warning Scrooge against it: " 'These are but shadows of the things that have been,' said the Ghost. 'They have no consciousness of us' " (71). But the text's emphasis is on the "reality" of these "shadows," and that emphasis is reinforced by an insistence on the reality of an even more removed level of representation: the characters of Ali Baba and Robinson Crusoe, products of the young Scrooge's imagination, not only appear in the first scene but are "wonderfully real and distinct to look at." And their realism seems both to produce and to be evidence of the spectator's ability to identify with representations; exclaiming about the adventures of these fictional characters, Scrooge "expend[s] all the earnestness of his nature . . . in a most extraordinary voice between laugh-

---

the corner of the court, some labourers were repairing the gas-pipes, and had lighted a great fire in a brazier, round which a party of ragged men and boys were gathered" (52). At stake in this description is less an attempt at mimesis than an evocation of desire for light (and heat). Other scenes, discussed in the body of the paper, similarly depend not so much on minute description as on a "strip-tease" effect that fetishizes the visual (Metz, *Imaginary Signifier*, 77). Dickens resembles numerous other Victorian novelists in his interest in the interrelations of vision and power. For more on this topic see D. A. Miller, *The Novel and the Police* (Berkeley: University of California Press, 1988), and Audrey Jaffe, *Vanishing Points: Dickens, Narrative, and the Subject of Omniscience* (Berkeley: University of California Press, 1991). The ability of "A Christmas Carol" to make readers "see" is further associated with a mechanics of projection and dynamic of spectatorial desire that produce in readers a condition of consumer desire and construct the text as commodity.

ing and crying," his face "heightened and excited" (72). Subsequent scenes produced by the spirit similarly evoke desire and compel identification. The scene of Fezziwig's ball takes Scrooge "out of his wits": "His heart and soul were in the scene, and with his former self"; he speaks "unconsciously like his former, not his latter, self" (78). If Scrooge's relation to the scenes from the *Arabian Nights* and *Robinson Crusoe* is analogous to his response to other scenes from his past and both are analogous to the reader's relation to the text of "A Christmas Carol," then literature is here imagined as spectacle, and both are defined as compelling identification while precluding participation.

Although temporal distance and fictionality separate observer from observed in these scenes, the story's emphasis on the realism of what is seen blurs the difference between a spectacularity literature finds and one it creates. Similarly, what the spirits choose to represent as "scene" is often, in effect, already one. Davis has described the story's construction as a series of scenes in its use of dream and projection and its allusions to popular Victorian images. But its scenes are also related to what Mary Ann Doane calls "scenarios": constellations of objects or persons charged with cultural significance, they are images of images displayed to evoke desire in a spectator who recognizes the values embedded in them.[11] The scenes of Scrooge's boyhood friends, for instance, compel spectatorial desire through their temporal distance and through Scrooge's evident, immediate pleasure in apprehending them. Indistinct as they are, however, they serve chiefly to signify youth and boyhood fellowship and to gesture toward an idealized preindustrial world in which work resembles play. In the description of Fezziwig's ball, similarly, desire is signaled by absorption, the disappearance of both the spirit and Scrooge while the scene is being described. But desire is also inscribed in the display of the dance itself, with its stylized emphasis on couples and courtship. Encoding specific cultural values in visionary scenes, surrounding with a golden or rosy light the images that convey them, the story identifies those values with light and vision themselves, and ultimately, as I argue below, with what it calls "spirit."[12]

[11] Davis, *Lives and Times,* 65–66; Mary Ann Doane, *The Desire to Desire: The Woman's Film of the 1940's* (Bloomington: Indiana University Press, 1987), 13–14.

[12] The cultural value placed on masculine virility, for instance, is conveyed by the detail that, as the old merchant danced, "a positive light appeared to issue from Fezziwig's calves" (77).

Encoded in these scenes, then, are some of Victorian culture's dominant values—youth, boyhood fellowship, heterosexual desire, and familial
pleasure—their naturalness asserted by means of a strategy that identifies
seeing with desiring. For embedded in the scenes are screens of their own:
cultural frames that define the contents as desirable. In perhaps the most
powerful example, a scene after the ball, the narrator models desire, moving into the spirit's position and, imaginatively, into the scene itself. He
supposes himself one of several "young brigands" playing a game at the
center of which is a young woman who might in other circumstances, it
seems, have been Scrooge's daughter.

> As to measuring her waist in sport, as they did, bold young brood, I
> couldn't have done it; I should have expected my arm to have grown
> round it for a punishment, and never come straight again. And yet I
> should have dearly liked, I own, to have touched her lips; to have ques-
> tioned her, that she might have opened them; to have looked upon the
> lashes of her downcast eyes, and never raised a blush; to have let loose
> waves of hair, . . . in short, I should have liked, I do confess, to have had
> the lightest licence of a child, and yet to have been man enough to know
> its value. (81–82)

The merging of narrator, spirit, and Scrooge in the speaker's "I" is the narrative's characteristic way of dramatizing the power of its own representations. And the subject of the passage—the impossibility of touching an
image whose status as image provokes the desire to touch (and holds out
a promise of "value")—might itself serve as a definition of spectacle. But
this seductiveness is a function not only of the image's status as representation but also of what Laura Mulvey calls the "to-be-looked-at-ness" of
what is represented.[13] What prevents the narrator from touching the
woman's skin—the "skin" separating spectator from spectacle—defines

---

[13] As Mulvey explains, "In their traditional exhibitionist role women are simultaneously
looked at and displayed, with their appearance coded for strong visual and erotic impact so
that it can be said to connote *to-be-looked-at-ness.*" "Visual Pleasure and Narrative Cinema,"
in *Visual and Other Pleasures* (Bloomington: Indiana University Press, 1989), 18–19. This
effect is what I refer to as circularity: in representing woman, "A Christmas Carol" (and,
of course, not only that text) highlights a figure already coded for visual impact, culturally
defined in representational terms.

both the reality of what is seen and the spectacle's condition as representation; the combination of desire and inaccessibility hints, as well, at woman's status in the real *as* representation. By framing the scene as fantasy, the text doubles and eroticizes the image's spectacular quality. It is not just projection that makes the idea of touch—of breaking the skin of representation—seem faintly transgressive here; what is presented is already defined as spectacle in Victorian culture.

And as transgressive. For this image is also desirable and untouchable because of the prohibition embedded in the imagined desire of the father for his own daughter. The woman's presence in the dream or fantasy thus echoes and encodes other prohibitions against touch, prohibitions marking gender codes and familial relations. Desire is both elicited by these prohibitions and inscribed in them; participating in that desire, observers become complicit in the scene's cultural dynamics.

Along with mode of representation and content, temporal distance gives the images of Scrooge's past an inherent spectacularity. But what the story offers as everyday reality—Christmas Present—possesses the same projective or illusory quality. It is as if, in order to make Scrooge and the story's readers desire the real, the text has to offer not everyday life but rather its image: everyday life polished to a high sheen.

> The poulterers' shops were still half open, and the fruiterers' were radiant in their glory. There were great round, pot-bellied baskets of chestnuts, shaped like the waistcoats of jolly old gentlemen, lolling at the doors, and tumbling out into the street in their apoplectic opulence. There were ruddy, brown-faced, broad-girthed Spanish Onions, shining in the fatness of their growth like Spanish Friars; and winking from their shelves in wanton slyness at the girls as they went by.... There were pears and apples, clustered high in blooming pyramids; there were bunches of grapes, made in the shopkeepers' benevolence to dangle from conspicuous hooks, that people's mouths might water gratis as they passed. (89–90)

Figs are "moist and pulpy," French plums "blush in modest tartness"; there are "Norfolk Biffins, squab and swarthy, setting off the yellow of the oranges and lemons, and, in the great compactness of their juicy persons, urgently entreating and beseeching to be carried home in paper bags and eaten after dinner" (90). These objects carry the same erotic charge as did the woman in the game-playing scene (and desire is once again modeled, in the image of watering mouths); they also similarly suggest temporal distance, with the spectator positioned as not yet in possession of what he sees. But they have these qualities not because they are framed as projections, although they appear in the scenes shown by the Spirit of Christmas Present, but because they are behind a screen already in place: the shop window. As in the earlier scene, what the text situates within its literary and phantasmatic frames is already culturally framed. Indeed, the idea of "framing" Christmas Present has as its premise the proposition that the real is only desirable—in fact, for Scrooge, only visible—when made into representation.[14]

It makes sense, then, that Victorian England's most important site of value—the home—also appears as image, framed by a perception from without that invests it with longing. There is no difference between the frame imposed by the spirit's presence and what a passerby in the streets would ordinarily see: "As Scrooge and the Spirit went along the streets, the brightness of the roaring fires in kitchens, parlours, and all sorts of rooms, was wonderful. Here, the flickering of the blaze showed preparations for a cosy dinner, with hot plates baking through and through before the fire, and deep red curtains, ready to be drawn, to shut out cold and darkness.... Here, again, were shadows on the window-blind of guests assembling" (99). The representational frames Dickens uses to set fantasy apart from reality—the dynamics that give "A Christmas Carol" its mythic or fairy-tale quality—turn out to be fully operative in the "real" world: for Scrooge and the spirit as they walk through the streets, the world is a series of such frames, of windows and projective screens.

The reality Dickens re-presents is, thus, already encoded as spectacle; it is "to-be-looked-at." And in this way the text, by emphasizing the real quality of its projections and the projective quality of what it offers at the level of the real, dissolves any sustainable difference between the real and

[14] Thomas Richards discusses the way the Great Exhibition synthesized, in the manufactured commodity, techniques associated with spectacle, such as the play of light on the object and the imposed distance between spectator and object. But the presence of these techniques in the "Carol" suggests that both Dickens and the Exhibition drew upon forms of representation widely present in everyday life, ones influenced perhaps most significantly by the use of plate glass. See Richards, *The Commodity Culture of Victorian England* (Stanford: Stanford University Press, 1990).

the image. Structuring desire through the imposition of fictionalized projections, on the one hand, and showing that desire is already structured by such everyday frames as windows and blinds, on the other, the story effectively demonstrates that the real already possesses the quality of image and shadow—if seen from the point of view of someone positioned outside it. And defining the real as spectacle, the text positions all of its readers outside it. Focusing on objects already fetishized visually (women, home, and food) and framing the already culturally framed, the story defines reality as spectacle—what one watches and remains outside of; investing its representational surface with desirability, the story turns its readers into spectators and positions them outside of everything. At Christmas (when, in Dickens's imagining of the holiday as in contemporary America's, the dominant fiction seems to be the only available reality), the story seems to say, the world is an image; moreover, it is an image in which spectators must seek to see themselves.[15]

This imperative to locate the self within the story's spectacles, associating as it does the representation of the self with the story's other representations, ultimately defines sympathy in the "Carol" in spectatorial terms: as a relation to representation. Scrooge typically loses himself in the "reality" of what he sees, imitating, for instance, the younger Scrooge's manifest identification. The story presents his watching of these scenes not only as the production, witnessing, and loss of self in spectacle (and, analogously, in reading) but also as the taking on of the image's desire. But the scenes prompt compassion as well: Scrooge's identification with his former self leads to sympathy for that self, and, in turn, to sympathy with others, and not only with images. "There was a boy singing a Christmas Carol at my door last night. I should like to have given him something: that's all," he says after witnessing the first scene of his boyhood self (73). The narrative of the development of fellow feeling offered here makes the two kinds of sympathy (identification and compassion) appear to be continuous, as if the opening up of a space between the self and its representation produces a general desire to identify, which can then be detached from the

---

[15] This collapse of reality and illusion suggests Jean Baudrillard's simulacra. But I am arguing not that the commodity form dominates culture, but rather that commodity culture draws its power from its status as an exemplary form of culture—its identity with culture as a system of representations.

self and shifted to some other identity. Indeed, throughout the story the presence of visual representation is identified with the presence of Scrooge's former self (the sight of Fezziwig's ball renders him "unconsciously" like his former self), and representation takes on a nostalgic quality, as windows or screens define a temporal distance between observer and observed. The scenes of Scrooge's past always possess more "presence" than he does; the younger Scrooge has a natural ability to identify with representations that the older Scrooge recovers as soon as the scenes are presented to him. In several ways, then, the story ties the ability to sympathize with images to the restoring of a past self to presence.

Positioning Scrooge as a reader and interpreter of cultural scenes, Dickens's story recalls Geertz's definition of culture as a system of signs to be read. But reading in "A Christmas Carol" also includes an element of internalization—or more precisely what Louis Althusser has called interpellation, a process he imagines "along the lines of the most commonplace everyday police (or other) hailing: 'Hey, you there!' " In this theoretical street scene, "the hailed individual will turn round. By this mere one-hundred-and-eighty-degree physical conversion, he becomes a *subject*."[16] As Althusser maintains, the individual can respond to the policeman's hailing only if already a subject. According to this narrative, if Scrooge learns his lessons with astonishing quickness, he does so because what is represented as learning in fact demonstrates that in his heart he knows them already. Reading, for the spectator of the story's scenes, is staged as the recovery of knowledge the reader once possessed.[17]

Althusser dismisses the apparently tautological structure of his narrative (the problem that the subject must already be a subject in order to respond); for the sake of "convenience and clarity," he writes, he has presented in sequential form what "in reality" is not sequential.[18] But Dickens's location of spectatorial desire in the speaking commodities be-

---

[16] Althusser, "Ideology and Ideological State Apparatuses: Notes toward an Investigation," in *Lenin and Philosophy* (New York: Monthly Review, 1971), 174.

[17] This interpretation offers a solution to what Elliot Gilbert has dubbed "the Scrooge Problem": "the unconvincing ease and apparent permanence of Scrooge's reformation." Scrooge's "ease" also suggests a projection of the text's ideal reader, compelled, as Scrooge is throughout, by the power of the story's representations. See Gilbert, "The Ceremony of Innocence: Charles Dickens's *A Christmas Carol*," *PMLA* 90 (1975): 22.

[18] Althusser, "Ideology and Ideological State Apparatuses," 174.

hind the shop window suggests that the narrative structure of Althusser's example exposes a similar narrativity in the capitalist subject's identity. The images of Christmases Past invite Scrooge's identification and imitation, but access to their reality is blocked by their status as representation. The objects Scrooge sees in the "real" world, however—such as the Norfolk Biffins that ask to be "carried home in paper bags"—*are* conscious of the spectator, and they explicitly invite participation in the form of possession. Visual representation inscribes the spectator as absence or lack and, in their fullness, these images emphasize that lack. But the relation between spectator and image is reversed, as these commodities call out to the spectator to complete them.

In the scenes of Christmases Past, Scrooge's (and by implication any spectator's or reader's) relation to representation is articulated in terms of absorption and self-loss: to supplement his own lack, Scrooge desires the presence projected by the image. But the images in the window are presented as desiring the spectator, now figured as consumer, whose completion of the scene depends on recognizing and identifying with their desire. Indeed, the logic of Dickens's speaking commodities seems contradictory at first. When one desires the objects that "speak" to one, the speaking appears to manifest either the external world's acknowledgment of one's individuality (as if, when a commodity says, "Hey, you there!" something essential about the self is being confirmed) or a recognition that the self requires something beyond itself to become individual or complete. In fact, this narrative may be said to display the same "convenient" logic as Althusser's, demonstrating that the individual who becomes a subject already is one. But the apparent contradiction might also be said to elaborate modern capitalism's construction of a temporally diffuse, or narrativized, subject—the kind implicit in the temporal division and reconstruction of Scrooge's life. For such a subject, that is, only the moment of consumption offers an illusion of presence, giving the self that consumes the opportunity to coincide, phantasmatically, with the idealized and temporally detached self projected into the object consumed. In a never-ending narrative of self-creation and transformation, that is, commodity culture may be said to work its effects by making its subjects feel incomplete without the objects they may purchase to complete themselves. Through the purchase of commodities, spectators become present to themselves, expressing an identification with representation and perhaps, like Scrooge, seeking the presence projected in images of a former self.[19] Sympathy with representation, then, links sympathy as compassion with the construction of the subject as spectator and consumer.

Dickens's speaking commodities thus literalize and dramatize Scrooge's implicit relation to representation throughout the story. All the scenes Scrooge is shown "speak" to him, positioning him as spectator and as desiring subject. But unlike the other images he sees, the commodities provide him with something to do, enabling him to participate in the circulation of representations the text defines as participation in culture.[20]

———

By the time Scrooge gets to the third of the series of scenes shown to him by the spirits, he has become an accomplished reader. He knows he should seek some meaning, as well as his own image, in these scenes, and he does so with confidence. "Scrooge was at first inclined to be surprised that the Spirit should attach importance to conversations apparently so trivial; but feeling assured that they must have some hidden purpose, he set himself to consider what it was likely to be. . . . [N]othing doubting that to whomsoever they applied they had some latent moral for his own improvement, he resolved to treasure up every word he heard, and everything he saw; and especially to observe the shadow of himself when it appeared. . . . He looked about in that very place for his own image" (113).

[19] The scene after the ball similarly imagines a consolidation of past and present: its fantasy of "presence" combines "the lightest licence of the child" with a man's knowledge of value.

[20] My interest lies in asserting not that readers have no agency—that the story's claims are irresistible—but rather that "A Christmas Carol," like any other text, will interpellate those subjects who respond to its call, those for whom the text compels or affirms belief in the feelings and cultural truths it represents. My reading thus participates to some extent in the "always already" structure of Althusser's narrative. I do not mean to suggest that such readers cannot read otherwise; my own argument, as well as discussions by Teresa de Lauretis and Kaja Silverman about the way considerations of gender complicate arguments about interpellation, may contribute to such revision. Silverman's discussion of Jacques Rancière's term "dominant fiction," as a story or image "through which a society figures consensus" (Silverman, *Male Subjectivity,* 30) helps elucidate the claim I want to make about the "Carol"—that it figures consensus in the process of identification I outline here. But the best evidence for the story's success at interpellation is the spectacle of social cohesion that takes place around its images each December. Those who resist the spirit of the "Carol" and of the holiday are, after all, nothing but a bunch of old Scrooges.

But his image does not seem to be there; instead there is the shrouded body and a conversation about the profits that can rightfully be made from it, given the way the living person had profited from others. "I see, I see," says Scrooge, thinking he has absorbed the lesson. "The case of this unhappy man might be my own" (117). In a moment, however, the thankful distance implicit in the conventional Christian formula for sympathy—"there but for the grace of God"—is exposed by a startlingly literal literary identification: the case of this unhappy man *is* his own. The scene projected by the spirit is now the place in which Scrooge doesn't want to identify. The text teaches not only the need to project the self into the consciousnesses of others but also the potential unpleasantness of doing so: the desire *not* to be in the other's place.

And that desire points toward what occupies the position of the real in this text: the images that pose an alternative to the story's scenes of cultural value. For although the story collapses the difference between reality and illusion, turning both into image, the scene of Scrooge's death (and indeed all scenes in which Scrooge appears as his present-day, undesirable self) signifies the real, pointing as it does toward the end of the narrative of Scrooge's actual life rather than toward the ideal life that will replace it. "Yet to come," like serial publication, seems to promise plenitude; indeed, Dickens's text dramatizes what Metz calls the ability of cinematic representation to construct a spectator who both identifies with an image and feels temporally distant from it—who, paradoxically identifying with his image, can only "catch up with himself at the last minute."[21] But Christmas Yet to Come projects a grim scene by contrast with the seductive images offered previous to and alongside it. Scrooge is offered the end of the series, the inevitable consequence of a life lived outside the representations presented to him and to readers as life, or as cultural life—indeed, as the identification of the two. "A Christmas Carol" accomplishes its interpellation of its readers not, finally, by modeling spectatorship in the person of Scrooge, but rather by identifying culture with images and scenes to be absent from which is, effectively, not to exist. Scrooge's death is a metaphor for his absence from representation; more powerfully, it is a metaphor for his absence from culture, defined *as* representation: as a series of images and structure of significations in relation to which, as he

---

[21] Metz, *Imaginary Signifier*, 96.

learns to "read" them, his own image takes on meaning. His death realizes, and teaches him to fear, the absence from the world of representations he—and we—have been shown.[22]

Dickens's text doubles, by framing, the scenes the spirits project or otherwise show and other kinds of frames, such as the windows of shops and of homes. Habituating readers to frames and focusing on the already spectacular, it presents the real as a series of images that exist even in the absence of any visible picture-making technology. Moving its frames in and out of visibility, the story reproduces the logic of the relation between cultural representation and ideology, in which frames are sometimes literal—in pictures, literary texts, or movie screens—and sometimes appear as an inherent effect on objects and vision. "A Christmas Carol" thus provides an anatomy of the way in which, in a print culture and even more emphatically in a "society of the spectacle," cultural values become manifest in—and as—a collection of images. More precisely, they become a way of seeing in which the real is filtered through cultural frames that precede any particular manifestation of it. Making the Christmas spirit visible and presenting visibility as a threat, the story dramatizes the coerciveness inherent in a culture's ability to endow certain artifacts, persons, and activities with "presence." And the conversion of Scrooge's feeling provides an analogue for the story's commodifying power: while alluding to the recovery of the natural, both reveal the absence of anything outside the frames of culture.

———

The culture from which Scrooge has been absent is, of course, commodity culture; his failure to participate in human fellowship is signaled by his

---

[22] Vicki Goldberg discusses the idea of images as collective culture in an article about the use, in advertising, of news photographs of catastrophes. "Whole populations," she writes, "have the same mental-image files, which constitute a large part of the common culture." "Images of Catastrophe as Corporate Ballyhoo," *New York Times*, 3 May 1992, sec. 2, p. 33. Such image repertoires, while obviously increased by the existence of cinema and television, would exist as soon as and wherever images are circulated. Elizabeth Eisenstein also suggests as much: e.g., *The Printing Revolution in Early Modern Europe* (Cambridge: Cambridge University Press, 1983), 37. The identity between culture and a series of visual images is reinforced by Dickens's description of his memories of Christmas as a series of images (see Davis, *Lives and Times*, 66–67).

refusal of, and need to learn, a gift giving defined as the purchase and exchange of commodities.[23] The need for conversion the text stresses and the form Scrooge's awakening takes resemble what Thomas Haskell has described as the social discipline and character modification effected by modern capitalism, which created the cognitive conditions that made humanitarianism (in particular, the abolition of slavery) possible, conditions such as the development of conscience and the necessity of living "partly in the future," anticipating the long-term consequences of one's actions. For Haskell, the conditions for humanitarianism were created by the "lessons" of the market.[24]

Scrooge lacks, Marley's ghost informs him, "the spirit within him [that] should walk abroad among his fellow-men, and travel far and wide" (61). The awakening of this spirit promises him affective relations where he previously had none, as well as improved business prospects. Scrooge's ability to project into past and future teaches him, and is concurrent with, his ability to project himself into the consciousnesses of others; both skills indicate possession of a spirit that travels far and wide—what might be called a spirit of capitalism, a capitalist sensibility.[25] The investment that commodities require in this text is the same as that which spectacle (and literary identification) invite—indeed, compel: each attests to the possession of a dispersed self capable of being in several places at once. As the story illustrates in an exemplary fashion, the extension of self required by the humanist ideology of "A Christmas Carol" also characterizes the capitalist subject's relationship to representation.

[23] Scrooge does participate in the economic system; Davis discusses the idea that before his conversion Scrooge promotes a "supply side" economy (*Lives and Times,* chap. 7).

[24] Thomas Haskell, "Capitalism and the Origins of the Humanitarian Sensibility," *American Historical Review* 90 (1985): 551, 560.

[25] The serialization of Scrooge's life (its division into past, present, and future) reflects the link between capitalism, serial publication, and the need for "projection"—living partly in the future—that Haskell defines as necessary to a capitalist sensibility.

Haskell quotes Defoe on the connection between business and metaphorical travel: "Every new voyage the merchant contrives is a project, and ships are sent from port to port, as markets and merchandizes differ, by the help of strange and universal intelligence; wherein some are so exquisite, so swift, and so exact, that a merchant sitting at home in his counting-house, at once converses with all parts of the known world" ("An Essay upon Projects"; quoted in Haskell, "Capitalism and the Origins of the Humanitarian Sensibility," 558).

Dickens's text draws out further implications of the connection between capitalism and the spirit that travels far and wide, implications that reintroduce an idea of circularity into an understanding of capitalism's projective effects. Like women, home, and food, the poor in Dickens's text are projections or spectacles of the already spectacular; fittingly, the images most frequently cited as evidence of the story's affective power are the children displayed by the Ghost of Christmas Present, allegorical figures named Ignorance and Want. If, in Haskell's formulation, capitalism produces a spirit that travels far and wide, it also creates the distance between classes that makes such traveling necessary, incorporating distance into daily life and turning immediate surroundings into allegorical figures or projections.[26]

The story's most famous icon, Tiny Tim, reproduces its economy of representation and consumption. Scrooge's macabre remark that the Cratchits' Christmas turkey is "twice the size of Tiny Tim" associates such plenitude with the object of sympathy in a manner that has become paradigmatic for "A Christmas Carol" itself. Exemplifying the feeling that leads to the gift, Tiny Tim appropriately enough imagines himself, at one point, as sympathetic spectacle: "he hoped the people saw him in the church, because he was a cripple" (94). Cratchit's family dines off the image that has become, for Dickens's text, the emblem of an inexhaustible fund of sympathetic capital. And the name for that capital, here, is "spirit." The gift is a visible manifestation of spirit, of a reader's willingness to enter into and identify with the text's circulation of representations. That identification accounts for the story's apparently limitless capacity for transformation: capturing the commodity's potential for sympathy, "A Christmas Carol" constitutes itself as an endlessly sympathetic commodity, its variable surface reflecting an unchanging ability to embody readers' and spectators' desires.[27]

---

[26] These images reflect the sense in which, by the time of Dickens's story, poverty was a spectacle rather than a visible reality for many members of the middle and upper classes. See Gareth Stedman Jones's discussion of the "separation between classes" in *Outcast London: A Study in the Relationship between Classes in Victorian Society* (New York: Pantheon, 1971), part 3.

[27] "A Christmas Carol" is, of course, concerned with relations between employer and employee—between the businessman and his clerk. But this story of class relations is mapped onto the symbolic context of a patriarchal Christian order, and its cross-class

In a cultural scenario of its own making, the marketing of "A Christmas Carol" consolidates and elaborates upon the text's interweavings of consumerism and sympathy. If vision's ability to evoke presence serves as a primary way of naturalizing ideological effects in the "Carol," the story's annual return may be said to perform the same function by making specific feelings and activities, including reading or viewing the story itself, seasonal imperatives. The "Christmas book" (for the "Carol" initiated a series of Christmas books) naturalizes literary production, linking text and author to holiday and season—a season already bound up with ideas of resurrection and eternal presence.[28] With the metaphorical deaths and rebirths of Scrooge and Tiny Tim echoing its annual return, the story associates the idea of Christian renewal with its own form of production. And in a way that further associates natural life with textual production, Scrooge's life—its ending rewritten by the reader-spectator, who thereby becomes his life's owner and producer—displays all the malleability of the serially published text. Indeed, Scrooge's exchangeable identity, and the story's emphasis on Christmas as a time when identities become exchangeable, may have given both Dickens and Christmas new currency by revealing the fungibility of self and time implicit in both Christian conversion and modern consumer culture.

A capitalist sensibility is perhaps most evident in the story's external and internal refusals of temporality: in the identification with a time of year that ensures its annual return and the offer—to Scrooge, to its readers or viewers, and, theoretically, to the poor themselves—of an endlessly repeatable cycle of failure and recovery, figured as an alienation from, and reacceptance into, an ever-forgiving culture. The reader-spectator who identifies with the Christmas spirit identifies with a culture in which that spirit will

---

appeal attests to the consensus achieved thereby. The story allegorizes and, in its own terms, ideally effects the inscription of its readers into Victorian culture's dominant ideological structures. To the extent that those structures remain the same for contemporary readers and spectators, the story may be said to achieve the same effects. But in that context it also serves as a different kind of culture-text, successfully representing Victorian England for present-day readers precisely because of its ability to condense culture into a series of representations. "A Christmas Carol" exemplifies the way in which, in a spectacular society, images mediate cultural memory.

[28] "We cannot remember when we first knew this story. It is allied in our consciousness to our awareness of day and night, winter and spring" (Davis, *Lives and Times*, 238).

always be necessary; the self as image is a renewable self, forever holding out the possibility of a new ending. Such an interpretation depends not on the idea that the story has no effect on the external world, but only that such an effect is never conceived as an ending; it is, rather, part of a cycle to which the story's own representation—having become a part of the culture it represents—also belongs. For Dickens, the term *spirit* jokingly yet insistently signals the weakness of the boundary between the invisible and the visible—and warns of the likelihood that the former will manifest itself as the latter.[29] Thus "A Christmas Carol" returns annually and, more often than not, visibly, with an emphasis (and a relentlessness) it has itself projected. In the story's identification with Christmas and in the repetition this identification ensures, Dickens's culture-text promotes its own endlessness as well as that of the culture it has helped to create.

[29] "A Christmas Carol" was the first, and the most frequently performed, of Dickens's public readings. Although the text varied from night to night, the crucial feature of the readings was reportedly the author's impersonation of his characters and his evident identification with the "spirit" of both book and holiday. See Philip Collins, *Charles Dickens: The Public Readings* (London: Oxford University Press, 1975), 4-7.

2

Detecting the Beggar:
Arthur Conan Doyle, Henry Mayhew,
and the Construction of Social Identity

"A Christmas Carol" renders visible the connections between
sympathetic identification and the consuming subject, showing how both
are consolidated in an identification with representation. Arthur Conan
Doyle's "The Man with the Twisted Lip" (1891) provides a late-century
unraveling of that same structure: confusing and confounding the identities of gentleman, beggar, and capitalist, the text literalizes the metaphor of
sympathetic identification as an investment of self in other by aligning that
identification with, and identifying it as, economic exchange. In Conan
Doyle's narrative of mistaken identity, in which the discovery is made that
the beggar really is a gentleman, the attenuation of self required by social
sympathy reproduces the structure of exchange that both defines and dismantles identity under capitalism.

In "The Man with the Twisted Lip," Sherlock Holmes is uncharacteristi-
cally baffled by the disappearance of Mr. Neville St. Clair, a well-to-do gentleman who, for years, while traveling to the City each day ostensibly to look
after his interests, has been disguising himself as a beggar named Hugh Boone,
having found begging to be less arduous and more profitable than other professions available to him. Holmes, seemingly relying on his expectation that
the case will yield the usual murder victim, advances the idea that St. Clair is

dead—just as Mrs. St. Clair produces a letter she claims was recently written by her husband. Wedded to his interpretation—appearing, almost, to desire the death he has theorized—the detective attempts to explain away the clues that suggest St. Clair is still living: St. Clair's ring, included with the letter, "proves nothing," as "it may have been taken from him"; the letter itself may "have been written on Monday and only posted to-day."[1] The ease with which Holmes detaches the signs of St. Clair's identity from St. Clair, and the fact that it is his job to reattach them, point toward the problematic of identity the story uncovers: Inspector Bradstreet's solemn insistence, at the end of the case, that there be "no more of Hugh Boone" reflects a determination to eliminate precisely the kind of instability Holmes here acknowledges. For the possibility that identity can be dissociated from its signs undermines, even as it provokes desire for, the stable categories of identity both detective fiction and Henry Mayhew's studies of the urban poor seek to construct.

Holmes is called to investigate after Mrs. St. Clair, returning from an excursion into the City, looks up to see in the window of an opium den (where St. Clair puts on and off his disguise) what appears to be an assault upon her husband, but is actually his manifestation of surprise at seeing her. The story describes not a crime but a disturbance in the social field, a confusion of social identity, which it becomes Holmes's task to resolve. That such a disturbance should appear as a crime makes sense given the fantasy of knowledge and social control detective fiction represents: St. Clair's indeterminacy—the mobility that allows him to occupy two social spheres at once—disturbs the possibility of fixing social identity on which detective fiction, and Holmes's cases, rest.[2] And that indeterminacy is expressed both in St. Clair's ability to transform himself and in the figures between which he oscillates—the gentleman and the beggar—who were, for the Victorians, ambiguous and sometimes interchangeable entities.

———

The scenario wherein a beggar is revealed to be a gentleman or nobleman in disguise is a familiar one; behind "The Man with the Twisted Lip," ac-

---

[1] All quotations from "The Man with the Twisted Lip" and other stories have been taken from Arthur Conan Doyle, *The Complete Sherlock Holmes* (New York: Doubleday, 1930). Titles will be noted in parentheses in the text.

[2] The definitive work on this topic is D. A. Miller, *The Novel and the Police* (Berkeley: University of California Press, 1988).

cording to Donald A. Redmond, lies Victor Hugo's *L'homme qui rit,* which tells of a nobleman stolen as a child and disfigured, so he won't be recognized, with a scar across the mouth that makes him appear to be smiling or laughing.[3] In the late nineteenth century, the oppositions and similarities mobilized by a pairing of these figures were particularly charged: in the context of changing ideas about gentlemanliness, for instance, popular ideology had it that a beggar might very well be a gentleman; at the same time an increase in financial speculation and unexpected, devastating crashes made it appear likely, at least from the gentleman's perspective, that a gentleman might someday have to beg. But rather than simply place a familiar tale in a new context, Conan Doyle's story demonstrates that the new context suggestively expands the problematic of identity implicit in the tale. For even as it does away with Hugh Boone, restoring St. Clair to his proper identity, "The Man with the Twisted Lip" dismantles detective fiction's fantasy of social control, establishing social identity only to disclose, simultaneously, the absence of the identities it seeks to expose.

The figure of the finance capitalist confounds the attempt—central to both Mayhew's project and Conan Doyle's—to define identity in relation to work.[4] The person of the finance capitalist remains detached from the system of production in which he participates; where the laborer might suffer "in his existence," Elaine Scarry writes, the capitalist suffers only "in his money."[5] The legalizing of joint-stock companies in 1844 and the institution of limited liability soon after increasingly separated businesses from those who invested in them, enabling capital, effectively, to carry on by itself, with "not so much as a sign of the Capitalist to be seen."[6] And

---

[3] Donald A. Redmond, *Sherlock Holmes: A Study in Sources* (Montreal: McGill-Queen's University Press, 1982), 55.

[4] Holmes characteristically identifies individuals by their professions: "By a man's fingernails, by his coat-sleeve, by his boots, by his trouser-knees, by the callousities of his forefinger and thumb, by his expression, by his shirt-cuffs—by each of these things a man's calling is plainly revealed" (*A Study in Scarlet*).

[5] Elaine Scarry, *The Body in Pain* (New York: Oxford University Press, 1985), 263.

[6] Leland Jenks, *The Migration of British Capital to 1875* (New York, 1927); quoted in Barbara Weiss, *The Hell of the English: Bankruptcy and the Victorian Novel* (Lewisburg, Pa.: Bucknell University Press, 1986), 139.

because of the detachment of "his own embodied psyche, will, and consciousness" from the manner in which he produces his income, as Scarry puts it, the capitalist might well be called an "exempted person": "it is that absence of self, that liberating relation, that attribute of nonparticipation," which "is summarized by the word 'capitalist.' "[7]

Such an exempted person is Charles Dickens's Alfred Lammle, who, in place of the usual markers of identity and gentlemanliness, has "Shares":

> The mature young gentleman is a person of property. He invests his property. He goes, in a condescending amateurish way, into the City, attends meetings of directors, and has to do with traffic in Shares. As is well known to the wise in their generation, traffic in Shares is the one thing to have to do with in this world. Have no antecedents, no established character, no cultivation, no ideas, no manners; have Shares. Have Shares enough to be on Boards of Direction in capital letters, oscillate on mysterious business between London and Paris, and be great. Where does he come from? Shares. Where is he going to? Shares. What are his tastes? Shares. Has he any principles? Shares. What squeezes him into Parliament? Shares. Perhaps he never of himself achieved success in anything, never originated anything, never produced anything? Sufficient answer to all; Shares.[8]

"Shares" substitute for cultivation, manners, principles, and production, replacing what had appeared to be substantive with what doesn't appear at all. In *Our Mutual Friend,* the sinister implications of such absence are manifest in Lammle's deceitfulness, as well as in the novel's paradigmatic image of the bodies Gaffer Hexam pulls from the river, devoid of any distinguishing characteristics but for their clothing and the money he retrieves from it. And it is in the atmosphere created by the novel's intertwining of finance and identity that Boffin engineers his "pious fraud"; in such a context, Dickens seems to say, not even well-intentioned characters need adhere to any notions novel readers might hold of consistency or legibility.

---

[7] Scarry, *Body in Pain,* 265.

[8] Charles Dickens, *Our Mutual Friend* (Harmondsworth, England: Penguin 1977), 159–60.

The identity of the "man who does something in the City," then, seemed as ungrounded as the City's prosperity itself did to many nineteenth-century observers—a perception no doubt enhanced by the frequency with which, in the second half of the century, prominent businessmen were revealed to have built their empires on foundations of nonexistent capital.[9] (Of the seemingly unbounded proliferation and circulation of wealth in the City, one contemporary observer wrote, "We find many thousands who live by supplying one another's wants; and the question arises, whence comes the original means by which such a state of things is rendered possible? What, in fact, is the primary fund of which these persons manage to secure a share?")[10] In his passivity and detachment, in the disinterested relation he bears to his interests, the "man who does something in the City" exemplifies the kind of fungible identity that, his contemporaries feared, inhabited a realm of exchange divorced from production.[11]

The middle classes in the nineteenth century regarded the unproductive gentleman in a dubious light. Since neither he nor the beggar put in what they regarded as an honest day's labor, both were subject to general suspicion—the suspicion, in particular, of attempting to deceive those who did. A section of Mayhew's *London Labour and the London Poor,* included under the rubric "Those Who Will Not Work" and written by Andrew Halliday, discusses those "beggars and cheats" who, although physically sound enough to perform "honest" labor, choose instead to make their livings by deceiving the charitable. This "false beggar," as Mayhew represents him, is a kind of actor, taking on specific costumes and mannerisms for the performance of his roles. Of one type of "street campaigner," for example, Halliday writes: "He is imitative, and in his time plays many parts.... His bearing is most military; he keeps his neck straight, his chin

[9] See Weiss, *Hell of the English,* chap. 7.

[10] Francis Sheppard, *London, 1808–1870: The Infernal Wen* (Berkeley: University of California Press, 1971), 81–82.

[11] On identity and exchange see Catherine Gallagher, "George Eliot and *Daniel Deronda:* The Prostitute and the Jewish Question," in *Sex, Politics, and Science in the Nineteenth-Century Novel,* ed. Ruth Bernard Yeazell (Baltimore: Johns Hopkins University Press, 1986), 39–62.

in . . . he is as stiff as an embalmed preparation, for which, but for the motion of his eyes, you might mistake him."[12] And in order to see through
this deceptive surface, the man on the street requires Holmesian powers of
detection. In one instance Halliday, in the company of a friend who had
once been a sailor, comes across what appears to him to be "a brother sailor
in distress." "Of course you will give him something," he says to his friend,
to which remark the friend responds negatively: "Did you see him
spit? . . . A real sailor never spits to wind'ard. *Why, he could'nt*" (415).
Unmasking the "false beggar" involves knowing the "true" version of the
character he attempts to impersonate, and it is the purpose of Mayhew's
work to codify these types, granting the public the ability to distinguish
"true" identity from "false."

Halliday is particularly offended by the figure whose pose conflates the
beggar and the gentleman. The begging-letter writer, who "is the con-
necting link between mendicity and external respectability,"

> affects white cravats, soft hands, and filbert nails. He oils his hair, cleans
> his boots, and wears a portentous stick-up collar. The light of other days
> of gentility and comfort casts a halo of "deportment" over his well-
> brushed, white-seamed coat, his carefully darned black-cloth gloves, and
> pudgy gaiters. . . . Among the many varieties of mendacious beggars,
> there is none so detestable as this hypocritical scoundrel, who, with an
> ostentatiously-submissive air, and false pretense of faded fortunes, tells his
> plausible tale of undeserved suffering, and extracts from the pockets of
> the superficially good-hearted their sympathy and coin. (403)

For Halliday, the link between mendicity and mendacity is more than
merely linguistic. But why should the begging-letter writer offend more
than other beggars who, through various schemes, deprive the charitable
of their "sympathy and coin"? Halliday's dislike of this character seems related to his pretense to respectability: the "intuitive knowledge" of the
"nobility and landed gentry" that aids him in his deceptive practice. The
begging-letter writer implies by his behavior that gentlemanliness is

---

[12] Henry Mayhew, *London Labour and the London Poor* (New York: A. M. Kelley, 1967),
4:418. Subsequent references included in the text.

merely a matter of surfaces, disturbingly suggesting, in his capacity for imitation, the gentleman's own imitability.

Such a possibility had already been explored in Lord Chesterfield's *Letters to his Son* (1774), in which the author tells his readers how to "act" the gentleman. "When you go into good company... observe carefully their turn, their manners, their address, and conform your own to them. But this is not all, neither; go deeper still; observe their characters, and pry, as far as you can, into both their hearts and their heads. Seek for their particular merit, their predominant passion, or their prevailing weakness; and you will then know what to bait your hook with to catch them."[13] As the general dislike with which Chesterfield's work was received in the eighteenth and nineteenth centuries demonstrates, the notion that the gentleman was imitable touched a particularly sensitive nerve. Robin Gilmour points out that the behavior Chesterfield recommends was in fact necessary for social advancement in eighteenth-century society. But by recommending particular forms of behavior rather than the cultivation of moral qualities, Chesterfield showed "how easily civilised behaviour could be reduced to the lowest common denominator," and revealed "how weak the links between manners and morals" might be.[14] Chesterfield's advice about "catching" members of "good company" closely resembles Mayhew's account of the begging-letter writer's scheme: both the gentleman, in Chesterfield's view, and the "false beggar," in Mayhew's, use knowledge of a group or class to imitate it and to advance themselves by means of that imitation. Both figures take dissimulation as their means of livelihood, cultivating exterior rather than interior; neither works in any sense Mayhew is willing to call work. Both, therefore, stand outside the wide realm of ordinary middle-class life, which made work into a moral imperative and accused both the gentleman and the "false beggar" of "living off the toil of others."[15]

Potentially productive individuals not engaged in productive labor—regarded, as Mayhew's "will not work" implies, as refusing work—not only

[13] Quoted in Robin Gilmour, *The Idea of the Gentleman in the Victorian Novel* (London: Allen & Unwin, 1981), 15–17.

[14] Gilmour is quoting Sheldon Rothblatt, *Tradition and Change in English Liberal Education* (London: Faber, 1976), 31; Gilmour, *Idea of the Gentleman,* 19.

[15] How Mayhew articulates this for the beggar is described below. Ruskin wrote that "Gentlemen have to learn that it is no part of their duty or privilege to live on other people's toil." *Modern Painters;* quoted in Gilmour, *Idea of the Gentleman,* 7.

offended the age's emphasis on energy and productivity, but they also presented the Victorians with a constant threat of social unrest. Describing the Poor Law's inability to meet the needs of those in want, Halliday cites a letter to the *Times* that expresses this anxiety: "It is an admitted and notorious fact, that after a fortnight's frost the police courts were besieged by thousands who professed to be starving.... It was the saturnalia if not of mendicancy, at least of destitution. The police stood aside while beggars possessed the thoroughfares.... We had thought that the race of sturdy vagrants and valiant beggars was extinct, or at least that they dared no longer show themselves. But here they were in open day like the wretches which are said to emerge out of darkness on the day of a revolution" (398). The New Poor Law of 1834 had as one of its main objectives the separation of the able-bodied beggar from others who could not raise themselves out of poverty. Mayhew's system of identification, separating those who "cannot work" from those who "will not work," fulfills the state's need to bring into the light of "open day" figures who represent a threat before they themselves choose to emerge. And it is the function of Mayhew's labor and of Sherlock Holmes's, in this story, to put both the gentleman and the able-bodied beggar to work.

But the anxiety about "false" beggary is also an anxiety about the theatricality of the social world: about the potential falseness of social surfaces, the susceptibility to manipulation of social identity. The "true beggar," "who has no means of livelihood," Halliday writes, "has invariably commanded the respect and excited the compassion of his fellow men." But "the beggar whose poverty is not real, but assumed, is no longer a beggar in the true sense of the word, but a cheat and an impostor, and as such he is naturally regarded, not as an object for compassion, but as an enemy of the state" (393). What, however, is a beggar "in the true sense of the word"? What, indeed, is a "false" beggar? For Mayhew, the "false beggar" is not just a corrupter of images but a corrupter of language: the desire for a "true sense of the word," like the desire for a "true beggar," is a wish for an absolute correspondence between sign and referent. A "false beggar" is, more precisely, a professional: one who knows the code of beggary and seeks to manipulate it, to sell a salable identity. Both "true" and "false" beggars deal in images, exchanging identity for coin. The term "false" is important, however, because it maintains the possibility of locating "true" identity: identity not subject to the vicissitudes of representation.

As part of the apparatus of the Poor Law, the concern with "true" and "false" beggars reflects a desire to locate the truth of identity in the body by means of the separation of productive from unproductive bodies. (The comment made by Halliday's friend—"Did you see him spit"—defines identity in terms of the body's adaptation to labor.) Mayhew locates the truth of the beggar's identity in the presence or absence of the potential for production: the "true beggar" is one who cannot, for reasons of physical disability or illness, work. And if the unproductive body is true, it follows for Mayhew that the productive body is at least potentially false; the capacity for productive labor without any sign of a product suggests that the impulse toward productivity is directed toward the body itself. On the one hand, a choice of profession may be regarded as a choice of identity. But, on the other, the very idea of choice opens up the possibility of multiple identities—an instability that the idea of an identity divided between work and home attempts to resolve, as I will discuss later. Productivity poses the threat of multiple identities; for Mayhew, the "false beggar" epitomizes this problem by making the production of identity a profession in itself.[16]

But the "false beggar" also disturbs because, in his capacity for producing representations, he endangers the identities of those who encounter him. As David Marshall has argued, sympathy—defined as the imagined reproduction of another's feeling within an observer's mind—is inherently bound up with representation and theatricality."[17] The beggar may be the focus of such intense concern about the possibility of separating "true" identity from "false"—for us as well as for the Victorians—because his confrontation with the potential charity-giver presents an exemplary moment of theatricality in social life: a moment in which, in Marshall's words, individuals "face each other as actors and spectators" (136). And that confrontation involves an exchange not only of money but also of identity— identity already implicated in a system of representation and exchange.

Halliday's linking of sympathy and coin implicitly connects identity with exchange: the offer of money acts as a sign that the observer has in-

---

[16] On individualism and the choice of a profession, see Fredric Jameson, *The Political Unconscious* (Ithaca: Cornell University Press, 1981), 249.

[17] David Marshall, *The Surprising Effects of Sympathy: Marivaux, Diderot, Rousseau, and Mary Shelley* (Chicago: University of Chicago Press, 1988), 21.

volved his own identity—including his belief in his own ability to tell "true" from "false"—in an exchange with the beggar's. Sympathy and coin, themselves within the realm of representation, are presented as guarantors of authenticity in the transaction between charity-giver and beggar, offering evidence of the charity-giver's belief in the truth of the beggar's image, as well as in his ability to read that truth. (Hugh Boone is supported by the public, and tolerated by the police, because they know him to be a "professional"; less important than the truth or falsity of the beggar's identity is the comfort they receive from being reassured of their ability to tell the difference.) What happens, then, when the observer discovers that he has unwittingly identified with a representation? The category of "false beggar" not only reveals the observer's failure to read identity correctly, but it also reveals sympathy, coin, and identity to be mere currency: no single one of these, offered in exchange, can guarantee the authenticity of the others. The "false beggar" makes visible a system of exchange wherein sympathy, coin, and identity can circulate endlessly, never drawing upon any fund of truth.

But the "false beggar" also takes advantage of the exchange between himself and the potential charity-giver as exchange. Adam Smith argues that while sympathy involves the observer's projection of himself into the sufferer's situation, it also requires the sufferer who desires sympathy to imagine how he would appear to a spectator: "As they are constantly considering what they themselves would feel, if they actually were the sufferers, so he is as constantly led to imagine in what manner he would be affected if he was only one of the spectators of his own situation."[18] Both figures in the "scene of sympathy," Marshall writes, "play the roles of spectator and spectacle" (173). The potential charity-giver's power inheres both in his ability to give money and in his imaginative projection: the former, in fact, depends upon the vividness and perceived truth of the latter. But that power is undermined by the charity-giver's susceptibility to representation: his imaginative re-creation of the sufferer's situation is matched by the sufferer's need to imagine what will provoke his sympathy. And it is this reciprocity that underlies the anxiety about false

[18] Smith, *The Theory of Moral Sentiments*, 22; quoted in David Marshall, *The Figure of Theater: Shaftesbury, Defoe, Adam Smith, and George Eliot* (New York: Columbia University Press, 1986), 172.

beggary: the "false beggar" endangers the charity-giver's identity by encouraging him to identify with a mere representation. The fiction of the "true beggar" is consolatory, therefore, in its construction of a figure who not only will not, but cannot, project: a figure seen as nothing more than a vessel for the charity-giver's projection. The "false beggar" and the finance capitalist, then, prove to be not only exchangeable figures but also figures *for* exchange—figures whose identities seem to inhere only in representation. And while Mayhew's project would protect the observer's identity by establishing the beggar's, his work finally undermines the safety of both. Similarly Conan Doyle, in a story not only destined for the popular market but to be sold in railway stations to businessmen commuting between home and City, simultaneously assures his readers that false identities can be done away with and implicates those readers, and himself, in the processes of exchange that bring such identities into being.

Just as Mayhew's work pits the beggar and the journalist against each other, so too does Conan Doyle's story associate Holmes and St. Clair through their use of disguise. In its opening section, Watson and his wife receive a visit from Kate Whitney, whose husband Ilsa has disappeared for two days, and who is known by his wife to be in an opium den in the City. Visiting the den to seek him out, Watson there encounters Holmes, disguised as a regular customer. "He sat now as absorbed as ever, very thin, very wrinkled, bent with age, an opium pipe dangling down from his fingers. . . . It took all my self-control to prevent me from breaking out into a cry of astonishment. He had turned his back so that none could see him but I. His form had filled out, his wrinkles were gone, the dull eyes had regained their fire, and there, sitting by the fire and grinning at my surprise, was none other than Sherlock Holmes." Like St. Clair, whose beggar's disguise originally served him when he was a reporter writing a series of articles on begging, Holmes's disguise helps him penetrate the opium den unnoticed. Both Holmes and St. Clair employ disguise in their professions; for both, disguise becomes a metaphor for profession. The transformation undergone in the opium den has its correlative, in Victorian life, in the imagined transformation of the husband and father who disappears mysteriously into "the City" in the morning and returns at night to a family which has no firsthand knowledge of what he does there.[19] And the idea of opium, like that of disguise, allows for a literalization of and play upon the idea of transformation: where Whitney enters the den a "noble" man and emerges "pale, haggard, and unkempt," St. Clair finds that he "could every morning emerge as a squalid beggar and in the evenings transform [himself] into a well-dressed man about town." As Holmes describes him, even though St. Clair "had no occupation," his regular departure for and return from the City every day substitute for one, confirming his good character: he "was interested in several companies and went into town as a rule every morning, returning by the 5:14 from Cannon Street every night." And, indeed, St. Clair gets along very nicely without any evidence of a profession; as he describes his situation, it was possible to continue this activity for years without anyone's actually knowing what he did during the day: "As I grew richer I grew more ambitious, took a house in the country, and eventually married, without anyone having a suspicion as to my real occupation. My wife knew that I had business in the City. She little knew what."

In moving back and forth between the City, the opium den, and the St. Clair home, the story plays St. Clair's various identities against one another: the figure who plies his trade as a beggar in the City every day, through the use of disguise—a painted face, a scar, a shock of red hair—and skillful acting, "a facility in repartee, which improved by practice, and

---

[19] It is useful here to think of Florence Dombey's adventure in the City: having lost, or been lost by, Susan Nipper, Florence finds herself alone, knowing only that she could look for "her father's offices," and that Dombey and Son was "a great power in the City." It is here that she encounters Good Mrs. Brown. Dickens registers the strangeness and bewilderment the City arouses in those who never go there. In the following passage, Florence in her anguish is suspected of "false beggary": "Tired of walking, repulsed and pushed about, anxious for her brother and the nurses, terrified by what she had undergone, and the prospect of encountering her angry father in such an altered state; perplexed and frightened alike by what had passed, and what was passing, and what was yet before her; Florence went upon her weary way with tearful eyes, and once or twice could not help stopping to ease her bursting heart by crying bitterly. But few people noticed her at those times, in the garb she wore: or if they did, believed that she was tutored to excite compassion, and passed on." Charles Dickens, *Dombey and Son* (Harmondsworth, England: Penguin, 1981), 132. Though "altered state" clearly refers to Florence, it also suggests that Florence might find Dombey "altered" in the city.

made me quite a recognized character in the City," versus the domestic
St. Clair, whose concern about "exposure" manifests itself as concern for
his appearance in his children's eyes:"God help me, I would not have them
ashamed of their father." The alignment of disguise with travel into the
City recalls the Victorian commonplace that the husband's and / or father's
true self could be found only at home: that profession was a mask, a false
self put on during the day but gladly relinquished "on the stroke of seven,"
when the husband and father became "himself" again.[20] ("When we
come home, we lay aside our mask and drop our tools, and are no longer
lawyers, sailors, soldiers, statesmen, clergymen, but only men.")[21] But while
St. Clair's disguise reinforces this notion of profession as mask, the story
also implies that his true self may be located in his City life—a possibility
enhanced by his desire to keep that life secret, as well as by the use of his
talents begging allows.

But if St. Clair's true identity is located in the City, in what does that
identity consist? The City appears here not as a place where the Victorian
husband goes to take on a social role, but rather as a place where he goes
to lose one—where, in the anonymity of the financial world or the opium
den, he can find privacy, freedom from the constraints of social and familial roles. Mrs. St. Clair's discovery of her husband results in what looks like
an actual crime—an assault on St. Clair—but it also appears as *her* violation of *his* privacy: she sees him while walking in the City, where he
doesn't expect her to be.[22] (Earlier, another wife acts as spy: Kate Whitney
had "the surest information" that her husband had "made use of an opium
den in the farthest east of the City.") The City and the opium den resemble each other as places where the usual constructions of identity can be
abandoned, together mediating and dismantling the opposition between
City and home: first, by providing a place where identity consists of freedom from identity—freedom found in exchange, in representation—and,

[20] *Mark Rutherford's Deliverance;* quoted in Walter Houghton, *The Victorian Frame of Mind* (New Haven:Yale University Press, 1957), 346.

[21] James Anthony Froude, *The Nemesis of Faith;* quoted in Houghton, *Victorian Frame of Mind,* 345.

[22] On surprise as assault, see my "Omniscience in *Our Mutual Friend:* On Taking the Reader by Surprise," in *Vanishing Points: Dickens, Narrative, and the Subject of Omniscience* (Berkeley: University of California Press, 1991), 150–66.

second, by implying that places serve not as loci of true or false identity, but rather as switching points along a path of multiple identities. (When Mrs. St. Clair recognizes her husband's writing, what she recognizes is "His hand when he wrote hurriedly. It is very unlike his usual writing, and yet I know it well." Identifying this writing as St. Clair's because it is uncharacteristic, she points toward the same fluidity of identity literalized in her husband's changing of places.) The den resembles the City as a place where identity is replaced by habit—a habit, moreover, of consumption associated with the loss of identity. We have already seen that Holmes, lacking an occupation with which to identify St. Clair, defines him by his habits and his finances: St. Clair is "a man of temperate habits," whose "whole debts... amount to £88 10s., while he has £220 standing to his credit in the Capital and Counties Bank." It makes sense, then, that when the police search the opium den for his body they find only a coat filled with coins—a coat more substantial, its pockets weighted with pennies, than the body which had inhabited it.

———

A former actor, St. Clair uses his skill with makeup to devise the beggar's disguise; as Hugh Boone, he thus resembles one of Mayhew's "false beggars." But his journalistic background—which leads him to put on the beggar's disguise in the first place—connects him with Mayhew as well. Disguised as Hugh Boone, St. Clair expresses his culture's ambivalence about the activity of "the man who does something in the City." But his transformation also reveals what underlies the social scientist/journalist's project: the sympathy and identification responsible for Mayhew's success in collecting and transcribing the stories of those he interviews in London's slums also account for St. Clair's success as "false beggar," and both amount to a dealing in representation, a selling of the beggar's identity. Indeed, by making Hugh Boone the beggar and Neville St. Clair the (former) investigative reporter one and the same, Conan Doyle erases the distinction between identification and exploitation: to "know" the beggar is to trade in his identity, and to trade in his identity is to sell—as both Mayhew and St. Clair do—his words. (There is a difference, however: St. Clair finds reporting to be "arduous labor" but has no difficulty with the labor involved in creating Hugh Boone. In fact, he takes pleasure in his role. "Arduousness," here, would seem to stand for the visibility of labor, which can be perceived as difficult only after having been perceived in the first place. Since labor is only what a culture recognizes as labor, the refusal to see that begging involves labor keeps society from having to acknowledge its complicity in the creation of begging as an activity. The ease with which St. Clair takes on the identity of Hugh Boone, and his pleasure in doing so, represent an effacement of labor that makes it all the more necessary to put the "false beggar" to work.)

And yet while unmasking the exploitative nature of Mayhew's project, Conan Doyle's story performs the same function as Mayhew's social science: in detecting the beggar, and making the "false beggar" confess the "truth" of his identity, it purports to distinguish true identity from false. And, maintaining the opposition between "true" and "false" in the figure of the beggar, both works appear to support the possibility of doing away with the world of representation the "false beggar" implies. It is this possibility, however, that they also finally undermine, since both Mayhew's structure and Holmes's reproduce the system of representation they find so troublesome.

In his section on beggary, Halliday describes an encounter with a one-armed beggar claiming to be a soldier wounded in battle. Quizzing the man, Halliday catches him in a factual error and, after accusing him of lying, proceeds to offer him a shilling—and his freedom—in exchange for his true story (418). In initiating and reproducing the business of the "false beggar"—the trading of identity, as narrative, for coin—Halliday exposes the ideology underlying Mayhew's project: not the desire to undo the system of exchange wherein identity is offered for money but rather the desire to maintain it, reinstating the hierarchy the beggar's imposture has upset by reaffirming the social scientist's position as arbiter of social identity. The end of Conan Doyle's story, similarly, has St. Clair telling his tale to Holmes and the police in exchange for a guarantee of confidentiality—a guarantee that will enable him, in spite of adjurations to the contrary, to keep "Hugh Boone" secret from his wife.

The conclusion of Doyle's story revolves around the question of whether or not a crime has been committed. What St. Clair most fears—"exposure"—is exactly what the case requires, for Holmes discovers the solution to the crime in one of the most private of bourgeois spaces: "In

the bathroom." St. Clair's violation of bourgeois values is represented as
dirt; what is needed to restore him—to make him come clean—is a
sponge and water.

> The man's face peeled off under the sponge like the bark from a tree.
> Gone was the coarse brown tint! Gone, too, was the horrid scar which
> had seamed it across, and the twisted lip which had given the repulsive
> sneer to his face! A twitch brought away the tangled red hair, and there,
> sitting up in his bed, was a pale, sad-faced, refined-looking man, black-
> haired and smooth-skinned, rubbing his eyes and staring about him with
> sleepy bewilderment. Then suddenly realizing the exposure, he broke
> into a scream and threw himself down with his face to the pillow.

Holmes's washing reveals what might well be taken, for all its lack of
specificity and interest, as a description of no one in particular; the passage's fascination lies with what it repeatedly invokes as "gone" rather than
with what remains. As in the description of Holmes in the opium den, the
narrative lingers over the moment of transformation, the moment at
which identity is revealed to have been—and to be—mistaken. Indeed,
those moments suggest that the pleasures of identity (and, for the story's
reader as for St. Clair, of identification) lie not in one position or the other
but in the detachment from both and the possibility of movement between; when Boone's face (not mask) peels off, it reveals a man whose
identity possesses little interest when he isn't being someone else.

The suspected crime—murder—is found not to have taken place; what
did occur was rather what Holmes calls an "error." And that error seems to
have been in essence a crime against the family: "You would have done better to have trusted your wife," advises Holmes. But what does Holmes
mean here—that, if St. Clair had confided in his wife, the beggar's disguise
would have been acceptable? That Mrs. St. Clair, apprised of her husband's
plans, would have acted as the police, and prevented the situation from occurring? The actual crime of begging is regarded very lightly—"What was
a fine to me?" More serious, it seems, is St. Clair's violation of the rules of
bourgeois family life: his failure to confide his true identity to his wife.

But the story only seems to resolve the problem of St. Clair's identity
by entrusting it to his wife: in fact, while returning her husband to her,
Holmes and the police keep their knowledge of his activity to themselves.

("If the police are to hush this thing up," says Inspector Bradstreet, "there must be no more of Hugh Boone.") "The Man with the Twisted Lip," like the Poor Law, seems to resolve the problem of the indeterminacy of social identity by locating identity in the body: a cut on the hand assures us that Boone and St. Clair are the same. But it goes a step further, requiring the subject to tell his story, to constitute his identity in (and as) narrative. And, trading the confidentiality St. Clair desires for that story, the police and the detective protect the system they accuse St. Clair of having perpetuated, reasserting their power to control an exchange that will remain, necessarily, in the realm of representation. For, having divested himself of his multiple identities at the police station, St. Clair will have to invent another before he gets home, thus beginning life again on a foundation of representation. Rather than determining the truth or falsity of any particular identity, then, these texts perpetuate a system wherein a subject is free to inhabit the identity designated as acceptable for him or her by the authorities. (Hence the unresolvable tension between fluidity and hierarchy in all these examples: Halliday's authority, for instance, lies not in his ability to discern the truth of the beggar's second story but in his ability to have the beggar tell it. Only the storyteller knows whether the narrative he tells is true, but that knowledge is not accompanied by power. The tale told by the beggar, like St. Clair's writing—and like the hand that identifies Hugh Boone as St. Clair—may well be merely "one of his hands.") Truth matters less than the production and maintenance of the proper fiction, or rather truth lies not in the story but in the system of exchange that requires the storyteller to tell it: a system which unmasks that man, and then requires him to unmask himself, before the police, the detective, the social scientist, the journalist. What is understood as stable identity in these works is constituted within and produced by the very system of exchange Mayhew and Conan Doyle condemn.[23]

And it is that system of exchange which links the "false beggar" to his detractors—Mayhew, Conan Doyle, Holmes, and finally St. Clair himself—as versions of the writer, not unlike the begging-letter writer whose

---

[23] This supports a definition of truth offered by Michel Foucault: " 'Truth' is to be understood as a system of ordered procedures for the production, regulation, circulation and operation of statements." *Power / Knowledge,* ed. Colin Gordon (New York: Pantheon, 1980), 133.

profession it is to trade stories of poverty and decline for cash, providing
the public with an opportunity to winnow "false" identities from "true"
ones by means of narrative. Since Mayhew (actually Halliday, who, appropriately enough, allowed his professional identity to be subsumed within
Mayhew's) includes himself as a character in his own story, he too is implicated in the exchange with his "false beggars": he constitutes himself as
social scientist at the same moment that he constructs the identities of his
subjects. It is more characteristic of the writer, however, to hide that implication, and no writer is more famously effaced behind his creation than
Conan Doyle—who, as a world of Sherlockiana attests, seems to have created an actual person rather than a fictional character. And, as fictional
character, Holmes is also famous for self-effacement: for the skill with
which he projects himself into "the criminal mind" while at the same time
remaining aloof from it, as if his identity inhered, like the writer's, in nonidentity: in the ability to project himself into the identities of others.
Mayhew, Conan Doyle, St. Clair, and Holmes are all, literally or
figuratively, writers, and the figure of the "false beggar" is a figure for the
writer, involved in a sympathetic taking on of identity that is also an act of
self-effacement, placing its instigator in an ambivalent relationship not
only with the other into whose identity he projects himself, but with identity itself, so easily slipped in and out of.

───────

Both Mayhew and Conan Doyle began to write out of financial need.
Mayhew, in particular, may be said to have deliberately differentiated himself from his subjects precisely through the act of writing about them: the
sympathy and identification that enabled his work kept away the possibility that he would actually occupy the beggar's place. And Conan Doyle
discusses his decision to write in terms that parallel St. Clair's decision to
beg: "It was in third year [1879] that I first learned that shillings might be
earnd in other ways than by filling phials."[24] (St. Clair says, "You can imagine how hard it was to settle down to arduous work at £2 a week when I
knew that I could earn as much in a day by smearing my face with a little paint, laying my cap on the ground, and sitting still.") Upon discovering that he could make more money selling stories than as a medical as-

---

[24] Arthur Conan Doyle, *Memories and Adventures* (Boston: Little, Brown, 1924), 24.

sistant, Conan Doyle—like St. Clair—simply exchanged one profession for another, more lucrative one. According to at least one critic, however, Conan Doyle felt degraded by the writing of mystery stories: Stephen Knight maintains that "The Man with the Twisted Lip" expresses Conan Doyle's shameful feelings about writing "vulgar potboilers" rather than the historical novels by means of which he hoped to establish himself as a respectable author. Publishing in the *Strand*—a magazine sold, appropriately enough, in railway stations "to catch the commuting white-collar market"—Conan Doyle felt (according to Knight) that he was taking "profits made in the street from City workers."[25]

Knight's reading depends upon a number of elements—Hugh Boone as "degraded," mystery-story writing as an "accidental discovery" which suddenly supplies Conan Doyle with large sums of money—that the story, and the biography, do not necessarily support. But the connection he emphasizes between writing and beggary may be drawn out in a number of ways: in terms, for example, of the need to appeal to an audience characteristic of both, or in terms of the movement from "filling phials" to "sitting still" that describes Conan Doyle's progression as well as St. Clair's—a movement, that is, from more to less visible labor. If Conan Doyle identified with his subject, as Mayhew appears to have identified with his, both suggestively turned that identification to account. An identification with illegitimate production is legitimated in a form of production—writing—that allows for vicariousness, for both imaginative participation and professional "disinterest."

On the one hand, stillness suggests the achievement of gentlemanly respectability; on the other, it evokes the degradation and loss of identity associated with the opium den. The identity Holmes and the police desire for St. Clair, in contrast, seems to depend upon incessant movement. And yet even as it seems to create such identity, this movement also dismantles it—and as he transforms contemporary readers of "The Man with the Twisted Lip," commuting between home and City, into a *mise-en-abîme* for his story, Conan Doyle challenges the polarity between true and false identities the story seeks to establish. For what is the identity of the man on the train, reading? Conan Doyle's story may indeed express an opposition between "true" and "false" selves he felt himself to be living: a structure in which the true, respectable self feels it necessary to trade on a false

[25] Stephen Knight, *Form and Ideology in Crime Fiction* (London, 1980), 70, 98.

identity in order to survive. And yet if Holmes's creator maintained, along with many of his contemporaries, a notion of a true self that could be supported only at the expense of participation in the false identities of the marketplace, this passage between high and low culture has the same implications as St. Clair's changes of identity: in a characteristically Victorian movement between the poles of respectability and nonrespectability, the subject must continue to strive for the former because he is always kept from complete adherence to it by participation in the latter. The question the story poses is thus not, What is identity? but rather, Where, at any moment, is identity? since it illustrates perhaps best of all the way the idea of respectability keeps identity in motion: the way the social self circulates endlessly as it imagines itself nearing the image of a desired, culturally valued self that will finally (and paradoxically) sit still.

The irresistible continuity between "filling phials" and "sitting still" recalls the opium den, which evokes the same images of passivity and loss of identity that the figure of the City man does—and that also surround Holmes. The story displays anxiety about labor that appears not to be labor, often mentioning the fact that, when working, Holmes appears to be doing nothing. Both Holmes and St. Clair live by their wits; neither is perceived to be working when he is actually hardest at work. Thus Holmes, at work on the case,

> took off his coat and waistcoat, put on a large blue dressing-gown, and then wandered about the room collecting pillows from his bed and cushions from the sofa and armchairs. With these he constructed a sort of Eastern divan, upon which he perched himself cross-legged, with an ounce of shag tobacco and a box of matches laid out in front of him. In the dim light of the lamp I saw him sitting there, an old briar pipe between his lips, his eyes fixed vacantly upon the corner of the ceiling, the blue smoke curling up from him, silent, motionless, with the light shining upon his strong-set aquiline features."

Indeed, Holmes at work resembles nothing so much as the habitué of an opium den. Producing the solution to the case in a scenario which highlights the absence of visible labor, Holmes resembles the "man who does something in the City," as well as the professional whose productivity the Victorians could not easily locate.

The beggar, the finance capitalist, and the detective are unproductive in the same sense in which Adam Smith found many entertainers and professionals to be, since they produce no "vendible commodity...for which an equal quantity of labour could afterwards be procured."[26] The figure who professes rather than produces—whose speech, writing, or self is his commodity—blurs the easily readable relationship between producer and product, laborer and commodity; the professional performs services whose merit, at least to some extent, the client has to take on faith. Having, as Harold Perkin writes, "a professional interest in disinterest," the professional also aroused suspicion for his "Protean" ability to "assume the guise of any other class at will."[27] It is therefore appropriate that it is in the figure of the professional as well as by means of professionals—the detective and the writer—that, in this story, the beggar and the gentleman meet and become indistinguishable from one another.

When Watson first meets Holmes, in *A Study in Scarlet,* he has difficulty figuring out his future comrade's profession; given what Holmes seems to know, it's not clear what he's suited for. Watson actually draws up a chart, listing such items as "Knowledge of Literature—Nil...Knowledge of Chemistry—Profound," and, when finished, throws it into the fire in despair: "If I can only find what the fellow is driving at by reconciling all these accomplishments, and discovering a calling which needs them all.... I may as well give up the attempt at once." What is baffling about St. Clair, similarly, is his failure to fit into any obvious profession. But Holmes's profession, of course, depends upon exactly the kind of indeterminacy he finds inappropriate for St. Clair. Holmes, it has often been pointed out, is a model of the "gentlemanly amateur," "relaxed and disinterested."[28] His lack of specialization is his chief asset, since his work requires a collection of arcane bits of knowledge that would not appear necessary to a member of any other profession. Yet Holmes does not simply accumulate random

[26] Adam Smith, *An Inquiry into the Nature and Causes of the Wealth of Nations,* ed. R. H. Campbell and A. S. Skinner (Oxford: Clarendon, 1976), 1:330.

[27] Perkin, *The Origins of Modern English Society, 1778–1880* (London: Routledge and Kegan Paul, 1969), 260, 253. Perkin is referring here to the new professional class, in the process of differentiating itself from the older professional class—represented here by Whitney and Watson—and from the capitalist middle class, more directly vulnerable to market fluctuations.

[28] Dennis Porter, *The Pursuit of Crime* (New Haven: Yale University Press, 1981), 156.

information: indeed, by his own account his methods are supremely practical. His theory of the mind is based on an analogy with material labor:
"I consider that a man's mind is a little like an empty attic, and you have
to stock it with such furniture as you choose. A fool takes in all the lum-
ber of every sort that he comes across, so that the knowledge that might
be useful to him gets crowded out.... Now the skillful workman is very
careful indeed as to what he takes into his brain-attic. He will have nothing but the tools which may help him in doing his work" (*A Study in
Scarlet*). In fact, Holmes's apparently scattered knowledge signals his professionalism. When Watson meets him, for instance, he has invented a
process for distinguishing bloodstains; he also reveals that he "dabbles with
poisons a good deal." The one element that signals "gentlemanly amateur"
in its apparent lack of professional value is Holmes's violin playing. Yet
even that, as Watson describes it, is geared not toward the ordinary production of music as a means of relaxation, but rather toward cogitation:
"When left to himself... he would seldom produce any music or attempt
any recognizing air. Leaning back in his arm chair of an evening, he would
close his eyes and scrape carelessly at the fiddle which was thrown across
his knee.... Whether the music aided these thoughts, or whether the playing was simply the result of whim or fancy, was more than I could deter-
mine."

Despite his practicality, however, Holmes maintains an attitude of gentlemanly disinterest; while asserting that "the theories... which appear to
you to be so chimerical, are... so practical that I depend upon them for
my bread and cheese," he also claims that he may get nothing out of a case
but a laugh at the expense of the inspectors who fail to solve it. Asserting
his economic interest in his work almost at the same time that he disavows
it, Holmes maintains professionalism's characteristic tension between productivity and unproductivity. The idea of the detective as amateur
mystifies, even as it transforms, the idea of professional labor: his capital,
Holmes suggests, is purely intellectual, his work a function of desire and a
source of pleasure rather than a necessity. It makes sense, then, that in "The
Man with the Twisted Lip" Holmes confesses to a fascination with that
other professional who manifestly enjoys his work: "I have watched the
fellow more than once," he says of Boone, "before I ever thought of making his professional acquaintance, and have been surprised at the harvest
which he has reaped in a short time." Intrigued by Boone's apparently

effortless production of income, Holmes boasts, at the end of the story, that he solved the case merely "by sitting upon five pillows and consuming an ounce of shag."

From the nonprofessional's perspective, such effortlessness is only a step away from doing nothing, and professionals are found in the opium den, in this story, because both professionalism and opium focus Victorian anxieties about unproductivity. The opium den was a fantasy about unproductivity: explicitly citing this threat, the anti-opium movement in the nineteenth century encouraged the idea that opium represented a particular danger for the working classes and raised anxiety about its spread to the middle classes; opium, wrote one physician in 1843, rendered "the individual who indulges himself in it a worse than useless member of society."[29] The lascar, similarly, was a figure of "surplus" population associated with unproductivity: considered, paradoxically, to be "indolent" himself— that is, likely to be a "false beggar" (for Mayhew, Asian beggars were figures of "extraordinary mendacity")[30]—this figure also aroused anxiety for his potential to take the place of English or Irish laborers, thereby producing unemployment (and "false beggars") in the native population. In his fictional role as proprietor of the opium den, the lascar is an entrepreneur of passivity and unproductivity, his appellation encoding the kind of information—about "race," profession, and social position—such labels are meant to supply.

The opium den undermines the possibility that St. Clair's "true" identity can be located either at home or at work; situated between the two, the den provides a place for transformation, for the constitution of identity in, or as, exchange. But the den also suggestively associates opium addiction with professional identity. Like disguise, which functions throughout the

[29] Anxiety about opium use in the late nineteenth century was associated with theories of the degeneracy of the middle class; the anti-opium movement helped spread the belief that "opium smoking was somehow threatening in its implications for the indigenous population." See Virginia Berridge and Griffith Edwards, *Opium and the People: Opiate Use in Nineteenth-Century England* (New Haven: Yale University Press, 1987), 175, 198–99, and *passim*.

[30] See Mayhew, *London Labour*, 4:423–24; also Rozina Visram, *Ayahs, Lascars, and Princes: Indians in Britain 1700–1947* (London: Pluto, 1986).

story as a metaphor for profession, opium transforms appearance. Yet is does so more profoundly than disguise: opium makes Whitney into "a slave to the drug...with yellow, pasty face, drooping lids, and pinpoint pupils." Where disguise points to the existence of the authentic identity underlying it, evoking an easy movement between true and false, Whitney's slavishness implies an inability to move back and forth—a fixedness and loss of identity. Indeed, while the story invites us to imagine disguise, profession, writing, and, here, reading (Whitney begins his opium addiction in deliberate imitation of DeQuincey) as analogous movements in and out of identity, the idea of opium addiction deconstructs that movement, suggesting that the individual in motion may become stuck, not in one identity or another, but in that very detachment from identity figured here both in the addict's stillness and the City man's incessant movement. Although the professional, or the City man, fancies himself moving freely between identities, his very movement registers his enslavement. Whitney's addiction—the presence of which disturbs the story's regular movement between suburb and City—thus represents the other side of the coin on whose face St. Clair and, preeminently, Holmes enact the pleasures of disguise. And in fact when the police and Holmes require St. Clair to remain, visibly, in circulation, they insist upon exactly the kind of detachment from self that makes St. Clair into the entrepreneur of identities they accuse him of being. The professional, Whitney's addiction implies, is addicted not to one identity or another but rather to the detachment from self both opium, and profession, imply.

But the story establishes a difference between Whitney and St. Clair, on the one hand, and Holmes on the other. Holmes famously has no private life, only a bohemianism that dramatizes the absence of one; the uncovering of his "true" identity in the opium den requires no scrubbing but only, apparently, an act of will, a change of mood—or merely, on Watson's part, a slight change of perception. "His form had filled out, his wrinkles were gone, the dull eyes had regained their fire." Holmes "is" his professional identity: in him, enslavement to profession is disguised as the discovery of identity through it. (When, in the same scene, he remarks, "I suppose, Watson,...that you imagine that I have added opium smoking to cocaine injections," Holmes emphasizes the bohemianism that seems to draw him away from his profession but in fact registers the absence, in his life, of anything else.) Dedicated to a profession he himself has invented, and of which he is the only member ("I suppose I am the only one in the world. I'm a consulting detective"; *A Study in Scarlet*), Holmes is a fantasy of professionalism as unalienated labor: of the highly specialized professional as a figure for whom slavery cannot be an issue because his work so completely fulfills his nature, because his work is the complete expression of his nature. (Just as writing provides Conan Doyle with an alternative to medicine, so too is Holmes's professionalism contrasted here with the doctoring of Whitney and Watson.) His work, in fact, is no work at all, but rather—as the nightlong smoking session suggests—habit: "From long habit the train of thoughts ran so swiftly through my mind that I arrived at the conclusion without being conscious of intermediate steps" (*A Study in Scarlet*). In the figure of Holmes, addiction is the same as fulfillment; for him, losing the self in one's work is the same as finding the self in it.

Yet this fantasy of professional identity exists alongside, and depends upon the production of, everyone else's divided self; it is purchased at the expense of those who, imagining that they can wear one identity in public and preserve another, secretly, for themselves, provide their culture with the reassurance about identity it desires (Wilde's *Picture of Dorian Gray* articulates another version of this fantasy). Both Whitney and St. Clair become objects of official scrutiny, it is important to recall, not when they begin leading double lives but when they cease to do so; the police and Holmes require them not to abandon their double lives but to lead them in plain sight—and, above all, to keep moving. For Whitney's and St. Clair's cessations of movement reveal that the double life functions for them, and for Victorian culture, in the same way that disguise does for Holmes: it preserves the fiction of an authentic self. And that may be what Holmes—and Boone—are smiling about.

Having revealed this secret, however, the story must conceal it once again, if only to provide Holmes with something to do. For the detective's business is to find the strange in the commonplace: life, he claims, "is infinitely stranger than anything the mind of man could invent" ("A Case of Identity"). In "The Man with the Twisted Lip" he is momentarily baffled by what has proven to be not so commonplace: St. Clair's choice of profession. The point of the case is therefore to return St. Clair the beggar—and St. Clair the gentleman—to the ordinary, middle-class world of work and family: the world that stands still while Holmes moves about, and that provides the identities into which he will, temporarily, disappear.

PART II

Fear of Falling

3

Under Cover: Sympathy and Ressentiment in Gaskell's Ruth

Under the cover of sympathy with the dismissed labourers, Mr. Preston indulged his own private pique very pleasantly.

—Elizabeth Gaskell, *Wives and Daughters*

Elizabeth Gaskell's goal in *Ruth* (1853) was to elicit sympathy for the figure of the fallen woman by means of the detailed representation of an individual case. Yet as many readers have noted, the novel takes an ambivalent approach to the category and the character with which it is most concerned. Critical of the social barriers that would place Ruth outside respectable society, Gaskell at the same time devised a heroine who is naturally good—indeed, one whose innocence borders on (and is figured as) an "unconsciousness" of the social norms she violates. Ruth's claim on readerly sympathy thus seems to derive less from a critique of the idea of fallenness than from her status as not truly fallen. And yet, as if doubting her heroine's virtue, Gaskell requires Ruth to redeem herself. The novel remains unable to reconcile her supposed innocence with her deviation from it, and—as if to escape all the confusion—she dies at its end.[1]

---

[1] For a useful review of *Ruth* criticism, see Elizabeth Helsinger, Robin Sheets, and William Veeder, eds., *The Woman Question* (Chicago: University of Chicago Press, 1983),

Criticism of the novel has, understandably, been unable to leave the subject of the fallen woman behind. But in addition to being concerned with the fate of fallen women, *Ruth* expresses Gaskell's general interest in sympathy as a solution to divisive social problems; in *Mary Barton* and *North and South,* for instance, individual sympathy is her solution to class conflict. *Ruth,* however, enacts a drama of identity transformation that expresses and reenacts the tensions sympathy is meant to resolve. Offered as the representative of a social category—a type—Ruth exemplifies the way the sympathetic object not only represents but dissolves into a generalized social identity; like Daniel Deronda, as character she is inseparable from the imagining of a social type and the attempted resolution of a social problem. What follows is that the sympathy she is meant to elicit—sympathy for the fallen woman—takes a form that expresses the social anxieties of those in a position to feel "for" her: those members of the middle class for whom she embodies an ever-present fear of falling.

According to some critics, sympathy was Gaskell's own "cover story," the fiction that enabled her to write—as, disavowing a conventionally masculine knowledge of fact, she claimed the conventionally feminine authority of feeling.[2] *Ruth* too, in one of fiction's most peculiar sympathetic gestures, also figures sympathy as cover: the novel's plot concerns the way in which the Bensons—a minister and his sister, who sympathize with Ruth and take her into their home—invent a false identity for her, ostensibly to shield her from censure. Ruth becomes known as the respectable widow Mrs. Denbigh, and her eventual exposure causes outrage in the community and especially in Mr. Bradshaw, the wealthy manufacturer and stern Puritan who has employed her as a governess.

That sympathy should manifest itself as disguise brings out, not least, the way both involve an imaginative transgression of the boundaries of social

---

3:113–22. Angus Easson discusses the protestations that make Gaskell seem unconvinced of Ruth's innocence in *Elizabeth Gaskell* (London: Routledge and Kegan Paul, 1979).

[2] Terry Lovell writes that Gaskell claimed "the right to speak not from knowledge of 'the facts' but from an identification with the feelings of an oppressed and suffering workforce." *Consuming Fictions* (London: Verso, 1987), 87. See also Hilary Schor, *Scheherezade in the Marketplace: Elizabeth Gaskell and the Victorian Novel* (New York: Oxford University Press, 1992), 21–22. The phrase "cover story" comes from Sandra Gilbert and Susan Gubar, *The Madwoman in the Attic: The Woman Writer and the Nineteenth-Century Literary Imagination* (New Haven: Yale University Press, 1979), chap. 5.

identity. It suggests, in ways I will develop further in this chapter, the sympathetic object's status as a figure for imaginative appropriation, enlisted in the construction of a spectator's identity. And, most prominently, the deceit shifts the novel's focus from Ruth's fall to the Bensons' lie, pointing toward what becomes the novel's insistent concern: the inability of its middle-class characters to sustain their own tenuously constructed identities. Focusing not on the alleged crime but on the cover-up—creating transgression, in effect, where she insists none had existed before—Gaskell subordinates Ruth's situation to (and makes it appear no less than a displacement of) the situations of those members of the community for whom identity itself seems fundamentally little more than a form of covering up. The common critical view of the novel's ambivalence—that Gaskell attempted to construct an innocent character but could not escape her belief in that character's sexual guilt—may thus be expanded to include the way sexuality in *Ruth* becomes a figure, and cover, for issues of class identity. Like the Bensons, Gaskell attempts to protect Ruth's identity by distracting attention from it, moving away from the idea of sexual transgression as if to mitigate it by creating another kind of transgression on which to focus. But the movement away from sexuality produces more, rather than less, transgressive energy, as Gaskell's attempt to elicit sympathy for the fallen woman becomes a story about the the fallen identity of the Victorian middle class.[3]

Ruth is only one of many divided and uneasy characters in the novel. Thurstan Benson and his sister Faith are at odds with the conventional society dominated by the wealthy manufacturer Bradshaw, who patronizes them; the brother, in particular, suffers from a vague emotional distress that ultimately takes shape as a struggle of conscience over his role in the deceit. Bradshaw, who expresses his own status anxiety in his treatment of the Bensons, has a troubled conscience as well: embarked on a scheme to bribe voters to elect his candidate for Parliament (the candidate, Donne, is

[3] My use of the term "transgression" draws upon the work of Peter Stallybrass and Allon White, *The Politics and Poetics of Transgression* (Ithaca: Cornell University Press, 1969). The fallen woman is, of course, traditionally regarded as a site of dangerous feeling, particularly feeling perceived as disruptive to the family. Susan Staves argues that eighteenth- and nineteenth-century "seduced maiden" novels express anxiety about what Lawrence Stone has termed "affective individualism": the shift from an assumed traditional, patriarchal continuity and familial order to an emphasis on individual will and desire. Staves, "British Seduced Maidens," *Eighteenth-Century Studies* 14 (1980–81): 109–34.

the former Bellingham, Ruth's seducer), he warns himself to take care that "the slack-principled Mr. Bradshaw of one month of ferment and excitement, might not be confounded with the highly conscientious and deeply-religious Mr. Bradshaw, who went to chapel twice a day."[4] Farquhar, the man Bradshaw's daughter Jemima is to marry, seems to Ruth to possess "two characters": "the old one . . . a man acting up to a high standard of lofty principle, . . . [and] the new one . . . cold and calculating in all he did" (228). And Jemima herself is caught between "awe" at her father and a desire to follow her own "passionate impulses" (211).

Bradshaw's relationship to Donne suggests an underlying cause for this nearly universal condition of self-division. The politician's aristocratic manner makes Bradshaw aware of the "incontestable difference of rank and standard that there was, in every respect, between his guest and his own family. . . . It was something indescribable—a quiet being at ease, and expecting every one else to be so—an attention to women, which was so habitual as to be unconsciously exercised . . . a happy choice of simple and expressive words" (261–62). "In fact," it seems to Bradshaw, "Mr. Donne had been born and cradled in all that wealth could purchase, and so had his ancestors before him for so many generations, that refinement and luxury seemed the natural condition of man, and they that dwelt without were in the position of monsters" (265). The difference between Donne and Bradshaw, as the latter sees it, is one of consciousness versus unconsciousness, the natural versus the forced ("His mode of living, though strained to a high pitch just at this time . . . was no more than Mr. Donne was accustomed to every day of his life" [265]), and aristocratic identity versus "monstrous" and self-conscious self creation. Indeed, Bradshaw's "straining," his moral and economic uneasiness, is only one example of a moral and economic discontent that affects almost all the novel's characters: an awareness of and uneasiness about identity constructed and anxiously maintained rather than assumed as natural. In particular, the novel's characters are tormented by the way in which a rigid adherence to the conventions of middle-class behavior inevitably gives way to a determination to deviate from those conventions.[5]

[4] Elizabeth Gaskell, *Ruth* (New York: Oxford University Press, 1985), 307. Subsequent references included in text.

[5] See John Kucich, *The Power of Lies: Transgression in Victorian Fiction* (Ithaca: Cornell University Press, 1995), for a discussion of the role of transgression in the formation of Victorian middle-class identity.

If the character of Ruth has traditionally been regarded as the occasion for an impulse that leads the Bensons outside conventional moral boundaries, then, she may also be seen as the form such an impulse takes. A social outcast—requiring, as Faith Benson decides, a new identity—Ruth provides the Bensons with a blank slate on which to write. And what they write projects both a desire for natural identity (which here, as in Donne's case, manifests itself in aristocratic form: "she might be a Percy or a Howard for the grandeur of her grace!" thinks Donne / Bellingham [278]), and an identity constructed as a tension between an illicit self and its respectable cover. "Mrs. Denbigh," that is, embodies the problem Gaskell raises for all *Ruth's* characters. Hovering between a transgressiveness defined in terms of both sexuality and class and a respectability presented as both natural and artificial, Ruth embodies anxieties constitutive of Victorian middle-class identity: the fear that respectability is a masquerade, that the individual self is already and inevitably fallen—that, as Peter Stallybrass and Allon White have put it, in the construction of bourgeois identity, an "underground self" has "the upper hand." In *Ruth,* both middle-class identity and the fallen woman take shape in a tension between what Marjorie Levinson has called "the mythologically antagonistic upper and lower classes," and Stallybrass and White have described as the opposition between "high" and "low" central to the construction of bourgeois identity in the nineteenth century.[6]

Ruth's divided identity also serves as a conduit for a feeling the novel associates implicitly with sympathy: *ressentiment.* Like a number of Gaskell's heroines, and like Gaskell herself, the Bensons fictionalize in the name of sympathy. But when Bradshaw, taken in by Ruth's disguise, takes her into his home, the Bensons' lie implicates them in an act of aggression against their wealthy neighbor. Disrupting and confusing social boundaries in their transformation of Ruth's identity, and demonstrating the ease with which a woman from one social background may blend in with another, the Bensons—and Gaskell—play on commonplace Victorian anxieties about the fallen woman's ability to rise in society, in particular her ability to penetrate the protected boundaries of the bourgeois household. The use to which the fiction of Ruth's identity is put, as well as the ur-

---

[6] Marjorie Levinson, *Keats's Life of Allegory: The Origins of a Style* (Oxford: Blackwell, 1988), 176–77; Stallybrass and White, *Politics and Poetics of Transgression,* 5.

gency of the Bensons' desire to erase its alienating effects once it is discovered, recall Max Scheler's description of *ressentiment* as anger against the rigid categories of identity against which the socially disaffected struggle yet to which they remain bound.[7] The social boundaries that would exclude the fallen woman from the community also define the Bensons' own powerlessness in relation to Bradshaw; disguising Ruth, the Bensons construct a plot that expresses in disguised form their own social discontent. Social sympathy, figured as the imaginative crossing of social boundaries, is violently literalized here in the Bensons' violation of class boundaries. *Ressentiment* thus appears here as the expression and inevitable accompaniment of middle-class sympathy.

Held responsible for the emotional well-being of the family, Victorian women were typically represented as conduits for either salutary or dangerous feeling. Attempting to construct an ideal sympathetic object, Gaskell seems to create a character of pure receptivity—one whose receptivity is in fact the cause of her fall. But from the beginning of the novel, Ruth is noted as well for her ability to communicate feeling to others. When she arrives at the Bensons', their servant Sally declares her sorrowful feeling unacceptable since it threatens to "infect" others: Sally and Miss Benson "each had keen sympathies, and felt depressed when they saw anyone near them depressed." Sally takes Ruth's baby out of his mother's arms when, while looking at her face, "his little lip began to quiver, and his open blue eye to grow over-clouded, as with some mysterious sympathy

---

[7] Scheler writes: "Ressentiment is apt to thrive among those who are alienated from the social order.... These persons...hate the existing institutional arrangement but at the same time feel unable to act out this hatred because they are bound to the existing scheme of things." Max Scheler, *Ressentiment,* trans. William W. Holdheim (New York: Free Press, 1969), 29. The basic account of *ressentiment* is Friedrich Nietzsche's in *On the Genealogy of Morals.* I have used the terms "resentment" and "*ressentiment*" somewhat interchangeably, though the latter refers to what is explicitly a social emotion, one that exists within a social context in which mobility (the ability not just to identify with the other, but to occupy the other's place) is simultaneously offered and denied. Sympathy and *ressentiment* resemble each other: each depends upon social inequity and a theoretical possibility of "becoming" the other. Indeed, as an embodiment of sympathy *and* of *ressentiment,* Ruth enacts the other side of Adam Smith's equation: sympathy as imagined from the sympathetic object's point of view. *Ressentiment* in this account takes shape as a projection of class anxieties and desires: as the psychologization of class envy and a justification for social inequity.

with the sorrowful face bent over him" (173). In the novel, the term "infection" and the idea of infectiousness are frequently used to refer to feeling: Ruth is "infected" by Bellingham's amusement (15); Mr. Davis suggests that his wife has "infected" him with a desire for children (437). Leonard, Ruth's son, at one point develops a tendency to lie, the implication being that he has caught duplicity from his mother; he also "catches" her bravery later on (427). Gaskell's use of the infection metaphor suggests the way fallenness in the novel is everyone's problem. Literalizing the metaphor, later, as disease, Gaskell paradoxically isolates the infection: since only Ruth has been infected by Bellingham, only for her is fallenness the cause of death.

Sally's anxiety about the infectiousness of Ruth's feeling evokes the fear of contamination conventionally associated with fallen women; it also amplifies an anxiety about the power of the sympathetic object that suggests, again, the potential fluidity of class identity in the novel. These scenes dramatize not Adam Smith's general idea of sympathy—the imagining of the self if the other's place—but rather a fear of sympathy's reversibility, as if the other's identity might too easily become one's own. When, in an effort to assist in her disguise, Sally abruptly cuts Ruth's hair, what is ostensibly done to make her resemble a widow is in effect a test of submissiveness and an insistence on difference: a dramatization of the giving up of identity in exchange for sympathy. And the novel as a whole, like this scene, dramatizes sympathy's transformation—and, ultimately, complete appropriation—of its object.

Ruth's disguise—the covering of one identity by another—functions as an attempt to transform one kind of feeling into another, and as the novel progresses, Ruth becomes an instrument for allaying the disruptive feelings her "fallen" self represents. After Sally's warning, Ruth's potential to "infect" others is transformed into an "unconscious power of enchantment" (179), an unwilled communication of serene and harmonious feeling. (Significantly, the warning is delivered by a female servant who has undergone a similar transformation, learning to discipline resentful feelings and accept her "station" [176].) With this transformation, Gaskell implicitly defines as the novel's task not so much the alteration of characters' and readers' feelings about Ruth but rather Ruth's ability to alter their feelings about themselves and each other, an ability reminiscent of the kind of reparation for past transgressions one of Gaskell's early critics described as necessary for the fallen woman: "The sin of unchastity in the woman is, above all, a breaking up or loosening of the family bond—a treason against the family order of God's world—so the restoration of the sinner consists mainly in the renewal of that bond, in the realization of that order, both by and through and around herself."[8] "By and through and around herself"—but not for herself—Ruth radiates feelings of serenity and cheerfulness; without intention, "with no thought of self tainting it" (366), she disseminates familial harmony. Through tensions within the identities of Benson, Bradshaw, Farquhar, and Jemima, Gaskell displaces the issue of sympathy for the social or moral other onto the problem of unifying middle-class identity. And the reformation of character in which Ruth assists within the novel resembles the reformation of identity her author wished to effect outside it: with her peculiar power to transform the feelings of others, Ruth embodies the transformative power Gaskell hoped her novel would possess.

Ruth's influence comes to bear most significantly on the character who possesses "passionate impulses" reminiscent of conventional anxiety about fallen women: Bradshaw's daughter, Jemima. Resisting her father's desire to control her choice of a husband, Jemima is described as being in "silent rebellion" against him (215). In a central episode, Bradshaw asks Ruth to encourage Jemima to soften her behavior toward Mr. Farquhar, the man he wishes her to marry. Though Ruth never consents to Bradshaw's plan, and indeed disapproves of it, it works despite her: by "simply banishing unpleasant subjects, and throwing a wholesome natural sunlit tone over others, Ruth had insensibly drawn Jemima out of her gloom" (234). Dissolving ill feeling, Ruth reconciles unruly impulse with patriarchal design; what Jemima later describes, resentfully, as "admirable management" (241) is accomplished by Ruth's unconscious role in Bradshaw's plan.

When Jemima learns of her father's request, she is outraged at this attempt at management, and the novel seems to endorse her outrage. But it goes on to manipulate Ruth's feeling to achieve the same end. For Farquhar subsequently becomes attracted to Ruth as "the very type of what a woman should be" (308), and both through the influence that makes Jemima behave according to her father's wishes, and through

---

[8] *"Ruth:* A Novel by the Author of *Mary Barton,*" *North British Review* 19 (1853): 155.

Farquhar's attraction to herself, Ruth encourages the marriage the father desires. Described as "one who always thought before she spoke (as Mr. Farquhar used to bid Jemima to do) and who was never tempted by sudden impulse but walked the world calm and self-governed" (242), Ruth functions as a model for and unconscious influence on Jemima, focusing her feeling and taming her impulse. But—in a manner that connects the novel's authorial consciousness to Ruth's "unconscious"influence—the greater portion of that work is done by the plot of the novel itself.

Jemima's story, and Jemima's impulsiveness, are clearly a muted version of Ruth's: a warning about impulse that leads away from the family. The episode stages the solidification of Victorian middle-class feminine identity as a function of the recognition and externalization of one's "fallen" self: "standing," the narrator comments, "[Jemima] had learned to take heed lest she fell" (370). Sympathy mediates Jemima's internal conflict between passion and authority, as Jemima's resentment toward her father finds just cause in her sympathy for Ruth. And that same sympathy simultaneously enables her to come to terms with Farquhar, thus fulfilling her father's wish: "the unacknowledged bond between them now was their grief, and sympathy, and pity for Ruth." In a displacement similar to that of the Bensons, threatening identification is transformed into sympathetic difference. Redefining the nature of Jemima's passion and differentiating it from the unruly feeling it might seem to resemble, Gaskell both exposes the novel's undercurrent of disruptive feeling and resolves the conflict that feeling causes. By means of this solution—in which the unconscious dissemination of feeling and the deliberate attempt to manipulate it amount to the same thing (the novel's plot is the same as the father's plot)—Gaskell enlists Ruth's affective power in the service of a strengthened familial order. But that order, finally, has no place for her.

Throughout the novel, Gaskell returns repeatedly to the issue of economic and emotional debt. Her insistent detailing of such debt, along with her careful recounting of the discomforts of the Bensons' poverty and the Bradshaws' ostentatious wealth, links the Bensons' fictionalizing to their resentment; even more suggestive is the way Ruth's presence in Bradshaw's home disturbs the manufacturer's emphatic desire to maintain legible social boundaries. Breaking through social and economic barriers, the Bensons' deception constitutes their own "silent rebellion," expressing both a frustration at the fixedness of social boundaries and a resentment against Bradshaw's power in the community. Only a few things circulate between the Benson and Bradshaw households: money in the form of pew rents, gifts from Bradshaw, and Ruth. Ruth is the Bensons' gift to Bradshaw: their answer to his patronage. Both as Mrs. Denbigh, a character invented by Faith, and as Bradshaw's employee, she exposes the vulnerability of the home on whose security Bradshaw stakes his identity and that of his family, the home that would place her irretrievably outside it and define her as incapable of redemption.[9] A conduit for the feelings of others and a figure of silent rebellion herself, Ruth enables the expression of class feeling whose existence the Bensons cannot own. Figuring sympathy and resentment simultaneously, she exemplifies sympathetic identity as a form of currency: she is the means of payment, the coin offered to shore up the Bensons' fragile identities.

Gaskell has been praised for her own transgression of middle-class norms in her representation of the unconventional Benson household: the feminized minister, the strong sister, and the hearty servant represent social and moral alternatives to the Bradshaws, unhappy in their prescribed roles (Jemima rages against her father's dominance; Mrs. Bradshaw looks "as if she was thoroughly broken into submission" [153]). But in aligning Ruth with feelings of resentment, I am relying on the way in which the Bensons feel themselves to be outsiders in their own community and suggesting that their sympathy for her expresses that shared status. (Sympathy, the novel explicitly suggests, depends on secret likeness; late in the novel, Mr. Davis offers to raise Ruth's son in just such terms: "I knew Leonard was illegitimate—in fact, I will give you secret for secret: it was being so myself that first made me sympathize with him" [441].) The line Faith's lie draws between the Bensons and the rest of the community expresses their unconventionality and marks their alienation. Benson is deformed, his sister unmarried, and Gaskell repeatedly associates them with an older way of life, one that is now in ideological competition with the livelihood of the prosperous mercantile classes. Despite their function as the moral center of the book, they lack the vitality of the less scrupulous, more financially success-

---

[9] Note Gaskell's own metaphor for the fallen woman's fate: "Respectability shuts the door upon her." Quoted in Monica Fryckstedt, *Elizabeth Gaskell's "Mary Barton" and "Ruth": A Challenge to Christian England* (Uppsala, 1982), 138. On woman as mediator between inside and outside, see Janet Todd, *Sensibility: An Introduction* (London: Methuen, 1986), 100.

ful Bradshaw. Women—particularly unmarried women—and priests are among the figures Scheler singles out as likely candidates for feelings of *ressentiment;* in particular, Benson recalls Scheler's discussion of the priest, whose role requires that he "always represent the image and principle of peacefulness."[10] The Bensons' social fall is linked symbolically to Ruth's moral one; Benson even averts her suicide by literally falling to the ground while pursuing her. For the Bensons, feeling for Ruth is a way of not feeling for themselves: it is a way of gaining distance from, even as it implicitly acknowledges, an unstable social position. Expressing what Barbara Ehrenreich has called a "fear of falling" endemic to the middle class, the Bensons' sympathy acknowledges in displaced form—through identification with a figure publicly identified as an outcast—the marginality those with limited social power perceive in their own positions.[11]

Sympathy in *Ruth* is identified with a threatened disturbance in, and subversion of, the rigid categories of identity—particularly feminine identity—that would exclude Ruth from respectable society. And that subversion is possible only if Ruth's identity retains its transgressive force. It thus makes sense that the disruptive energy Gaskell attempts to eliminate by constructing Ruth as innocent returns via the mechanism of disguise. By displacing the novel's focus from Ruth's fall to Faith's lie, Gaskell alters the stakes of sympathizing with Ruth (and with *Ruth*) to include not just sympathizing, but fictionalizing, or, in the novel's terms, lying: there is no mistaking the analogy between Faith's pleasure in manufacturing details of Ruth's identity and Gaskell's own activity. For while Benson might be said to identify with Ruth's outsider status and vulnerability, or with her unconscious deviation from moral behavior, Faith seizes upon her as an opportunity for transgression, saying "I do think I've a talent for fiction, it is so pleasant to invent and make the incidents dovetail together. . . . I am afraid I enjoy not being fettered by truth" (150). Through her fictionalizing, Faith strikes a blow against the rigid roles that keep the Ruths and the Mrs. Bradshaws of the world "broken into submission"; she disrupts the home organized around the assertion of Puritanical values, and deceives the patriarch, Bradshaw, whose outrage anticipates that of

---

[10] Scheler, *Ressentiment,* 36.

[11] Barbara Ehrenreich, *Fear of Falling: The Inner Life of the Middle Class* (New York: Pantheon, 1989).

Gaskell's outraged male readers—and ultimately chastens Faith's pleasure in the production of narrative. The analogy between Faith's fictionalizing and Gaskell's—between getting Ruth into the Bradshaw home and getting *Ruth* into the homes of Gaskell's readers—affirms, however, the inseparability of Gaskell's plea for sympathy from the social discontent that plea expresses.[12] Like her author, Faith Benson transforms resentment into fiction; inventing character to gain authority, she suggests the potential fluidity of social boundaries and social authority. Her fictionalizing works to alter the balance of power in a community in which Benson's moral concerns had been increasingly marginalized, his financial dependence on Bradshaw undermining his moral position.

"I want to know how I am to keep remembering how old I am, so as to prevent myself from feeling so young?"
(Faith Benson, looking in the mirror, 206)

Sympathy in *Ruth* is an identification with the marginal, expressed in the falling that links Benson with Ruth and the disguise wherein he and his sister reproduce their own conflicted identities. But it is also a mechanism for eliding that identification, enabling the novel's characters to retain their places in the social hierarchy and remain unconscious, like Ruth, of the *ressentiment* she embodies. As we have seen, Gaskell insists upon Ruth's unconsciousness: her ignorance of social convention saves her from participation in her fall; the lack of deliberateness in her subsequent behavior underscores her essential value (both Benson and Bradshaw admire Ruth's "complete unconsciousness of uncommon power," the fact that "she did not think of herself at all" [187]). Her unconsciousness, I have suggested, defines her as a figure of *ressentiment:* one who cannot act on

[12] Gaskell connected her own feelings about the novel with the idea of sexual transgression, identifying with her heroine. In her letters, she describes herself as being in pain from the things people are saying about *Ruth;* she is ill, and says she believes she must be ill with a "Ruth fever." And in a comment reminiscent of Ruth's "unconscious" fall, she writes, "I think I must be an improper woman without knowing it." J. A. V. Chapple and Arthur Pollard, eds., *The Letters of Mrs. Gaskell* (Cambridge: Harvard University Press, 1967), letter 150 (1853).

her own behalf, and for whom others are invited to feel, she embodies the anger the Bensons cannot express directly.[13] The character who exists as pure receptivity is, as Amanda Anderson points out, "a mere slave to the other."[14] (And as such, Ruth's extreme passivity may be said to suggest its opposite: not just the Benson's *ressentiment* but, in a displaced fashion, her own: the rage of the fallen woman.)

But the novel also associates unconsciousness with a desire to escape middle-class identity and its seemingly inevitable transgressions. When Ruth first meets Benson, she is about to drown herself—in the novel's words, to "seek forgetfulness." Benson saves her by enabling her to replace one form of self-forgetfulness with another; he falls, and his fall "did what no remonstrance could have done; it called her out of herself" (97). That initial meeting connects the capacity for sympathy with self-forgetfulness, and throughout the novel, the possibility of Ruth's redemption is identified with Ruth's forgetting of her former self. Indeed, she is most herself when most "out of herself," helping the poor and the sick in an effort "to forget what had gone before this last twelve months" (191). (Benson too strives "to leave his life in the hands of God, and to forget himself" [142].) It is as if the absence of consciousness Ruth exemplifies, and for which Benson longs, expresses a desire for relief from consciousness, identified in this novel with an almost unbearable sense of self-division. Indeed, it may be in her unconsciousness—identified with her unselfconsciousness—that Ruth best exemplifies middle-class identity: sympathy here resembles a state of forgetfulness that serves to assure the sympathizer of the unquestioned, secure nature of his or her identity. After all, the issue for middle-class identity, as the novel worries it (and Faith's comment implies) is "remembering" who one is, as if identity inheres in its active maintenance. But while sympathy here may seem to offer middle-class identity a welcome unselfconsciousness, it also suggests the absence

---

[13] Amanda Anderson argues that Ruth's character represents an antidote to determinism, especially the determinism of social construction. What the novel reveals, however, is the identity of character *with* social construction: social identity may be a fiction, even a lie, but the transformation of Ruth's character into pure receptivity results in the creation of a character whose boundaries finally dissolve completely. *Tainted Souls and Painted Faces: The Rhetoric of Fallenness in Victorian Culture* (Ithaca: Cornell University Press, 1993), 127–40.

[14] Ibid., 138.

of an essential self: the way in which identity built on identification with others may be imagined as no identity at all.

As Ruth takes on the fallen woman's traditional role and moves toward death, the novel insists even more emphatically on her emptiness. On her deathbed, as she becomes literally unconscious, she also becomes literally selfless: lying ill, "She could not remember the present time, or where she was . . . she was stretched on the bed in utter helplessness, softly gazing at vacancy with her open, unconscious eyes, from which all the depth of their meaning had fled" (444, 448). Lying "in utter helplessness, softly gazing at vacancy," Ruth becomes an emblem both of the vacancy of the ideal sympathetic observer, who forgets herself in her devotion to others, and of sympathy's object, displaced by the spectator's projection. In attempting to construct an ideally sympathetic character, Gaskell develops the sympathetic object to its logical extreme, finally exposing her character as a palimpsest of the cultural desires and anxieties that surround the figure of the fallen woman. "She could not remember who she was now, or where she was" (444). Mrs. Denbigh, the novel seeks to reassure us, was never anything more than a fantasy about social mobility; moving easily from one social position to another, Ruth gives up the hold on identity she might have possessed had she stayed in one place.

The exposure of Ruth's "true" self is thus only another move in the novel's continual construction and dismantling of her identity. It clarifies her function in the novel, legitimating and solidifying—even as the history of her identity may be said to undermine—the identities of the novel's other characters. As we have seen, Gaskell initially establishes social and moral uncertainty as norms of middle-class identity: the novel's characters are perpetually self-divided, guilt-ridden about the moral laxness and social uneasiness they seem unable to avoid. But the narrative works to efface such discomfort; though it rejects Bradshaw's desire for firm principles ("She has turned right into wrong, and wrong into right, and taught you all to be uncertain whether there be any such thing as Vice in the world" [339]), somehow events transpire so as to leave no uncertainty about everyone's feelings toward Ruth. The novel transforms social identity into emotional unanimity, as social difference gives way to shared feeling and an unconsciousness of the tensions Ruth's presence made visible.

The novel's plot demands the working out of the conflict between Benson and Bradshaw, and the breach Ruth's discovery causes between them—Bradshaw had refused to continue attending Benson's chapel (hence denying him his pew rents)—immediately effects a transmutation of resentment into affection: "He [Benson] felt acutely the severance of the tie which Mr. Bradshaw had just announced to him. He had experienced many mortifications in his intercourse with that gentleman, but they had fallen off from his meek spirit like drops of water from a bird's plumage; and now he only remembered the acts of substantial kindness.... [H]e had never recognized Mr. Bradshaw as an old familiar friend so completely, as now when they were severed" (352). But Benson's guilt about his failure to recognize Bradshaw merely suggests guilt about his own *ressentiment;* the novel's plot, rather than dissolving class boundaries, has characters appear to forget that such boundaries ever disturbed them. But sympathy, in the end, demands a series of falls: Bradshaw's son, for instance, is first revealed to be a forger and then injured in a coach accident.[15] And when Bradshaw sits in Benson's church with his head "bowed down low in prayer" where once "he had stood erect, with an air of conscious righteousness," his demeanor convinces Benson that "the old friendly feeling existed once more between them" (422).

As these scenes suggest, the novel remembers everywhere what it claims its characters can forget; Gaskell's language continues to invoke the hierarchical structure it insists has disappeared. The novel's end finds Benson at the "apex" of the community: preaching about Ruth after her death, he surveys around him "one and all—the well-filled Bradshaw pew—all in deep mourning, Mr. Bradshaw conspicuously so...the Farquhars—the many strangers—the still more numerous poor—one or two wild-looking outcasts, who stood afar off, but wept silently and continually" (456–57).[16] Moving from center to margins, high to low, the minister's eye defines the

---

[15] The elimination of uncertainty—of differences in feeling—thus requires a certain violence. For Bradshaw to be made part of the community—part, spiritually, of Gaskell's middle class—he must fall; it is not enough that his son turns out to be a forger, but the son must suffer a serious accident to awaken the father's humanity. Indeed, the novel's obsessive literalization of the falling metaphor suggests the violence with which Gaskell imagines the social or moral fall. Benson's deformity is "owing to a fall he had had" (135); Richard Bradshaw is seriously injured in his coach accident. The latter case in particular literalizes Bradshaw's unspoken fear: that self-forgery will lead to a fall.

[16] In 1849 Edward Miall described the way old parish churches, and in particular the pew system, reproduced social inequalities: "The poor man is made to feel that he is a poor

congregation as an idealized microcosm of the social whole, its members' ability to share the same feelings unaffected by social difference. Finally, the novel's model for the circulation of feeling is no longer an infectious blurring of boundaries but an assertion of harmony in social difference, of personal relationships disturbed by no feelings arising from social inequities. Sympathy provides a way out of immediate social conflicts and produces a fiction of both individual and communal unity here, not because it resolves conflict, but rather because it enables the evacuation or forgetting of conflict in the manufacture of sympathetic subjects and objects.

The invention of Mrs. Denbigh might be read as a sign of Gaskell's awareness of the difficulty, even impossibility, of gaining sympathy for her heroine: an implicit acknowledgment that sympathy for the fallen woman *as* fallen woman is impossible to achieve. The disguise might be considered a strategic ploy, an attempt to encourage readers, aware as they are of Ruth's "true" identity, to position themselves in opposition to the narrow-minded Mr. Bradshaws of the world. In either case, the Bensons' lie raises the same suspicion as Ruth's death: the suspicion that, if she is to win sympathy, Ruth cannot be "herself." For in what would such a self consist? In *Ruth*, Gaskell describes an identity so enmeshed in the projections of others, and in literary convention (her name tells us her story), that it becomes a kind of exposure of the power of the type—an assertion of the capacity of cultural identity to annihilate any sense of individual identity altogether. In this novel, as in other fallen woman novels, unconsciousness is the author's way of protecting her heroine from sexual knowledge. But it is also the manifestation in character of the way sympathy denies its object agency and intention, making it not at all surprising that, on her deathbed, Ruth "could not remember who she was now."

―――

Early in the novel, Gaskell foregrounds the naturalness of Ruth's sympathetic identity: her responsiveness to nature, her lack of self-consciousness,

―――

man, the rich is reminded that he is rich, in the great majority of our churches and chapels.... the arrangements are generally such as to preclude in their [the poor's] bosoms any momentary feeling of essential equality. We have no negro pews, for we have no prejudice against colour—but we have distinct places for the pennyless, for we have a morbid horror of poverty." Quoted in Fryckstedt, *Elizabeth Gaskell's Mary Barton,* 58–59.

her innocence of the social world. When Bellingham beckons her to look at her image in a pond, "She obeyed, and could not help seeing her own loveliness; it gave her a sense of satisfaction for an instant, as the sight of any other beautiful creature would have done, but she never thought of associating it with herself" (74). Ruth's inability to associate her image with herself, and the tension between what she "could not help" and what she "never thought"—between the natural and the social—appear again in a similar set piece at the novel's end. When Bellingham returns, Ruth finds herself in church being observed by him, and "in this extreme tension of mind to hold in her bewildered agony" focuses on a gargoyle in one corner of the room.

> The face was beautiful...but it was not the features that were the most striking part. There was a half-open mouth, not in any way distorted out of its exquisite beauty by the intense expression of suffering it conveyed. Any distortion of the face by mental agony, implies that a struggle with circumstance is going on. But in this face, if such struggle had been, it was over now. Circumstance had conquered.... And though the parted lips seemed ready to quiver with agony, yet the expression of the whole face, owing to these strange, stony, and yet spiritual eyes, was high and consoling.... Who could have imagined such a look? Who could have witnessed—perhaps felt—such infinite sorrow, and yet dared to lift it up by Faith into a peace so pure?...Human art was ended—human life done—human suffering over; but this remained; it stilled Ruth's beating heart to look on it. (282–83)

The gargoyle projects Ruth's struggle into the future, suggesting at the same time the future the novel has in store for her: the fulfillment of her objectification in death. A vision of suffering transmuted—lifted up ("by Faith")—into art, it also crystallizes the aestheticizing process in which the novel is engaged and recapitulates the structure of sympathy on which it depends. In this scene, Ruth reflects upon an external image she nowhere explicitly names as a reflection—an image that, in effect, embodies her own emotional history. The emphasis is on an image that collapses narrative: an image in which nothing is left of the character's history but opposing images of suffering and its transcendence. Focusing on that figure, Ruth focuses, for the novel's readers, the tensions she herself embodies; as she does so, she becomes—like the statue—"still." Moving beyond Ruth's consciousness to seek the "look" that transformed hers into art, Gaskell's narrator locates an understanding of the gargoyle's significance in the consciousnesses of the novel's readers, unifying them around the doubled image of Ruth. Here, as in *East Lynne*—as my next chapter argues—class identity is figured as emotional unanimity, as subjects are "stilled" by an image of their social identifications and the conflicts to which those identifications lead. In this "unconscious" act of identification, the sympathetic observer—like the fallen woman, and like Sherlock Holmes—gains identity in the act of losing it. Middle-class identity itself, by this account, is *Ruth*'s scene of sympathy.

4

Isabel's Spectacles:
Seeing Value in East Lynne

"The world goes round and round by rules of contrary.... We
despise what we have, and covet that which we cannot get."

— Ellen Wood, *East Lynne*

Toward the end of Ellen Wood's *East Lynne* (1863), Barbara
Carlyle recounts to her family's governess, Madame Vine, the story of
Isabel Vane's elopement—not knowing that the governess actually is Isabel,
Carlyle's first wife, transformed by the combined effects of a disfiguring
railway accident and a disguise. Barbara includes the one detail of which
Isabel is unaware: that Francis Levison, the man for whom Isabel left her
husband, is now known to be a murderer. Isabel responds to that detail, and
to the cumulative effect of hearing the entire story, immediately and physically: "In spite of her caution, of her strife for self-command, she turned of
a deadly whiteness, and a low sharp cry of horror and despair burst from
her lips.... 'I beg your pardon, Mrs. Carlyle,' she shivered: 'I am apt to picture things too vividly. It is, as you say, so very horrible.' "[1]

[1] Mrs. Henry Wood, *East Lynne,* ed. Sally Mitchell (New Brunswick, N.J.: Rutgers
University Press, 1984), 417. Subsequent page numbers are included in the text. See Mary
Ann Doane, *Femmes Fatales: Feminism, Film Theory, Psychoanalysis* (New York: Routledge,

Isabel might be regarded here as a model for sensation fiction's ideal reader: one for whom that genre's too-vivid pictures provide an occasion for the experience and release of powerful affect. Indeed, spending considerably more time detailing Isabel's response to representations of her experience than it does recounting that experience itself, the novel suggests the superiority of representation and sensational narrative over the experience represented to produce affect and sensation. Positioning Isabel as audience to her own story—asking her, in effect, to sympathize with herself as a fictional character—Wood reproduces both the reader's relation to Isabel and the divided structure of Isabel's own experience in the novel's latter half, which finds her situated as spectator to the familial life of Mr. and Mrs. Carlyle: to the life she might have led, that is, had she not run away with Levison. In doing so, the novel renders Isabel's sympathy for a fictional character inseparable from her identity as that character (this is the same literalization of identification found "A Christmas Carol," in which the shock of recognition stems from the fact that the character in the story *is* you), and it implicates its readers in her identification: sympathy with Isabel is aligned with reflection on, and horror at, the story she now recognizes as her own. In this way, as, later, in Isabel's active reconstruction of her body and identity, the novel defines her, has her define herself, and implicitly defines its readers as effects of sympathetic identification. To sympathize with Isabel, in Wood's novel, is manifestly to sympathize with representation.

Recent criticism of sensation fiction finds in the genre's reliance on what might be called bodily sympathy (as in the communication of nervousness from character to reader) an erasure of representation, an evocation of the real and the natural in somatic responses that seem to efface the boundary between reader and text.[2] But Barbara's narrative and Isabel's spectatorship stage this ostensible erasure as a response to representation, affirming less the immediacy of sensation's effect on the body than the role of cultural representations—such as *East Lynne*'s own sensational narrative—as mediators of sensation and its meanings. Isabel's response to

---

1991), 19, on the way the absence of spectatorial distance characterizes the construction of female subjectivity—the way in which women always "picture too vividly."

[2] See D. A. Miller, "Cage aux folles," in *The Novel and the Police* (Berkeley: University of California Press, 1988), 146–91; Ann Cvetkovich, *Mixed Feelings: Feminism, Mass Culture, and Victorian Sensationalism* (New Brunswick, N.J.: Rutgers University Press, 1992).

Barbara's narrative, like the agony of suffering she endures in her position as spectator, aligns her embrace of middle-class values with the mediation of her experience by representation—or, in the novel's term, "reflection." Rather than grounding affect directly in the body, that is, *East Lynne* highlights the cultural construction of ideological effects—a highlighting for which the eyeglasses Isabel wears as part of her disguise (which both frame the scenes she witnesses and make a spectacle of Isabel herself) will serve as my metaphor. Despite the novel's reliance on the idea of unmediated bodily response (as in Isabel's sexual response to Levison), then, I wish to argue that experience in *East Lynne* counts most heavily and leaves a more lasting impression when filtered through Isabel's spectacular lenses. In particular, framing its representations of domesticity through and as Isabel's spectacles, the novel reveals them to be, precisely, vivid pictures.

Meeting Frances Levison in Boulogne, where Carlyle has sent her for her health, Isabel "shrank from self-examination" (175). No sooner has she left East Lynne with Levison, however, abandoning husband and home, than she develops a capacity for "reflection," simultaneously recognizing the "true" nature of her action: "The very hour of her departure she awoke to what she had done: the guilt...assumed at once its true, frightful colour " (237). "The terrible position in which she found herself, had brought to Lady Isabel *reflection*. Not the reflection, so called, that may come to us who yet live in and for the world, but that which must, almost of necessity, attend one whose part in the world is over" (249). Much of the remainder of the novel is taken up with this process of reflection, in which Isabel reimagines—in their "true colors"—events she has witnessed or experienced (the best example is the scene of Carlyle and Barbara walking in the moonlight, a scene to which the novel returns repeatedly and which, appearing to confirm Isabel's suspicions of her husband's infidelity, prompts her departure). Indeed, the entire second part of the novel, which finds Isabel installed as governess to her own children in the Carlyle home, in essence constitutes such a reflection, as Isabel, wearing the tinted spectacles some Victorian actresses used to indicate the entire none-too-flattering disguise, entertains vivid pictures of what would have been her life had she remained.[3] "Then came another phase of the pic-

---

[3] On the glasses, see Sally Mitchell, introduction to *East Lynne*, xiv.

ture," she imagines before returning: "How could she bear to see Mr. Carlyle the husband of another?—to live in the same house with them, to witness his attentions, possibly his caresses?" (333). "The old scenes passed through her mind, like the changing pictures in a phantasmagoria" (493).

In this process of reflection, things Isabel initially observed through an ostensibly distorted lens are said to assume their true colors, as in the following account of the transformation of her consciousness: "As her eyes opened to her folly and to the true character of Francis Levison, so in proportion did they close to the fault by which her husband had offended her. She saw it in fainter colours; she began to suspect—nay, she knew—that her own excited feelings had magnified it in length, and breadth, and height.... She remembered his [Carlyle's] noble qualities; doubly noble did they appear to her, now that her interest in them must cease... her esteem, her admiration, her affection for him, had returned to her fourfold. We never know the full value of a thing until we lose it" (249). Her eyes opening and closing at once—opening to an inward scene as they close to the external world—Isabel weighs her losses and readjusts her vision. Registering changes in moral value as shifts in visual values, this passage illustrates both the bourgeois nature of perception in the novel (its relentless attempt to measure, to value, everything) and the *embourgeoisement* of Isabel's consciousness: as the passage slides effortlessly from "appear" to "know," swelling Carlyle's retrospective value, Isabel's body and vision serve (as they do throughout the novel's latter half) as instruments for the recalibration of social value.[4]

Defining the acquisition of knowledge as a readjustment of vision—giving Isabel colored glasses through which to view things in their "true" colors—the novel both suggests that she needs corrective lenses and offers a metaphor for its own ideological coloring. For rejecting what she now perceives as "magnified," Isabel simultaneously expresses her discovery of truth in equally exaggerated terms: "she remembered his noble qualities; doubly noble did they appear to her... her affection for him had returned fourfold." But if, indeed, "her own excited feelings had magnified" Carlyle's fault in "length, and breadth, and height" (as if measuring for a carpet, or piece of furniture), who is to say that her current feelings are

---

[4] On the calibrations or rationalizations of the middle-class household, see Anne McClintock, *Imperial Leather: Race, Gender, and Sexuality in the Colonial Context* (New York: Routledge, 1995), 168.

any less the result of magnification, or, as the passage has it, multiplication? Making visible what it quickly moves to repress—the difficulty of separating value from the "color" with which one sees it (or of separating "knowledge" from "suspicion," with the suggestion that the former is nothing but the fulfillment of the latter—"she began to suspect—nay, she knew")—the passage calls attention to the instability of its ideological calculus: its claim that "doubly" and "fourfold" add up to "full."

Grounding truth in the need for Isabel to re-see and revalue the events of her life, Wood aligns Isabel's "discovery" of the truth of bourgeois verities with representation in several forms. Mental "reflection" conjures up "pictures" and "phantasmagorias," all of which, aligned with the characteristic visual intensity of sensation fiction and melodrama, suggest the representational function of the novel itself. And in *East Lynne*'s second half, the projection of domestic spectacles through Isabel's eyeglasses in effect renders them indistinguishable from productions of her own consciousness and, by implication, the consciousness of readers who "see" through her eyes. In a process that mirrors the self-alienation and desire projected on the novel's readers, then, Isabel's newfound interiority and the interiorities of her readers are represented as effects of the ability to project the self into representations. "Reflecting," Isabel comes to know her true self; seeing "correctly," she attests to her possession of proper values.[5] Isabel's interiority *is* cultural representation: experience filtered through the categories of bourgeois ideology.[6] And, indeed, to

---

[5] This despite Margaret Oliphant's assertion that sympathy for Isabel would lead to "moral confusion." *East Lynne* disturbed Oliphant because—like Gaskell's *Ruth*—it seemed to her to direct feeling to the wrong place; in encouraging readers to sympathize with Isabel, Oliphant writes, Wood makes "the worse...the better cause" ("Novels," *Blackwoods'* 94 [1863]: 170). But to sympathize with Isabel at this point in the novel is to identify with her desire to occupy Barbara's place: Readers who identify with Isabel imaginatively invest themselves in a consciousness emptied of everything but a gaze; the spectacles through which they look are filled with the domestic scene that has become the novel's locus of value.

[6] Susan Stewart describes a similar effect as characteristic of nostalgia: "The inability of the sign to 'capture' its signified, of narrative to be at one with its object, and of the genres of mechanical reproduction to approximate the time of face-to-face communication leads to a generalized desire for origin, for nature, and for unmediated experience that is at work in nostalgic longing." *On Longing: Narratives of the Miniature, the Gigantic, the Souvenir, the Collection* (Baltimore: Johns Hopkins University Press, 1984), 23–24.

sympathize with Isabel is to sympathize with representation in several forms. Unable to participate in middle-class life by virtue of her aristocratic identity, figured as her oversensitive body, Isabel in the latter half of the novel "assents" (Wood's term) with all the intensity of her spectatorship and suffering to the value of that life. Eliciting readerly sympathy for Isabel largely through the mechanism of spectatorship—requiring readers, as a condition of sympathy for her, to gaze both at and through the eyeglasses that mark her as spectator and spectacle—Wood ties readerly sympathy to a condition of spectatorship. Sympathy for Isabel is identified with a relentless spectatorship that mirrors Isabel's own; it depends upon identification with the representations for which she comes to yearn, and with her yearning for them. Indeed, in several ways Isabel's story registers her social fall as a fall into representation: as an increasing involvement with spectacle, reflection, projection, dissimulation, and disguise. To identify with Isabel is to identify with Isabel's spectacles: those she sees, those she wears, and those in which she appears; it is also to sympathize with an identity in which, as in the fiction called the middle class, images of various class identities jostle against one another. As a fallen aristocrat, and in particular a woman in decline, Isabel-in-disguise emerges as a paradigmatic figure for a fractured middle-class identity, an image that captures the tensions between high and low, "nature" and artifice, out which this identity is constituted. Rendering sympathy a spectator's melodrama, *East Lynne* makes spectatorship a condition of sympathy and, in doing so, discloses the role played by sympathy and spectatorship, and sympathy with spectatorship, in the construction of middle-class identity.

Wood's reliance on a dynamic of scenes and spectators has, it has often been noted, obvious affinities with stage melodrama.[7] But that connection does not so much explain away her reliance on spectatorship as suggest the way both the popular novel and stage melodrama reflect and reproduce the increasingly spectatorial nature of experience in the 1860s. To describe the scenes Isabel imagines as a phantasmagoria, as Wood does, is to imagine a spectator *in* the mind: to include spectatorship in subjectivity's definition. As E. Ann Kaplan notes, *East Lynne* demonstrates the way the

---

[7] As Sally Mitchell notes of stage adaptations of *East Lynne,* "The essential scenes were in Wood's novel" (Mitchell, introduction to *East Lynne,* xv).

popular novel is "affected by the culture of the spectacle," revealing in turn the way that culture "transform[s] the subject's ways of perceiving and desiring."[8]

Here as in "A Christmas Carol," however, spectacular forms of cultural representation do not create but rather reinforce cultural values already in place. *East Lynne's* visuality amplifies the spectacular function of middle-class Victorian women, for whom visible details indicated status and value; the novel functions in large part as a feminine phantasmagoria, a portrait gallery in which women hone their ability to distinguish good feminine spectacles from bad ones and evaluate the pictures other women make. For Isabel embodies the contradictory tensions of a Victorian middle-class feminine identity that was, increasingly and preeminently in the mid-nineteenth century, a matter of keeping up appearances: of displaying the visible evidence of middle-class status.[9] Sympathy with representation, for instance, accurately describes Barbara's activity as she observes and imitates Isabel's manipulation of social codes (despite Isabel's ostensible function as a negative role model, she is, as Jeanne B. Elliot points out, very much a

---

[8] E. Ann Kaplan, *Motherhood and Representation: The Mother in Popular Culture and Melodrama* (London: Routledge, 1992), 62. Richard Altick dates the first London phantasmagoria as occurring in 1801 or 1802. But he also points out that the term "phantasmagoria," like "panorama," was "quickly was absorbed into the common vocabulary." *The Shows of London* (Cambridge, Mass.: Belknap, 1978), 219. "By the 1860's," he writes, "they were well on their way to becoming one of the most widely attended of all forms of Victorian entertainment" (220). No specific form of representation need be at stake here, then; "phantasmagoria" signifies the general way in which "dull" subjects are "glamorized" by means of technological projection (220). But the actual structure of the phantasmagoria (in which the size of images projected from a magic lantern behind a screen could be increased or decreased to simulate movement toward or away from the audience) may also be relevant since, as one observer noted in the 1830s, images in a phantasmagoria could seem enlarged and all encompassing (219). In a manner relevant to Isabel's experience at the Carlyle's, as well as to *East Lynne's* idealization of middle-class life, audiences at the phantasmagoria were deceived into thinking they could touch the figures projected, so close and so real did those figures seem. The point was to focus the audience's attention on the lighted figures: as Altick further remarks, "The ghostly figures were painted on glass 'sliders,' the extraneous portions of which were blacked out so as to concentrate the light...on the luminous images" (217).

[9] On middle-class feminine display, see Elizabeth Langland, *Nobody's Angels: Middle-Class Women and Domestic Ideology in Victorian Culture* (Ithaca: Cornell University Press, 1995), 33–34.

lady).[10] In several crucial scenes at the novel's beginning—especially that of Isabel's first appearance in West Lynne's church, which finds Barbara appointed in pink parasol, bonnet, and feather, and Isabel elegantly understated in white muslin—Isabel provides Barbara, and the novel's readers as well, lessons in the management of female spectacularity. If, for Isabel, an adjustment of values can lead to nothing but, as the novel puts it, "one long scene of repentance," for Barbara and potentially for Wood's readers as well an openness to the colors of class value translates into a new identity, a new social self. Indeed, by the end of the novel, Barbara—reproached in the novel's first half for her love of finery and for the failure of control that results in her emotional outburst to Carlyle—has, by watching Isabel, learned balance, and the ability to manipulate her own self-representation to achieve it. Her accession to her position as Carlyle's wife and mistress of East Lynne serves as a model for a fluid, socially mobile subjectivity able to perceive the hues and shades, codes and controls, that enable movement from one class to another.[11]

Seeming to value the identification that leads to social advancement, however, the novel also works to disavow the instability that identification suggests; while it values in Barbara the fluidity that leads to and defines middle-class identity, it disavows that fluidity in its scapegoating of Isabel, condemning her awareness of the codes of self-representation by associating that awareness both with aristocratic indulgence and with disguise. In Isabel's first public appearance at West Lynne's church, for instance, outdressing the local women by not dressing up at all, she avoids the "unnecessary profusion of splendour" Carlyle perceives that same day at the Earl's dining table (53–54). But subsequent events suggest that within her apparent modesty lies an undesirable canniness about self-presentation. Later,

---

[10] Elliott writes that despite Isabel's beginning as the Earl's daughter and ending as a governess, she remains a "lady" in whom "every Victorian female reader could encounter an idealized version of herself." See "A Lady to the End: The Case of Isabel Vane," *Victorian Studies* 19 (1976): 331.

[11] Of the construction of the "aristocratic bourgeoisie" in Victorian England, Elizabeth Langland writes, "The middling classes did not ape the economic practices of upper-class life, but, afflicted by status anxiety, set out to master its signifying practices." *Nobody's Angels,* 26. Kaplan writes, "The novel shows that the only class capable of the correct balance between desire and its release is the middle class" (*Motherhood and Representation,* 89). But Barbara has to learn "balance" from watching Isabel, and from losing her own at a significant moment.

for instance, she deliberately overdresses for a recital by Kane, the music master, in order to show "that *I* think the poor man's concert worth going to, and worth dressing for" (63). It is as if, in Wood's estimation, Isabel cannot fill the role of the liberal subject because she is unable to detach herself from her own spectacular class identity: she cannot, as she will soon have to, "lose" her self. Exhibiting sympathy, Isabel also displays her ability to manipulate self-display and her awareness of its consequences: "I feared it might be thought I had put them on to *look* fine," she says elsewhere of some diamonds she has chosen not to wear (12).[12]

Thus despite Wood's evident valuing of Isabel's feeling for Kane, the novel—as if rehearsing a characteristically middle-class response to this aristocratic gesture—expresses ambivalence about her mode of expressing it. And that ambivalence is reinforced when, summoned in all her finery from the concert to her father's sickbed, she refuses to pay attention to that same dress. However awkward it would be to change costumes for her father's death, she is nevertheless found to be inappropriately dressed for the occasion. The episode suggests the difficulty, for the aristocratic Isabel, of wearing the virtue she is condemned to lose; hard as she may try, she can never strike the correct balance between inner value and external display. For she cannot cease being on display: though her impulse in each instance is a sympathy of which Wood evidently approves, her unavoidable visibility suggests (and the novel continues to demonstrate) that the aristocratic heroine cannot truly sympathize because she cannot help but make a spectacle of herself: she cannot accurately read, nor can she be quietly absorbed into, the scenarios in which she finds herself. (And, indeed, the spectacle of degradation Isabel embodies as Madame Vine reproduces Isabel Vane's subjection to the relentless middle-class gaze—a gaze literally reproduced when, toward the end of the century, the novel was transformed into theater.) Only middle-class identity, the novel's ideology suggests, with its valorization of inwardness and intuition of the proper balance between feeling and its manifestations, is sufficiently mobile, sufficiently flexible, and—as its metaphorical figuration in the theater audience suggests, sufficiently invisible—for the proper exercise of sympathy.

---

[12] Elaine Hadley links Isabel's benevolent desire to display herself to her aristocratic identity. *Melodramatic Tactics: Theatricalized Dissent in the English Marketplace, 1800–1885* (Stanford: Stanford University Press, 1995), 170.

This episode also marks gender differences in sympathy's mode of operations. The novel's critique of Isabel's attempt to assist Kane designates the personal gesture as feminine and self-indulgent, well intentioned but insufficiently considered. This leaves room for the dispassionate, "professional" sympathy displayed in Carlyle's behind-the-scenes assistance to Barbara's brother James—and, presumably, in his later political life. When Isabel "mistakes" meetings between Barbara and Carlyle for love scenes, she is of course hardly mistaken; in these scenes, Carlyle's cool, rational business mode—ostensibly just a convenient cover for discussing how to help James—develops as the novel's alternative to Isabel's overheated and unpredictable emotion. In this way, as in its later evocation of mass sympathy in the theater, *East Lynne* distinguishes a practical, masculine sympathy from an ostentatious and impractical—if also admirable—feminine one.

———

The novel valorizes Barbara's self-presentation over Isabel's. But it does so in a manner that merely replaces the latter with the former as the novel's glamorous center. And in this replacement, an aristocratic "ethos of visibility" is adapted to and seamlessly merged with the visual modality of the Victorian marketplace, the Victorian bourgeois home positioned, in Andrew Miller's succinct characterization of the effects of Victorian commodity culture, "behind glass." Barbara's spectacularized home embodies what Thomas Richards has called "capitalist representation," and what, for Jürgen Habermas, marks a hollowing out of the private sphere, an "illusion of bourgeois privacy" in which the home in effect becomes an advertisement for a form of intimacy in the process of being displaced by popular culture. The value of West Lynne's domesticity, then, is located in Isabel's newly altered perception, and in ideological perception in general as it projects value onto everyday life.[13]

East Lynne allegorizes a social shift: the replacement of Isabel and her father by Carlyle and Barbara signals the replacement of the aristocracy by

———

[13] Thomas Richards, *The Commodity Culture of Victorian England,* 13; Jürgen Habermas, *The Structural Transformation of the Public Sphere* (Cambridge: MIT Press, 1994), 161; Andrew Miller, *Novels Behind Glass: Commodity Culture and Victorian Narrative* (Cambridge: Cambridge University Press, 1995). Hadley writes that *East Lynne* "projects its vision of a traditional social order and adheres to its ethos of visibility even as the novel celebrates

the professional middle class, and the novel's representation of bourgeois life is inseparable from its project of engendering desire for that life. And replacing the aristocracy with the middle class means, for Wood, substituting the one for the other as the object of the reader's desirous gaze. Thus while in the novel's first half the middle class envies the aristocracy, in its second the aristocracy is put in the position of envying the middle class, the former's characteristically heightened sensibility and emotional susceptibility given over to the incitement of middle-class desire. The novel's idealization of the middle class is thus rendered as a function of Isabel's gaze: if we begin by gazing at Isabel, we end by gazing—through and with Isabel—at Barbara. And as that gaze shifts from one woman to another and one class to another, the bourgeoisie seems less to replace the aristocracy than to become it. (Once she has become an expert at the bourgeois economics of feeling and its expression, Barbara exemplifies what Nancy Armstrong calls—referring to an ambiguously coded combination of character regulation and external display—"middle-class aristocracy.")[14] In *East Lynne*, spectacle, both naturalized and psychologized through Isabel's gaze, is identified with both aristocratic excess and an idealized middle-class domesticity. Even when the scenes Isabel witnesses seem to speak of nothing but surface, then—of the shallowness, for instance, of Barbara's managerial mothering—the intensity with which they are visualized figures the intensity of Isabel's longing and invites readerly longing as well. Indeed, the novel's pictures of East Lynne's domesticity exist chiefly as metonyms for Isabel's desire. And that desire, in turn, suggests the inescapably representational status of Victorian middle-class domesticity: the way its successful achievement is always in question. (And always in process: the necessity for active household maintenance—which goes largely unseen—reflects the perpetual identity-maintenance of middle-class consciousness, as it works toward a never-to-be-attained ideal. "We never know the full value of a thing until we lose it," says Wood's narrator, the "until" implying the inevitability of loss.) As the novel struc-

what we now recognize as the bourgeois virtues of modesty and prudence." *Melodramatic Tactics,* 169.

[14] In connection with Austen's novels, Armstrong describes the "middle-class aristocracy" as a formation that links middle-class moral and economic codes with aristocratic "nuances of emotion and ethical refinements." Armstrong, *Desire and Domestic Fiction: A Political History of the Novel* (New York: Oxford University Press, 1987), 160.

tures its representations, the reader who identifies with Isabel, like Isabel herself, remains hopelessly identified with the "pictures" she longs to inhabit.

Whereas early in the novel Isabel's perceptions are isolated, defined as excessive and overwrought, after her fall readers share her vision, witnessing Barbara's life through lenses that locate desire for bourgeois life in an overly sensitive aristocratic body—the body offered to readers for their sympathy and identification.[15] Here is Isabel being taken through East Lynne for the first time:

> On she followed, her heart palpitating: past the rooms that used to be hers, along the corridor, towards the second staircase. The doors of her old bed and dressing-rooms stood open, and she glanced in with a yearning look. No, never more, never more could they be hers: she had put them from her by her own free act and deed. Not less comfortable did they look now, than in former days; but they had passed into another's occupancy. The fire threw its blaze on the furniture: there were the little ornaments on the large dressing table, as they used to be in *her* time, and the cut glass of the crystal essence bottles was glittering in the fire-light. On the sofa lay a shawl and a book, and on the bed a silk dress, as if thrown there after being taken off. (336)

Desire produces a description already framed, by both Isabel's spectacles and the doorway through which she glances; it produces a path of glittering objects for the eye to trace, and ultimately a place—the discarded dress—with which both Isabel and the novel's female readers are invited to identify, and into which they may, imaginatively, insert themselves. As Mrs. Carlyle, Barbara becomes visible in the visual details Isabel glimpses. And throughout the novel's latter half, the lives of Barbara and Carlyle—

---

[15] John Kucich argues that *East Lynne* "is centrally concerned with middle-class apprehensions about its rising political and economic fortunes, and the way those fortunes had fragmented its own moral makeup." *The Power of Lies: Transgression in Victorian Fiction* (Ithaca: Cornell University Press, 1994), 161–62. For Kucich, the figure of the professional resolves tensions between middle-class and aristocratic values. In my view, Isabel's unstable identity, and in particular her governess disguise, perform similar "resolutions," suggesting middle-class ideology's simultaneous, contradictory reliance on both stable moral truths and fluid identity boundaries.

especially that of Barbara, whose desires, amply described earlier, seem now to have been fulfilled—similarly appear as image and spectacle. Isabel's vision overlays what she sees with painful intensity, perhaps, we are told, distorting it. Thus "inexpressibly more beautiful looked Barbara than Lady Isabel had ever seen her—or else she fancied it" (339). But where the "or else" might suggest a perception weakened or at least called into question by an acknowledgment of feeling's effect on perception, here it also seems to define a mode of seeing that, drenched in longing, expresses a more profound truth than any objective account could. Collapsing Isabel's consciousness into its own representational strategies, the novel generalizes her perception, as if to acknowledge that the expression of ideological truths requires a certain distortion. *East Lynne* gives middle-class life both specular and spectacular form by framing it through the eyes of an observer whose life has become, Wood puts it, "as one long scene of mortal agony" (516). Like "A Christmas Carol," the novel repeatedly—and relentlessly—positions readers, along with Isabel, outside the home, staging window-scenes that set a brilliantly lit East Lynne against a dark background: "In one of the comfortable sitting-rooms of East Lynne sat Mr. Carlyle and his sister one inclement January night. The warm, blazing fire, the handsome carpet on which it flickered, the exceedingly comfortable arrangement of the furniture of the room altogether, and the light of the chandelier which fell on all, presented a picture of home peace, though it may not have deserved the name of luxury" (284). (Scenes showing Barbara and Carlyle are usually framed through Isabel's eyes: "Lights were moving in the windows, it looked gay and cheerful, a contrast to her" [335]). The novel's readers, positioned along with Isabel as targets of these representations, are invited to perceive themselves as similarly dispossessed, and Isabel's distance from her "own" experience is thus inscribed as a division within bourgeois life itself: as the insurmountable but inevitable distance between the middle-class wife and the "scenes" in which she lives.

These pictures of idealized domesticity capture the tension between permanence and transience that marks the professional middle class's "inheritance" of aristocratic property, its attempted appropriation of aristocratic signifiers. For despite the sale of the house, despite the changes of master and mistress, everything—from the fire to the "little ornaments on the dressing table"—seems to Isabel "as they used to be in *her* time." One might think that a new mistress would have chosen new ornaments, or that the "crystal essence bottles...glittering in the fire-light" might now be different ones. But here every detail, including and perhaps especially the dress lying on the bed, tells readers that what is susceptible to change is not the house but its occupants, particularly its mistress. Describing what, in her view, constituted the moral misguidance of sympathy for Isabel, Margaret Oliphant wrote that "when she [Isabel] returns to her home under the guise of the poor governess, there is not a reader who does not feel disposed to turn her virtuous successor to the door, and to reinstate the suffering heroine, to the glorious confusion of all morality."[16] For Oliphant, sympathy for Isabel takes the form of a reader's wish for her reinstatement, into the house, the ornaments, the dress; what is rejected is not the place and not even the husband, but the other woman, who becomes—as any reader might imagine herself—just another temporary occupant ("as if thrown there after being taken off"). Indeed, given the permanence accorded to domestic objects here—even to the fire that, it seems, is always burning—this picture gives female readers a rather tenuous hold on their bourgeois paradises. Sympathizing with Isabel means sympathizing with the place in which she wants to insert herself, and with her desire to do so. (Wood stresses everywhere the identification between the two women; Barbara is what Isabel might have been; Isabel "almost regarded Mr. Carlyle as *her* husband" [497] [as, indeed, he is]. Emphasizing the reversibility of their positions, the novel makes clear the precedence accorded social identity: both Isabel and Barbara long to be, and identify with, the name "Mrs. Carlyle.")[17]

———

Barbara's and Isabel's gazes imbricate class desire and feminine envy; both define middle-class feminine consciousness as a condition of being inhab-

[16] Oliphant, "Novels," 170.

[17] Indeed, the idea of arousing envy, and of the attractiveness of the picture she would make, play no small role in Barbara's desire to be Mrs. Carlyle: "She saw herself, in anticipation, the wife of Mr. Carlyle, the envied, thrice envied of all West Lynne; for, like as he was the dearest on earth to her heart, so was he the greatest match in the neighborhood around. Not a mother but coveted him for her child; not a daughter but would have said 'Yes, and thank you' to an offer from the attractive Mr. Carlyle" (25).

Emphasis on the permanence of the house or name, rather than the individual who happens to inhabit it at the moment, is the aristocracy's traditional mode of asserting power through continuity. In the middle-class version, the individual is always in the process of attempting to assert the stability the aristocrat took for granted.

ited by and dependent on the class-inflected images of others. Seeing Isabel's and Carlyle's marriage from the inside, readers learn of the effects of "time and custom" on Carlyle, whose "demonstrative affection, shown so greatly for her in the first twelve months or so of their married life, had subsided into calmness.... Do we not all," Wood writes, "become indifferent to our toys when we hold them securely in possession?" (166). But such indifference never manifests itself in the marriage of Barbara and Carlyle. For while readers are invited to participate in the dissatisfactions of various female characters at various points, for instance—to see through Barbara's "covetous eyes," or to hear about Isabel's jealousy of Barbara and uncertainty about her own marriage—the woman who has achieved the novel's ideal position seems to have no interiority once she achieves it. This marriage is an idealized and nostalgic construction whose value Barbara perceives only because, living both literally and figuratively with Isabel's shadow hovering at her side, she does not fully possess it; in the novel's terms, it can be perceived as valuable only because (and this is in keeping with many critical assessments of Barbara's character) no one really inhabits it.

And yet Wood also suggests that what appears as distortion or magnification in East Lynne's domesticity is not only the product of the novel's representations or of Isabel's gaze: the staged quality of the domestic life Isabel observes in the Carlyle home is, we learn, inextricable from that home's successful functioning. Barbara offers her governess and *East Lynne*'s readers the following lesson in child rearing:

> "Now, what I trust I shall never give up to another, will be the *training* of my children," pursued Barbara. "Let the offices, properly belonging to a nurse, be performed by the nurse....let her have the *trouble* of the children, their noise, their romping.... But I hope I shall never fail to gather my children round me daily, at stated periods, for higher purposes: to instil into them Christian and moral duties; to strive to teach them how best to fulfill the obligations of life. *This* is a mother's task....a child should never hear aught from its mother's lips but persuasive gentleness; and this becomes impossible, if she is very much with her children."
>
> Lady Isabel silently assented. Mrs. Carlyle's views were correct. (341)

East Lynne is best known for its affirmation of natural maternal feeling: for Isabel's longing for her children, and (in the theatrical versions) the deathbed melodrama of recognition. But what Isabel approves here is not nature, but rather a theatricality fully ingrained in ordinary life, and made possible by a division between the mother's emotional and the governess's physical labor: motherhood in this account is the effect of an image making orchestrated by the mother herself. This explanation of the machinery whereby middle-class domesticity produces itself as ideology—what John Kucich calls "professional motherhood," and what constitutes the underlying condition for Joseph Litvak's description of the home as a stage set (see below)—might, like the representational excesses of the passage discussed earlier, be said to undercut the novel's idealizations. Whether or not Wood herself agrees with Barbara's words, that is, Isabel herself unequivocally endorses a life defined as representation and a motherhood that consists of knowing how to play the part.[18] Indeed, in a formulation that resolves the confusing tension between what appears to be Wood's simultaneous approval and disapproval of Barbara's methods, Isabel may be said to assent not necessarily to Barbara's exact methods but rather to her demonstrations of the *value* of representation: to an ideal of ideological representation she herself, as aristocrat or as governess, can only clumsily manage. In other words, the novel registers here a perverse admiration for the emptiness of its domestic images, for the exposure of the bourgeois home as theater—and for the way in which, to a desiring if ambivalent spectator (and these images project no other kind) the scenes of Barbara's marriage celebrate the impossible cancellation of the distance between self and image so relentlessly inscribed in Isabel's experience.

Litvak describes the representational excess of *East Lynne*'s domesticity as the novel's transformation of domestic space into "one big stage set" (138). Of Wood's theatricalization of the home, he writes: "If the narrative can reinforce 'home control' only by casting the home itself in an enthrallingly theatrical light, the spectacle thus staged may be compromising in more ways than one. To reframe the home as a desirable site, glittering with crystal and silk, is to make it all the more intelligible as a site of desire" (140). Wood's novel sketches the Victorian home's own fall into representation—a fall that reveals, by virtue of the home's reframing, the

---

[18] Kucich argues that Wood endorses neither version of motherhood on display here (*Power of Lies*, 193).

weakness of the "controls" imagined therein. Similarly, suggesting that the correct practice of motherhood is indistinguishable from the mother's good image, and reconfiguring that image in her own novel's spectacular closure, Wood at once exposes spectacle's workings and exploits its power as a mechanism for the transmission of bourgeois ideology.

And indeed, a fall into representation is precisely what Isabel's *embourgeoisement*—the discovery of her "natural" maternal feeling—requires. For if Isabel's spectacles give readers and audiences of *East Lynne* something to look through, they also give readers and audiences something to look at: seeing what Isabel sees, readers (and of course spectators) also find their attention relentlessly directed toward the figure cut by Isabel herself. On the one hand, *East Lynne* inscribes middle-class values on a body whose aristocratic complexion gives that inscription its ideological force; Isabel's assent to Barbara's idea of motherhood is reinforced by the pain inflicted on her oversensitive aristocratic body. But on the other, her railway accident, like the clothing and eyewear with which she enhances her disguise, transforms her body's class markers; Isabel's coming to bourgeois consciousness—more precisely, the violent infliction of middle-class consciousness upon her—is signaled by a confusion of the signs of class identity, an exposure of that consciousness's own vexed identifications.

The novel frequently points toward Isabel's essential self: without her eyeglasses, we are told, she is dangerously identifiable (Madame Vine resembles her, Miss Corny remarks at one point, "especially in the eyes" [392]). Shielding her identity, the spectacles point toward its irreducibility. But the gaps the glasses also demarcate—between Isabel and her surroundings, between her vision before and after her fall, and between the person behind them and the picture she presents to those who view her—focus attention on the reconstruction of her body and her experience. Indeed, Isabel's disguise, like her earlier skill at manipulating her appearance (for which her deformation seems an appropriate punishment), highlights her identity as a creature of representations, and opens up the same cultural space for identifying with representation that the novel itself does. Capturing the tension between claims to nature, on the one hand, and the constructedness of social identity, on the other, that characterized the Victorian middle class, disguise in *East Lynne* registers the same tension as disguise in *Ruth:* it points toward natural identity at the same time that it signifies a distance from it, a fall into a bourgeois world of representation.[19] With her numerous and ambiguous class signifiers, and her allegiances to ostensibly natural feeling as well as to a world of artifice and disguise, Isabel embodies the contradictions of Victorian middle-class identity.

And she also illustrates, in exemplary fashion, the construction of the sympathetic object. For in taking on the governess's disguise, Isabel willingly becomes a metaphor for a self seen primarily as spectacle (and the voluntary nature of her self-abnegation is important). Entering into her husband's household service, she not only accepts but actively assists in the construction of her own image as the dominant ideology would construct it. In doing so, she reveals the indistinguishability of the object of degradation from the object of sympathy. As Isabel reconstructs her body, enhancing the deformation wrought by her railway injury—and as she becomes the agent of her own suffering, willfully entering into service in the Carlyle household—she emerges as a paradigmatic sympathetic spectacle, not only accepting but actively embracing the punishment her actions would suggest to her Victorian readers. And the overdetermined nature of her spectacularity registers her as an object of sympathy *par excellence* as well, since spectacle itself—in the context of Victorian sensation fiction and theater—is a signifier of degradation, reminiscent of other, "cheap" entertainments in which the visual predominates. Constructing herself as a middle-class fantasy of degradation and decline, Isabel is, again in an exemplary manner, a figure about whom it feels good—indeed, virtuous—to feel bad. Readerly sympathy in *East Lynne* is thus inseparable from the taking of some pleasure in her punishment. Fashioning Isabel's character as a series of images that foreground identity's social and cultural configuration, the novel reveals the object of sympathy to be a projection of the dominant culture's gaze, and sympathy for Isabel to be inseparable from sympathy against her.

By the end of the novel, outcast, wearing victims' clothing, deprived of her children, and physically as well as emotionally scarred, Isabel in all her discomfort fits comfortably into the category of sympathetic object.

---

[19] For a reading that stresses the multiplicity and instability of Isabel's identity, see Nina Auerbach, *Private Theatricals: The Lives of the Victorians* (Cambridge: Harvard University Press, 1990), 22. On construction of a myth of middle-class identity, see especially Samuel Smiles, *Self-Help* (London, 1859).

Ostensibly sympathetic because no one sees or recognizes her, she is so garishly appointed as victim—as if she were wearing a sign—that she is the inescapable object of everyone's gaze. Clumsily dropping her eyeglasses, a device that in its most banal form calls attention to the eyes it conceals, Isabel works at shattering the illusion of her false identity as assiduously as any stage actress wishing to leave a distinct mark on the role. And the awkwardness—what might be called the staginess—of her disguise functions in the same way her spectacles do: pointing toward the "true" self, it simultaneously suggests the painful self-consciousness of a self-constructed identity. Underneath the disguise, say the glasses, lie true identity and true worth—not incidentally, in aristocratic form—if only someone will recognize them. Indeed Isabel's painful self-consciousness exposes a yearning for recognition that (certainly according to *Jane Eyre*) underlies the governess's stereotypically self-effacing facade. In its final, spectacular moments, *East Lynne* affirms a bourgeois publicization of supposedly private values, as if true feeling can only *be* true when ratified by the public gaze.

Isabel's sexual fall leads to, but also displaces, a class saga in which the aristocratic Isabel, confident in her ability to control the terms of her self-representation, is refashioned as Madame Vine, a figure self-alienated but also and somehow simultaneously at one with herself. The governess disguise thus effects a kind of solution to the claims made by *East Lynne,* and by Victorian middle-class culture, to both stable moral values and fluid identity boundaries: Isabel is both a victim of disguise (deformed by the accident) as well as the manipulator of her own image. Signifying the kind of fate that awaits those who violate bourgeois morality, the disguise marks her as having paid, and continuing to pay, for her behavior; if Isabel appears to become aware of her tragic mistake, simply by virtue of the power right thinking has over evil, she is also made to feel and to represent—in her bodily injuries, the loss of her child, and the painful self-consciousness she experiences as governess—how inescapably she has left happiness behind. Indeed, with the accident (as with the hard labor to which the novel gleefully sentences Levison) Isabel is made to bear the burden of middle-class *ressentiment;* her aristocratic sensibility has bourgeois verities violently impressed upon it. In Isabel, a figure of aristocratic ease experiences her class's decline in physical and emotional terms as her own personal narrative.

But the novel's sacralization of Isabel as mother distracts from and ultimately overshadows the class drama her various identities enact; class confusion gives way to phantasmatic unanimity in the novel's insistent claims for maternal feeling. Emphasis on the priority and passion of that feeling conceals the more socially complex division of labor the novel also exposes: the way the role of mother is created here by two actors, one acknowledged and the other not. As Barbara's lesson in motherhood suggests, Madame Vine is the repressed "other" of this maternal scene—the figure who, absorbing children's (and readers') anger, makes idealization of the mother possible. The unrecognized mother, Wood's plot suggests, is not just Isabel Vane but rather the Victorian governess. But if for the Victorian middle classes motherhood required more than one player, sympathy with Isabel's maternal feeling sweeps aside that class reality. Behind Isabel's disguise readers are meant to perceive true maternal feeling—feeling belonging to a mother significantly not allowed to live, as if the intensity of her feeling renders her unsuited to the world of representations that, if she did live, she would have to inhabit. And the placelessness of Isabel's feeling—the novel's refusal to install the true mother in her true home—contributes to its peculiar power. For in the social context in which the novel was translated into theater, Isabel's homelessness corresponds to the displacement of the bourgeois home itself: the removal of domestic feeling to the public sphere.

———

Sympathy generally entails an attenuation of self in a spectator's disturbing identification with the marginal. In the shift from Vane to Vine, one marginal self becomes another in a transformation that, characteristically, elides the middle. Isabel Vane the aristocrat is favored, elite, but in decline; Madame Vine the governess would, in another novel and by other means, be the predictable result of that decline. Sympathy here involves the creation of a self positioned on the margins, yet occupying a place at the center, of the consciousnesses of the middle classes who, policing the borders of their cultural centrality, find themselves preoccupied with—and imagining the spaces they construct invaded by—the very characters they would exclude. (Though Isabel wears her governess disguise on the outside, sympathy with her appeals to the governess "within" Wood's female readers: the ever present middle-class anxiety about degradation and decline.) The novels I have discussed sometimes literalize the invasion: Isabel, like Ruth, penetrates the sanctified boundaries of the bourgeois home, while in Madame Vine the body the middle class wishes to see as foreign to that home is rewritten as, literally, a foreign body. And in a scenario that captures the way imaginative space legitimates, and displaces, an increasingly segregated physical space, theater audiences watching stage adaptations of *East Lynne* during the latter decades of the nineteenth century would—by feeling for a character previously excluded from middle-class sympathies—have expanded their emotional horizons as they occupied an increasingly exclusive space: one more and more hostile to any but the respectable middle classes.[20]

East Lynne's home-as-stage-set sets the scene for the novel's actual transformation into a work of theater at the precise historical moment when the theater was being reconfigured in the image of the middle-class home. The novel's suitability for stage adaptation has already been noted; apart from scenes and dialogue modeled on stage melodrama, its voyeuristic structure duplicates the relation between theater audience and stage. And presenting home as image and Isabel as envious looker-on, the novel foregrounds the late-nineteenth-century theater's thematics of exclusion ("*East Lynne*'s central emotion," writes Sally Mitchell, "is the pain of exclusion").[21] The period saw the transformation of the English theater's class associations: theaters were restructured to make both attendance and enjoyment more difficult for members of the lower / working classes, and their surrounding areas were similarly (in Russell Jackson's term) "cleansed." By the 1880s, Jackson writes, theater "had established itself as a rational entertainment for the middle and upper classes."[22] Thus the putative expansion of audience sympathy signaled by a willingness (indeed an eagerness, suggestive of a cohesiveness founded as much on class resentment as on sympathy) to sympathize with Isabel Vane was accompa-

---

[20] The novel was first dramatized in 1863 and "almost constantly acted" in subsequent years (Mitchell, introduction to *East Lynne*, xiii–iv). Adeline Sergeant writes of this supposed extension of sympathy in modern life in *Women Novelists of Queen Victoria's Reign* (London: Hurst & Blackett, 1897), 182–83.

[21] Mitchell, introduction to *East Lynne*, xvi.

[22] Jackson describes these changes in *Victorian Theatre* (London: A. & C. Black, 1989). Aside from "smaller, more comfortably appointed and socially exclusive theatres," he describes "such 'cleansing' as Macready's banishing of prostitutes from the precincts of Drury Lane...made it a safer place for the middle class" (11–12).

nied by a contraction of the place in which that sympathy was to be felt, as the newly intimate and comfortable theater grew to resemble the home it (at least in the case of *East Lynne*) depicted. Exclusion from the theater took a subtle form, however, affecting not so much members of a particular class as their theatergoing culture; lower- or working-class audiences were not eliminated but rather were conscripted into an imagined middle-class solidarity. As theaters gained in "legitimacy," so too, it seems, did their audiences participate in and reinforce a unanimity of feeling and behavior: despite being literally relegated to the margins, working-class audience members enthusiastically enforced the new theater's codes and conventions.[23] The diffuse gaze of the theater audience embodies the fictional gaze of the dominant culture.

As public versions of private space, then, both play and theater suggest what Habermas calls "the floodlit privacy of the new [bourgeois] sphere . . . [an] externalization of what is declared to be the inner life" that reflects consumer culture's domination of family life and leisure time as it disseminates and universalizes images of cultural value.[24] The theater becomes, in effect, an imaginary home, redeeming Isabel's solitary spectatorship by binding its spectators together as consumers and producers of an emotional surplus. For despite the story's adjurations toward emotional balance, the extravagant sympathy *East Lynne* evokes is a luxury all can afford. *East Lynne*'s most important scene of sympathy, then, occurs not in the novel or on the stage but rather in readers and audiences, for whom Isabel serves less as an object than as an occasion for (to adapt Raymond Williams's phrase) a middle-class structuring of feeling.

Sally Shuttleworth argues that sympathy for Isabel undercuts *East Lynne*'s ideological prescriptions: readerly sympathy for Isabel's passion, she

---

[23] "Numerous individuals come literally together—assemble—in the space the theater furnishes in order to confront one and the same representation. It is as if the lines of sight that connect them to a common object also unite them in a common identification." David Lloyd and Paul Thomas, *Culture and the State* (London: Routledge, 1998), 56. Jackson points out that working-class audiences were often "more likely than others to insist on the strict observance of conventional morality and decorous behavior in plays" (*Victorian Theatre*, 13). I cannot say here—if it is possible to say at all—to what extent this insistence derives from the influence of middle-class ideology and to what extent it belongs to working-class culture, if indeed cultures are so easily distinguishable from one another.

[24] Habermas, *Structural Transformation*, 156–57.

claims, subverts the novel's moral condemnation.[25] But the injured, disguised Isabel is an image of the body Victorian sympathy produced for its own consumption. Sympathy for Isabel requires the monstrosity and deformity it seems to lament; rather than subverting the novel's condemnation of Isabel, sympathy is coterminous with it. The narrative of Isabel's punishment and decline constitutes the cultural narrative of sympathy for her: it is the narrative that invites readers to imagine themselves in her place. In a manner that recalls René Girard's accounts of sacrifice, Isabel seems to fall victim to her own sensibility and susceptibility: the violence inflicted upon her, ostensibly caused by no one but herself, purges her from the community, which then establishes its innocence by producing around her death a spectacle of emotional unanimity and class cohesion (a performance of cohesion brought to life, I have suggested, by the novel's translation into theater). Sympathy constructs an imagined class solidarity in which a phantasmatic bourgeois interior makes a home for an equally phantasmatic bourgeois interiority. "The leisure activities of the culture-consuming public," writes Habermas, "themselves take place within a social climate, and they do not require any further discussions."[26]

Assenting to her appropriate role and its generic consequences within the drama of bourgeois representation, Isabel does not die so much as fade; in keeping with the novel's phantasmagoria of vision and value, she diminishes in color and strength as a direct result of the "incessant irritation on the mind" (472) to which she has subjected herself, literalizing in her body the distance from value that becomes the defining feature of her experience. While Barbara, after her initial outburst of affection for Mr. Carlyle, learned to keep her feelings to herself, Isabel chafes against that restriction; as her response to Barbara's narrative shows, she is always on the verge of giving herself away. And her "rebellion" against her situation, in the novel's economic terms, "cost[s] her her life." (In fact, the entire second half of the novel is described as a kind of death: the effect of the accident

---

[25] Shuttleworth, "Demonic Mothers: Ideologies of Bourgeois Motherhood in the Mid-Victorian Era," in *Rewriting the Victorians,* ed. Linda Shires (New York: Routledge, 1992), 31–51.

[26] Habermas, *Structural Transformation,* 163.

is "little less than death itself"[270]; her experience since her return to East Lynne is "as one long scene of mortal agony." As in "A Christmas Carol," where the idea of Scrooge's death threatens him with irrevocable absence from the scenes of culturally sanctioned delight he witnesses, Isabel's death is identified with a spectatorial position that marks her as hopelessly identified with, yet forever excluded from, the scenes Wood identifies not just with health but with life.

PART III

The Aesthetics of Cultural Identity

5

Consenting to the Fact: Body, Nation, and Identity in Daniel Deronda

When, in George Eliot's *Daniel Deronda* (1876), the aged Jew Mordecai seeks a man to fulfill his nationalist and religious ideals, he fashions the mental equivalent of what today would be called a personal ad. Acting on what Eliot describes as "a mature spiritual need akin to the boy's and girl's picturing of the future beloved,"[1] Mordecai seeks the image of his protégé throughout the world and, specifically, in the museum:

> He imagined a man who would have all the elements necessary for sympathy with him, but in an embodiment unlike his own: he must be a Jew, intellectually cultured, morally fervid...but his face and frame must be beautiful and strong, he must have been used to all the refinements of social life, his voice must flow with a full and easy current, his circumstances be free from sordid need: he must glorify the possibilities of the Jew, not sit and wander as Mordecai did, bearing the stamp of his people amid the signs of poverty and waning breath. Sensitive to physical characteristics, he had, both abroad and in England, looked at pictures as well as men, and in a vacant hour he had sometimes lingered in the National Gallery

---

[1] George Eliot, *Daniel Deronda* (Harmondsworth, England: Penguin, 1986), 531. Subsequent references included in text.

in search of paintings which might feed his hopefulness with grave and noble types of the human form, such as might well belong to men of his own race. (529)

"He must be a Jew . . . but." The right man for the job will be the character the novel calls the "refined Jew"—the Jew whose background, education, and physical features "might well belong to men of his own race," or—this passage strongly suggests—might just as well not. Mordecai's museum search recalls Eliot's use of family portraits to describe Deronda's appearance: "He was handsomer than any of them, and when he was thirteen might have served as model for any painter who wanted to image the most memorable of boys: you could hardly have seen his face thoroughly meeting yours without believing that human creatures had done nobly in times past, and might do more nobly in time to come" (205). Though the absence of resemblance between Deronda's features and those of Sir Hugo's family tells of his lack of blood relation to them, it also seems to tell of an absence of relation to any ordinary human family. But the description, giving readers the opportunity to fill in Deronda's blank features with their own designs (imagine for yourself "the most memorable of boys"), is in fact more specific than it appears: the vacancy established by referring the business of description to "you," like the vacancy that characterizes Eliot's descriptions of Deronda, invites the constitution of a subjectivity in effect already constituted—a space to be filled with images whose specific referents, hanging on the walls of the National Gallery, are assumed to be the cultured reader's intellectual property.[2] As model and, implicitly, copy, Deronda occupies a niche less in a specific family history than in an aesthetic imaginary, as a descendant of idealized types and portraits rather than particular individuals.[3] Both passages, in fact, exemplify

---

[2] Hugh Witemeyer's discussion of the artworks to which the novel refers is relevant here, as is his quotation from W. J. Harvey that Eliot had "a mind like the National Gallery." *George Eliot and the Visual Arts* (New Haven: Yale University Press, 1979), 9.

[3] For Eliot's readers, sympathy with the individual presumably lays the groundwork for sympathy with the Jews. By letting readers get to know Deronda as an English gentleman first, and as Jewish only later, Eliot attempts to secure sympathy from English readers who then find, belatedly, that they have identified with a Jewish character. Prefacing the revelation of Jewish identity with an exploration of Deronda's English self, however, promotes the association of Englishness with individuality and Jewishness with type. Eliot's strategy

the novel's duck-rabbit, now-you-see-it-now-you-don't approach to Deronda's appearance, evoking stereotypes only to cancel them in their attempts to describe the character whose distinctive feature will be his ability to do the same: to evoke a type, belong to a group, without being constrained by that membership. Their convolutions convey the strain of trying to represent what is, in Victorian readers' mental portrait galleries as in Victorian novelistic representation in general, an impossibility: the Jew who does not look like one.

As Mordecai wanders through the National Gallery, he too becomes a hypothetical object of speculation: "Some observant persons may remember his emaciated figure, and dark eyes deep in their sockets, as he stood in front of a picture.... But spectators would be likely to think of him as an odd-looking Jew, who probably got money out of pictures" (529). As attempts to imagine sympathetic "others," Daniel and Mordecai figure in Eliot's imagination, and for each other, as types and relationships to types. But Eliot's use of the museum as a setting for these descriptions also puts the idea of type, as a simplification and aestheticizing of character, on dis-

---

is reminiscent of one criticism of a liberal idea about how to treat England's Jewish population, namely, the idea that Jews should efface their identities as Jews to win acceptance as individuals. See David Feldman, *Englishmen and Jews: Social Relations and Political Culture, 1840–1914* (New Haven: Yale University Press, 1994), 27.

Though she doesn't discuss the term "noble," Inderpal Grewal suggests that connections between ideas of classical form, the whiteness of white marble, and Englishness might be conveyed by that term. The "valorization of Greek art," she points out, "participat[ed] in creating an 'ideal' English subject, unquestioningly masculine but one who was receptive to a 'moral' art and who immediately recognized the 'purity' of classical forms." *Home and Harem: Nation, Gender, Empire and the Cultures of Travel* (Durham: Duke University Press, 1996), 108. Grewal quotes Sir Henry Ellis on the Elgin marbles—"The possession of this collection has established a national school of sculpture in our country, founded on the noblest models which human art has ever produced"—and refers to the "nobleman [Elgin] to whose exertions the nation is indebted for it [the collection]" (119, quoting Ellis, *Elgin and Phigaleian Marbles*, 10, 215).

For a similar scenario of looking for an aesthetically pleasing "norm" in the museum: in a *New York Times Magazine* article on plastic surgery, the author asks one Dr. Joseph M. Rosen "how a surgeon decides on the shape of a given altered part." Rosen replies, "I once asked that of a well-known plastic surgeon I work with, and he told me he went to the Louvre and studies art, and that while he was aware of many different standards and measuring systems, he ultimately decided by what looked right and nice." Charles Siebert, "The Cuts That Go Deeper," *New York Times Magazine*, 7 July 1996, 40.

play—revealing how, in the museum as in the novel, issues of race, like those of class and gender, are transmuted into the category of sensibility or taste.

The museum here figures, as it did in the late nineteenth century and still does today, as a place in which artworks are not the only things on display: one in which visitors, extending their license to look and seeking to become spectacles themselves, serve as spectators of and objects for one another. The art gallery in particular, whose visitors possessed (it was assumed) specific knowledge of the works they had come to see, provided a "key symbolic site for those performances of 'distinction' through which the *cognoscenti* differentiate themselves from the masses"—and, the passage cited above also suggests, the non-Jews differentiate themselves from the Jews.[4] Those spectators "capable of recognizing and appreciating those works [of art] as such" would also "recognize" that Mordecai's purpose in the museum must differ from their own; the examination to which he is subject is part and parcel of the museum's contribution to the observation (in both senses) of distinctions.[5] The National Gallery functions here as a version of the "imagined community" of the nation as *Daniel Deronda* finally envisions it, a community in which a fantasy of shared sensibilities produces a heightened consciousness of social and cultural differences.[6]

Mordecai's features, "bearing the stamp of his people," block the evocation of sympathy his religious and nationalist plans require. They also, for the spectators who characterize him, signify the limited scope of his observation: narrowly seeking his object, he embodies the refusal—projected on the Jews—to participate in the general cultural project of the nation. For Eliot and her hypothetical spectators, the Jew's gaze is focused elsewhere: on his nation but not on theirs. Lacking the whiteness that signifies a wide-ranging sympathy (like that of the novel's invisible omniscience), Mordecai necessarily lacks what Michael Ragussis calls "the practical power of the assimilated Jew."[7] Deronda, however, possessing the qualities Mordecai lacks (or more accurately, lacking the qualities Mordecai pos-

---

[4] Tony Bennett, *The Birth of the Museum* (New York: Routledge, 1995), 11.

[5] Ibid., 163.

[6] The term "imagined community" comes from Benedict Anderson, *Imagined Communities: Reflections on the Origin and Spread of Nationalism* (London: Verso, 1983).

[7] Michael Ragussis, *Figures of Conversion: "The Jewish Question" and English National Identity* (Durham: Duke University Press, 1995), 288.

sesses), possesses that power, and invites the sympathy Mordecai's project requires. For despite Mordecai's search for features that suggest "Jewish birth" (531), he seeks a Jew who "might or might not" look like one, and Eliot's narrator describes Deronda largely through references to historical, heroic types and by negation: he is "not more distinctively oriental than many a type seen among what we call the Latin races" (553).

———

"Discrimination" is the term Eliot uses in the Philosophers' Club chapter (chap. 41) for the ability to distinguish different degrees of Jewishness in its members—characters whose features are so marked that, the narrator relates, "even" Deronda, little practiced in this kind of "discrimination," can perform it (581). Establishing him as her inexperienced and impartial observer on the scene—"Deronda was well satisfied to get a seat on the opposite side, where his general survey of the party easily included Mordecai"—Eliot supplements his knowledge with her own: "In fact, pure English blood (if leech or lancet can furnish us with the precise product) did not declare itself predominantly in the party at present assembled." But despite skepticism about the idea of "pure English blood," the passage proceeds to establish a relationship between Jewishness and nationality for each of the club's members: "Miller, the broad man . . . had at least grand-parents who called themselves German, and possibly far-away ancestors who denied themselves to be Jews; Buchan, the saddler, was Scotch; Pash, the watchmaker, was a small, dark, vivacious, triple-baked Jew; Gideon, the optical instrument maker, was a Jew of the red-haired, generous-featured type easily passing for Englishmen of unusually cordial manners. . . . Only three would have been discernible everywhere as Englishmen" (581–82). This passage establishes Jewish identity, like all "discriminations," as a matter of degree; what defines the discerning observer is the ability to perceive the Jewishness nationality conceals. Yet while the club members emerge, in discussion as well as through observation, as different "types" of Jews, Eliot's emphasis with respect to Deronda falls, somewhat condescendingly, on his gracious ability to participate as one of the company. It is the task of manners to make him an equal, that is, because until he encounters Mordecai's wishful vision, Deronda is the Jew even the most discerning of observers can't discern: "He looked around him with the quiet air of respect habitual to him among equals, ordered whisky and water, and offered the contents of his cigar case" (582).[8]

Indeed, despite Eliot's disclaimer, "discrimination" is the mode of seeing on which this novel depends, both in its depiction of Jews said to be recognizable as such and in its characterization of the Jew who is not. For though Mordecai's purpose in the museum may not seem to its regular visitors likely to match their own, neither can it be said to differ greatly. Seeking the image of his "beloved" in a gallery that expresses something of the nature of belonging to the nation—as if misunderstanding the museum's function, but in fact understanding it all too well—Mordecai is also looking to discriminate, to find a cultural type "gathered from his memory of faces seen among the Jews of Holland and Bohemia, and from the paintings which revived that memory" (531). (Mordecai might be considered mistaken for pursuing not what the museum invites its visitors to consider—the abstraction "man"— but rather an image he hopes will lead him to an actual man.) Though he and the narrator establish different markers for Deronda's features—the one seeking some signs of Jewish identity, the other emphasizing the absence of such signs—both practice a mode of observation whose essential quality is a habit of noting the presence or absence of "Jewish" features.

The museum-goers struck by Mordecai's incongruous presence, these passages invite us to imagine, must be the kind of discriminating observers he is; for all Mordecai knows, Deronda himself might be among them. Appealing to a consciousness of social types in those same readers who would share an image of Deronda's "nobility," the novel links the museum-goer's sensibility not just to Mordecai's but to the reader's as well. For what Mordecai does in envisioning his beloved is what Eliot does in envisioning Mordecai, what Deronda does when he imagines the family he dreads discovering is Mirah's, and what Deronda will later counsel Gwendolen to do: "take hold of your sensibility," he tells her, "and use it as if it were a faculty, like vision" (509).

While the sensibility in question in this passage is fear (Daniel is advising Gwendolen to let her conscience be her guide), seeing with one's sen-

---

[8] The ease with which Deronda discriminates suggests that his ability to make himself comfortable is perhaps the result of the members' visible difference from him. As Lionel Trilling suggests in "Manners, Morals, and the Novel," manners allow one to discriminate while seeming not to. *The Liberal Imagination* (New York: Viking, 1950), 206.

sibility is in fact an excellent description of the novel's moral and aesthetic mode. For when sensibility is a faculty, taste becomes a sense, and in the racial and national context *Daniel Deronda* establishes, discrimination (or "discernment") signifies not only the ability to classify according to race, class, and nationality but also a visceral response to any or all of the above. This is what it means for Daniel to see with his sensibility: "he saw himself guided by some official scout into a dingy street; he entered through a dim doorway, and saw a hawk-eyed woman, rough headed, and unwashed, cheapening a hungry girl's last bit of finery; or in some quarter only the more hideous for being smarter, he found himself under the breath of a young Jew talkative and familiar...and so on." Suggestively ending thus, the narrative once more allows its readers to fill in the blank; as Eliot writes, confident in her readers' competence, such images are "the language in which we think" (247). Aligning sensibility with vision, identifying thought as a system of images, Eliot underscores the ease with which, in this novel's cultural context, moral judgments slide into aesthetic ones. In such a context, that is, it is impossible not to think in images.[9]

While Daniel generally escapes the examination to which the visibly Jewish are subject, the diffuse features that express his ethical nature—the "many-sidedness" of his sympathy—establish him as a recognizable cultural type.[10] It is not, in other words, that he is an absence, a "nobody," but that his features are such that they make no difference to a sympathetic reader's imagination—indeed, the lack of difference they make is what defines that imagination as sympathetic. The description of the object of Mordecai's search no less than Daniel's later decision to dedicate himself to "his own hereditary people" renders explicit what is implicit elsewhere in Eliot's work (and what I have argued throughout this book): that sympathy, ostensibly grounded for Eliot in personal knowledge and identification, is predomi-

---

[9] Tellingly, in a passage lauding the working classes for their good behavior when visiting the museum, and the museum for its civilizing powers, an 1852 guidebook to the British Museum uses the term "sympathy" to mean "taste": "Verily this is an age of progress, and the conviction of this truth...that the sympathies of the rich and the poor are identical." Quoted in Grewal, *Home and Harem*, 124.

[10] Possessed of "a fine person, no eccentricity of manners, the education of a gentleman, and a present income" (412)—Deronda resembles Conan Doyle's no-identity capitalist, the man with the twisted lip. Says Ezra Cohen, "I thought you might be the young principal of a first-rate firm" (442).

nantly a matter of cultural identification, as the sympathetic self seeks out a particular assemblage of social and cultural markers with which to sympathize. As Gwendolen says when she learns of Deronda's background, establishing credentials to sympathy more impressive, at that moment, than his own, "*You* are just the same as if you were not a Jew" (873).

Though Jewishness ostensibly functions in the novel as a signifier of difference, that is, it is the point of Deronda's Jewishness to make, with all the weight the narrative can bring to bear on the subject, no difference; just as Gaskell's Ruth is the fallen woman who is not "really" fallen, Deronda is the Jew who must be "just the same" as if he were not. For this reason alone, it would make no sense for Eliot to refer readers to any physical marker of his Jewishness. In considering this issue I necessarily refer to Cynthia Chase's 1978 essay, "The Decomposition of the Elephants: Double-Reading *Daniel Deronda*."[11] Despite Chase's insistence on the bodily nature of Jewish identity—"For Deronda not to have known he was Jewish until his mother told him means... 'that he never looked down'" (222)—the most important feature of Jewishness as an aspect of Deronda's cultural and physical identity is its invisibility.[12] A figure drawn

---

[11] Acknowledging the insights of Lennard Davis and Steven Marcus, Chase writes: "For Deronda not to have known he was Jewish until his mother told him means, in these terms, 'that he never looked down,' an idea that exceeds, as much as does magical metamorphosis, the generous limits of realism." "The Decomposition of the Elephants: Double-Reading *Daniel Deronda*," *PMLA* 93 (1978): 222.

[12] In this he resembles the "invisible" Jew of the latter half of the nineteenth century, as well as the one constructed by nineteenth-century liberal arguments: invisible unless he chooses not to be. On the invisibility of Jews in Europe in the latter half of the nineteenth century, see Sander Gilman, *The Jew's Body* (New York: Routledge, 1991), 99. David Feldman explains that in nineteenth-century England Jews were "not recognized" by the state as such; "they were disadvantaged as non-Anglicans and non-Christians." "The absence of statutory recognition in Britain meant that structures of communal authority and cohesion had to be manufactured entirely by Jews themselves." *Englishmen and Jews*, 23. See p. 27 for liberalism's idea of the Jew, based on its identity as a "universalist, bourgeois creed, concerned with the rights of individuals."

Both Michael Ragussis and Christina Crosby note Eliot's effacement—Christianization and secularization—of Judaism in *Daniel Deronda*. See Crosby, *The Ends of History* (New York: Routledge, 1991), 27; Ragussis, *Figures of Conversion*, 226.

It is the increasing invisibility of the Jew that makes it necessary for late-nineteenth-century race theorists to rely on the idea that difference is inscribed in blood; science takes on the task of "seeing" and quantifying what the untrained eye cannot easily discern.

from Eliot's portfolio of classically featured sympathizers (such as
Dorothea Brooke, also likened to a museum piece) and from the Victorian
novel's tradition of a liberal subject whose centrality and universality manifest themselves in an ability to identify with the narratives of others,
Deronda must possess the ability to invest his self in other selves.
Paradoxically, in order to identify himself with and as Western culture's
most "marked" other, he must be unmarked himself. Figured in the whiteness and blankness of the exemplary middle-class subject, his "representative subjectivity" is, in David Lloyd's words, a function of his ability "to
take anyone's place"; he is the figure "of a pure exchangeability."[13]

Yet by the end of the novel this figure of pure exchangeability has become a national subject, willing to devote his life to helping his "hereditary people" (724) found a nation. This development, encompassed in a
narrative that elicits Deronda's consent to what he is said incontrovertibly
to possess—a Jewish identity—situates him on both sides of a colonialist
imaginary. It participates in a Lawrence-of-Arabia-like mode of cultural
cross-dressing that is an expression of colonial power: an exemption from
the identity boundaries that constrain others. At the same time, it idealizes
an emotional attachment and commitment at odds with such freedom: the
narrative of Deronda's "discovery" produces an identity defined in narrowly national terms. Cultivating in her readers the kind of national and
cultural discrimination in which the narrator excels, Eliot constructs a
Jewish hero who ostensibly exemplifies yet is himself clearly exempt from
such discrimination, with an identity both global and narrowly national,
discerning but not generally discernible.

In *Daniel Deronda,* Eliot projects her exemplary bourgeois subject into
the context of late-nineteenth-century nationalism and contemporaneous
debates about the relationship between the English and the Jews. The idea
of nationalism allows her to play out in political and historical terms the

[13] David Lloyd, "Race under Representation," *Oxford Literary Review* 13 (1992): 70. In
the course of describing Eliot's use of portraits in *Daniel Deronda,* Hugh Witemeyer suggests that, modeling Mordecai on Italian portraits, Eliot "almost subliminally" encourages
her reader to "grant the Jews whatever tolerance and respect he is accustomed to grant the
Italians." "Eliot's pictorialism," he writes, "here becomes a sophisticated rhetorical device
employed in the service of a liberal social vision." *George Eliot and the Visual Arts,* 98. Note
the phrase "Hebrew dyed Italian" (*Daniel Deronda,* 748).

collapse between sympathy and identity that occurs elsewhere in her fiction: in the idea of national identity, as at the end of many of Eliot's novels, the limited field deemed sympathy's proper sphere defines the self's boundaries. If, as the novel seems to suggest, in the modern world there is no bourgeois subject without his or her developmental narrative, it also seems that the narrative that subtends bourgeois identity must be a national one: the emotional and ethical coherence of the bourgeois self depends upon knowing to what nation that self belongs. And yet nationality is itself subordinated here to a high-cultural ideal within which the Jew can also be the model English gentleman, and the model English gentleman the Jew. Because of these contradictions—and because sympathy, like national identity, has power to the extent that it seems to emerge from within—sympathy in *Daniel Deronda* is less a function of self than a rationale for self-construction, a narrative from which identity emerges apparently unwilled.[14]

———

> It was as if he had found an added soul in finding his ancestry—his judgment no longer wandering in the mazes of impartial sympathy, but *choosing,* with the noble partiality which is man's best strength, the closer fellowship that makes sympathy practical—exchanging that bird's eye reasonableness which soars to avoid preference and loses all sense of quality, for the generous reasonableness of drawing shoulder to shoulder with men of like inheritance. (814; emphasis mine)

Eliot devoted her artistic career to the expansion of her readers' consciousnesses through sympathy. But the ethical compulsion to embrace difference in an attempt to recognize in the other "an equivalent center of self" (in *Middlemarch*'s famous formulation) gives way, in Daniel Deronda's

---

[14] On the Jew and the gentleman as similar figures of exchange see Catherine Gallagher, "George Eliot and *Daniel Deronda:* The Prostitute and the Jewish Question," in *Sex, Politics, and Science in the Nineteenth-Century Novel,* ed. Ruth Bernard Yeazell (Baltimore: Johns Hopkins University Press, 1986), 39–62.

decision "to identify myself, as far as possible, with my hereditary people" (724), to an explicit compunction to seek out sameness: Daniel will live out his life, to paraphrase Gwendolen Harleth, not necessarily with no one he *does* not like, but with no one he *is* not like (says Gwendolen: "It came over me that when I was a child I used to fancy sailing away into a world where people were not forced to live with any one they did not like" [760]). Some years before Wilde exposes Victorian sympathy's exhausted state in *The Picture of Dorian Gray,* Eliot characterizes sympathy as a currency whose random expenditure engenders emotional paralysis and inhibits action. Giving us in Deronda a character who not only fails to save Gwendolen Harleth but also fails to sympathize with her as well (his final advice to her is, essentially, that she learn to sympathize with herself), Eliot rejects, or at least severely qualifies, the intersubjective ideal her novels have come to represent.[15]

In *Daniel Deronda,* the attenuated self that tends to trouble participants in the sympathetic exchange appears as a single character's sustained problem of self-definition. Deronda's too diffuse extension of self defines a sympathy that, Eliot claims, threatens sympathy's demise: "His plenteous, flexible sympathy had ended by falling into one current with that reflective analysis which tends to neutralize sympathy" (412). In particular, this kind of sympathy engenders not just emotional paralysis but an inability to act: Deronda's "many-sided sympathy . . . hinder[s] any persistent course of action." Sympathy's multiplication of selves leads, oddly, to a deficit; the capacity to sympathize with everybody renders Deronda a kind of nobody.

But the term "sympathy" serves as a confusing kind of catch-all here: in the phrase "that reflective analysis which tends to neutralize sympathy," one kind of sympathy is said to cancel another. Deronda's early sympathy is associated both with an exemplary personality and with a search for self that suggests he has not yet found his identity. In fact, the negative cast of Deronda's pre-Mordecai emotional life—the free-floating sympathy Eliot calls a "meditative interest in human misery" that "passes for comradeship" (219)—heightens the need for the emotion that forms its necessary antidote and for the narrative of discovery that will serve as that emotion's vehicle.

---

[15] Alexander Welsh notes Eliot's questioning of her "steady faith in sympathetic understanding." *George Eliot and Blackmail* (Cambridge: Harvard University Press, 1985), 302.

Replacing one brand of sympathy with another, the novel rejects Deronda's ability to identify universally in favor of the strong emotion that arrives, in a narrative of nationhood, to narrow his concerns. The sympathy Deronda possesses early in his life becomes passionate feeling when he finds the narrative in which he wishes to insert himself, one that allows him to define his identity in both individual and cultural terms and that he may imagine as thrust upon him rather than ambitiously sought after: "Since I began to read and know, I have always longed for some ideal task, in which I might feel myself the heart and brain of a multitude—some social captainship, which would come to me as a duty, and not be striven for as a personal prize" (819).

Deronda's Zionism is usually regarded as a development and expansion of his early sympathy. But in fact, the identity he "discovers"—a national and religious identity as leader of his people—is a rewriting of the attenuated self he is attempting to escape. For in this novel the substitution of one form of sympathy for another can replace one form of identity with another, or, more specifically, can replace an effect of nonidentity with an effect of identity only because, in nationalism's model of the self, the others with whom one identifies are, precisely, not "other." Nationalism draws its power from its ability to transform a certain kind of attenuated identity into identity's essence, saying "you are who you sympathize with." As Julia Kristeva writes, "in nationalism, 'I am' becomes 'I am one of them,' 'to be' becomes 'to belong.' "[16] The modernist tendency toward diffusion, anonymity, and anomie represented in the novel as an effect of imperialism, in the characters of Gwendolen and Grandcourt, and in the ever present metaphor of gambling is countered by a pull toward identity that, as if to ward off the "scattered" effect of internationalism, casts sympathy in the form of national identity, in effect collapsing any difference between the two.[17] It is this collapse that Eliot, startlingly, dubs "practical." (In this sense, Deronda's desire to give a

---

[16] As Franco Moretti notes, *Daniel Deronda* is the product of a period in which, "in ideology after ideology the individual figured simply as part of the whole." *The Way of the World: The Bildungsroman in European Culture* (London: Verso, 1987), 228. Julia Kristeva writes, "Subjectively, the issue of 'national' identity is that indistinct domain of psychic and historical experience which transforms identity into belonging." "Proust: In Search of Identity," in *The Jew in the Text: Modernity and the Construction of Identity,* ed. Linda Nochlin and Tamar Garb (London: Thames and Hudson, 1995), 140.

[17] Caroline Lesjack argues that the capitalist expansion for which the nation state serves as "motor" is also responsible for the sense of rootlessness and anomie from which Deronda

"centre" to his "scattered" people is the equivalent of locating a center for his own scattered identity [875]. And not only is individual identity based on national identity, but the nation itself is imagined as a kind of unruly character requiring emotional organization.) In *Daniel Deronda,* what is represented as sympathy with the other turns out to be sympathy with the self. Becoming and at the same time discovering that he already "is" the other with whom he sympathizes, Deronda provides a model of selective sympathy that, Eliot wished, would make it possible for her readers to sympathize with the Jews.[18]

"Then it is not my real name?" said Deronda, with a dislike even to this trifling part of the disguise which had been thrown around him.

"Oh, as real as another," said his mother, indifferently. "The Jews have always been changing their names." (701)

The narrowing of Deronda's identity into Jewishness may be said both to evade and to avoid the problematic topic of the Jewish body by simply leaving it aside. In fact, Eliot enlists both heredity and narrative in the construction of Deronda's identity. Despite language suggesting that for Eliot national feeling is "genetically based,"[19] and despite Chase's claim that *Daniel Deronda* self-deconstructs, Eliot's novel in fact produces what nineteenth-century and later nationalism requires: consent. *Daniel Deronda*

---

suffers; nationalism, Eliot's prescription for Deronda, is also at the root of his problems. Eliot's contradictory use of the term "sympathy" may thus be said to express nationalism's contradictory impulses. "Labours of a Modern Storyteller: George Eliot and the Cultural Project of 'Nationhood,'" in *Victorian Identities,* ed. Ruth Robbins and Julian Wolfreys (New York: St. Martin's, 1996), 25–42.

[18] It should be pointed out that while many modern critics discuss Eliot's effacement of Jewish identity in *Daniel Deronda,* this strategy did not universally succeed in persuading English readers to sympathize with the Jews; rather, what many saw as the novel's narrow concerns and intellectualism tended to alienate readers, some of whom pronounced it a failure. See the reviews collected in John Holmstrom and Laurence Lerner, eds., *George Eliot and Her Readers* (London: The Bodley Head, 1966), 122–58.

[19] Katherine Bailey Linehan, "Mixed Politics: The Critique of Imperialism in *Daniel Deronda,*" *Texas Studies in Literature and Language* 34 (1992): 345.

is less significantly about Deronda's discovery of his Jewishness than it is about what Eliot calls his "consent to the fact" (819). As his mother chides, bitterly but justifiably, "You are glad to have been born a Jew.... That is because you have not been brought up as a Jew" (693). *Daniel Deronda* is the narrative that makes Deronda "glad to have been born a Jew."

Chase's argument for the novel's self-deconstruction depends on the way its logic seems to require Deronda to discover that he is Jewish, rendering his identity, in Hans Meyrick's words, a "present cause of past effects" and disrupting the fundamental tenet of narrative realism, linear causality. For Chase, Mordecai's "coercive" identification of Deronda—the way in which Deronda seems to be a product of Mordecai's vision—violates both Mordecai's apparent recognition of Deronda and Paul de Man's definition of identity as something known rather than constituted.[20] Her interpretation might be said to work so well precisely because of its astounding literal-mindedness—one might also say essentialism—about Jewishness: a Jew must be circumcised; a Jew cannot become a Jew through conversion, and Eliot must have known these things; therefore the novel's account of Jewishness is contravened by Judaism's very nature. Writes Chase, "Conversion precisely does *not* apply to Jewish identity, which is inherited, historical, and finally, here, genetic"; according to Chase, Jewish identity cannot be the result of a speech act.[21]

---

[20] The phrase "present causes of past effects" appears in a letter to Deronda (704) and is cited by Chase ("Decomposition of the Elephants," 215). Chase's argument is based on what she calls an "identity principle" articulated by Paul de Man, in which knowledge of identity is received passively rather than imposed (221). As Chase writes, "Such a notion, that identity is the product of a coercive speech act, deconstructs the identity principle and the constative concept of language grounded upon it." And for Chase this "identity principle" applies, somewhat peculiarly, especially to Jews. More recent criticism argues that it is not the novel's logic but rather Eliot's idea of racial memory that renders Deronda's discovery of his Jewishness inevitable.

[21] Chase, "Decomposition of the Elephants," 222. Chase's "here" attributes any apparent racism to the novel. It is my sense, however, that what I have called "essentialism" inheres in her argument—a sense influenced, for example, by her use of de Man's identity principle as the abstraction by means of which identity is defined. I have been influenced as well by the way her argument echoes Sander Gilman's description of nineteenth- and twentieth-century racial theories, in which "the circumcision of the genitals is the outward sign of the immutability of the Jew within" (*Jew's Body*, 204).

Not only are these assumptions technically incorrect, however, but in fact speech plays a prominent role in both Eliot's and Deronda's imagining of Jewish identity. It figures, for instance, in Deronda's own consciousness of it: Mirah seems to him "a personification of that spirit which impelled men after a long inheritance of professed Catholicism to leave wealth and high place and risk their lives in flight, that they might join their own people and say, 'I am a Jew'" (426). And Deronda himself must declare his Jewishness if anyone is to know about it, especially given his wish to marry Mirah. Somewhat circularly, whether one considers these statements to be speech acts depends on whether one considers Jewishness inherent in, or ultimately detachable from, identity, or considers identity-for-others constitutive of identity. In any event, Deronda's consent to his Jewishness, like his mother's repudiation of hers, represents Jewish identity as characteristically embraced, repudiated, or at the very least altered.[22]

For Chase, two "identity principles" are in conflict in the novel; identity, she claims, cannot be both the result of recognition and its effect. But her own language suggests that these principles may in fact support rather than cancel each other. "On the one hand," she writes, "Mordecai's identification of Deronda is presented as a recognition, and for this reason his assertion of a claim on him has authority and appeal. On the other hand, Deronda's *assumption of the identity* of Mordecai's prefigured friend is shown to be a consequence of Mordecai's act of claiming him. He be-

---

For a response to Chase that challenges her deconstructive method but reads Deronda's body just as literally, see K. M. Newton, "*Daniel Deronda* and Circumcision," in *In Defence of Literary Interpretation: Theory and Practice* (London: Macmillan, 1986), 197–211.

[22] In response to Joseph Kalonymos's insistence that he "call [himself] a Jew and profess the faith of [his] fathers," Deronda asserts: "I shall call myself a Jew.... But I will not say that I shall profess to believe exactly as my fathers have believed" (792).

See Feldman, *Englishmen and Jews*, 23, on the idea that in Victorian England Jewish community "depended solely on voluntary association"—that is, on choice, the affirmation of identity.

As Ragussis notes, the idea that Judaism was "natural," and that converting a Jew was therefore a logical impossibility, arose from the new "science" of ethnology in the mid-nineteenth century. Robert Knox wrote that the Jews were "unaltered and unalterable," and that Jews could not be converted because "Nature alters not." See Ragussis, *Figures of Conversion*, 26; Knox, *The Races of Men: A Fragment* (Philadelphia: Lea & Blanchard, 1850), 206. Christina Crosby also discusses Deronda's assertion of Jewishness, though her reading differs from mine and supports Chase's (*Ends of History*, chap. 1).

comes what Mordecai claims he is."[23] But this "becoming" in no way conflicts with Deronda's account of his coming-to-Jewishness: as he tells Mordecai and Mirah, "If this revelation had been made to me before I knew you both, I think my mind would have rebelled against it. Perhaps I should have felt then—'If I could have chosen, I would not have been a Jew.' What I feel now is—that my whole being is a consent to the fact. But it has been the gradual accord between your mind and mine which has brought about that full consent" (819).

Indeed, the consent of his "whole being"—body and mind—is crucial to the construction of Deronda's identity, and the narrative that produces consent, activating readerly sympathy in the process, is arguably more crucial than the "fact" of Jewish birth. Devising a character who actively desires his national identity, Eliot produces in her hero an exemplary subject of late-nineteenth-century nationalist ideology. Accustomed early in his life to "a state of social neutrality" encouraged by "the half-known facts of his parentage," Deronda rejects success at Cambridge for the sentimental education travel will provide, "the sort of apprenticeship to life which would not shape him too definitely, and rob him of that choice that might come from a free growth" (220). And in that shapelessness, manifest in his ability to "[think] himself imaginatively into the experience of others" (570), he resembles nothing so much as the conventional liberal subject of the nineteenth-century novel. Just as important as—perhaps more important than—the knowledge of Deronda's maternal origin, that is, is the process by means of which he arrives at and comes to embrace that knowledge, and by means of which what is cast as shapelessness gradually gives way to what he, and Eliot, want to call shape.[24]

---

[23] Chase, "Decomposition of the Elephants," 221; my emphasis.

[24] The novel, and my argument, may seem to leave the body behind by emphasizing consent. But the novel returns to the body—and returns the body to the text—by way of its emphasis on feeling. In contrast with his mother and her "sincere representations" of feeling, Eliot pointedly has Deronda pale with "what seems always more of a sensation than an emotion—the pain of repulsed tenderness" (697). And for Deronda nationality is less as an accident of birth than something "throbbing in his veins" (411). If Deronda's identity, like nationalism, presents itself as "simultaneously open and closed" (Anderson, *Imagined Communities,* 146), simultaneously indeterminate and overdetermined, and simultaneously bodiless and embodied, it is because of the multiple and mutually contradictory tasks Eliot's sympathy requires it to perform.

In *Daniel Deronda* and in other writings, such as "The Modern Hep! Hep! Hep!" Eliot blurs the difference between constructions of nation and race, suggesting that "national life" springs from "nature" and blood; in the novel, she implies as well what Katherine Linehan calls a "genetically based ancestral memory."[25] But national identity in *Daniel Deronda,* as in the late nineteenth century, was made as well as found; constructions of national identity depended then as they do now on constructing the made *as* found. As E. J. Hobsbawm writes of "that characteristic formation of the nineteenth century, the nation-state," "the state not only made the nation, but *needed* to make the nation." Like Eliot, Hobsbawm conceives of Jewish identity as a paradigmatic version of nineteenth-century European nationalism; national identity, he writes, especially in the Hapsburg Empire and the Jewish diaspora, inhered "not in a particular piece of the map to which a body of inhabitants were attached, but in the members of such bodies of men and women as considered themselves to belong to a nationality, wherever they happened to live."[26] The phrase "considered themselves" bears directly on Eliot's account of Deronda's acceptance of his Jewish identity. Particularly toward the end of the century, when nationalist expansion and imperial conquest meant not only locating national subjects and institutions outside territorial boundaries but also frequently inculcating a sense of national identity in those who could not be said to have been born with one, the Jewish desire for a nation might well be regarded as a model for the idea of desiring the "national" component of one's identity. For at stake in late-nineteenth-century nationalism is the identification between the institutions that define the self and "identity" itself: what Terry Eagleton calls "that historically new form of power that Antonio Gramsci has termed 'hegemony'—that process whereby the particular subject so introjects a universal law as to consent to its imperatives in the form of consenting to his own deepest being."[27] Indeed, given the multidetermined nature of late-nineteenth-century Judaism (which, like an "ur" nationalism, encompasses and blurs distinctions between ideas of family, race, culture, religion, and nation), it makes sense that Jewish identity in *Daniel Deronda* be both discov-

[25] Linehan, "Mixed Politics," 345.

[26] E. J. Hobsbawm, *The Age of Empire, 1875–1914* (New York: Pantheon, 1987), 148–49.

[27] Terry Eagleton, "Nationalism, Irony, and Commitment," in *Nationalism, Colonialism, and Literature,* ed. Seamus Deane (Minneapolis: University of Minnesota Press, 1990), 32.

ered *and* chosen: that a narrative describing the long-awaited result of a family history of repression and denial and, above all, of the mystical prompting of feeling should produce a subject fashioned in an impossibly coincidental blending of chance and choice. Nationalism's magic is, as Benedict Anderson writes, "to turn chance into destiny,"[28] creating "consent" for identities also authorized as "fact."

In *Deronda*, as I have suggested, bourgeois identity emerges from national identity. Aware of his ethical duty to others, Deronda does not actively prosecute that duty until he perceives it to be part of his identity: until he knows, or feels, who he is. And knowing who he is means knowing to what nation he belongs. At that point, what prepares the ground for and in fact finally constitutes his identity is a sympathy so unwilled as to present itself as the result of a series of fortuitous events, events that are not actively desired but that simply overtake the self.

———

In the context of late-nineteenth-century nationalist expansion and discussions of Jewish identity, what Eliot's exemplary sympathizer must possess is the ability to "be at home in foreign countries" (220) and to "understand other points of view" (224), a phrase in which "other" signifies "other nations." But in the context of the novel, "other" points as well toward Western culture's perennial other—the Jew—and to the mutually constitutive and phantasmatic roles played by body and mind in nationalist constructions. Exploiting the ambiguous roles of birth and consent, accident and purpose in the construction of national identity, Eliot conceives of a subject who, though born a Jew, must come to desire Jewish identity through the gradual assumption of a feeling of likeness and belonging. And, when this feeling arrives, this subject discovers—in a circular fantasy of complete sympathy in which the physical body gives empirical weight to the feeling of belonging—that he *is* that other. Deronda's body is sympathy made manifest, identified in its essence—so the story has it—with the social and cultural other.[29] (Hence his body, invoked by critics from Chase on as the place where the novel's realism founders, has in fact little to do with re-

———

[28] Anderson, *Imagined Communities*, 12.
[29] What after all is "consent" but a merging of the willed and the unwilled? The term implies choice, but according to an essentialist reading Deronda would have no choice.

alism at all: as the exemplary sympathetic body in all the ways I have suggested, it is the novel's most phantasmatic construction.) But with his exemplary ability to sympathize, Deronda represents as well Eliot's ideal of high culture—the very culture to which her own novels belonged, and which they assisted in constructing. Thus the novel's "others" must remain other, with the capacity to arouse repulsion and disgust; their role in the construction of the hero's identity cannot be acknowledged. And thus Eliot's narrative of sympathy with the Jews takes shape as a narrative in which the obstacle of otherness vanishes. (Deronda's rationalization of his ready attraction to Mordecai's ideas *despite* their source, for instance—"what was there but vulgarity in taking the fact that Mordecai was a poor Jewish workman . . . as a reason for determining beforehand that there was not some spiritual force within him that might have a determining effect on a white-handed gentleman?"—testifies less to an egalitarian spirit than to the appeal of the romantic idea that "poverty and poor clothes" have, "in some remarkable cases," accompanied "inspiration" [571].) Deronda embodies an absolute merging of self and other (a merging suggested repeatedly by Mordecai's insistence that Deronda must "be not only a hand to me, but a soul—believing my belief—hoping my hope—seeing the vision I point to" [557]), but this complete sympathy is possible only when identity has been evacuated of everything but the self's projections. A subject can become "other," the novel's collapsing of sympathy and national identity suggests, only when identity equals identity politics: when self and other merge because they are already merged into an imaginary unified identity.

The wish-fulfillment structure that for Chase deconstructs the novel's realism may thus be seen as a consequence of a logic the novel shares with nationalism, in which desire for a particular identity becomes a crucial component of an identity said to be already possessed (what else might it mean to "consent" to one's identity?). In a move that conveys the way the pictorializing imagination assists in sympathy's mystifications, Deronda is described as the realization of Mordecai's wish: "the outward satisfaction of his longing" (550). Deronda's apparent production as an effect of Mordecai's desire is thus not most significantly (as Chase reads it) a violation of realism; it is rather an exposure of the way sympathy turns happenstance into fate and makes choices seem to be determined by the promptings of some unalterable essence at the self's core. (Gwendolen, telling Deronda of Grandcourt's death by drowning, uses a similar formulation: "I only know that I saw my wish outside me" [761].) In both instances, narrative is completed or fulfilled by a picture that collapses narrative in the seemingly inevitable materialization of unconscious desires. If, then, in Chase's words, "a reader *feels*" that "it is *because* Deronda has developed a strong affinity for Judaism that he turns out to be of Jewish parentage,"[30] this narrative convolution is less significantly "a deconstruction of the concept of cause" than a structural affirmation of the privileged status the novel accords to feeling, especially "national feeling." *Daniel Deronda* lays the groundwork for a consent not at odds with physical identity, but rather in support of it.[31]

In making Jewish identity grow out of feeling and require consent, Eliot substantiates the *mythos* of national identity on which nation-states would increasingly come to rely: the way in which, with the widening reach of empire, feeling increasingly becomes the ground of national identity. What, after all, is national identity but fellow feeling, a sympathy whose organizing principle is the country to which (and the fellows to whom) one considers oneself to belong? Simultaneously "natural" and capable of "naturalization," national identity is constituted as a sensibility in which, advantageously for the nation that wishes to command allegiance, the genealogical and the emotive or intellectual are suggestively confused. In John Stuart Mill's language, fellow feeling both follows from and leads to all the givens of nationality—race, descent, language, religion, geography and history, and "without fellow-feeling... the united public opinion, necessary to the working of representative government cannot exist." With reassuringly circular reasoning, *Daniel Deronda*—like nationalism—implies that feeling is also a given: the sympathy that affirms identity is also its consequence.[32]

---

[30] Chase, "Decomposition of the Elephants," 217; my emphasis.

[31] My concerns echo those of recent criticism, in which the salient question is, What is a Jew? See, for instance, Lawrence Lipking's review of Ragussis and others, "The English Question," *New Republic*, 26 February 1996, 33.

Controversy over whether Jews should take the Christian oath in order to serve in Parliament provides an interesting example of the requirement for "consent." As Feldman writes, "It was not until 1866 that the Parliamentary Oaths Act introduced a form of words for both Houses which required a conscientious speaker to believe in God but made no particular demands beyond this" (*Englishmen and Jews*, 46).

[32] J. S. Mill, *Considerations on Representative Government* (London, 1861), 287; quoted in Feldman, *Englishmen and Jews*, 73.

Rather than promoting sympathy as a means toward understanding difference, then—indeed, strikingly rejecting that principle in Deronda's rejection of Gwendolen—the novel valorizes sympathy as an identification with and affirmation of similarity. In this way *Daniel Deronda* may seem to naturalize or racialize sympathy: to suggest that Deronda's sympathy with Mordecai, like Mordecai's recognition of Deronda, is linked to the presence in both of Jewish blood (a version of the superstition, discussed by Sander Gilman, that Jews will always recognize one another).[33] Indeed, "sensibility" may seem to provide the key to the novel's idea of racial difference, if one agrees with Gilman's reading of the narrator's remark: "And one man differs from another, as we all differ from the Bosjeman, in a sensibility to checks, that come from a variety of needs, spiritual or other" (370).[34]

And yet by restricting Deronda's attraction to the more "refined" of Jews, Eliot reveals the weak point in this argument: it is not so much people of the same blood who will find one another as people of the same sensibility. In *Daniel Deronda,* the rewriting of nationality as sensibility enables the well-known scenario in which the novel divides Jews into two types, one degraded and one ideal, and insists that its hero can identify with, and establish an identity as, the latter but not the former. Deronda's discovery that he belongs to—is one of—the people with whom he most sympathizes substantiates the importance of taste (what Sir Hugo, nicely suggesting that the capacity to change identities is a matter of having the proper credentials, calls Deronda's "passport in life" [217]) in the formation of his identity; indeed, it subverts what the novel calls sympathy—an "early habit of thinking himself imaginatively into the experience of others" (570)—by making those others in whom Deronda finally decides to invest his feeling into projections of himself ("my hereditary people"). His newfound sympathy, as an expression of his identity, thus acts as a kind of quality control, "exchanging that bird's-eye reasonableness which soars to

---

[33] Gilman, *Jew's Body,* 242. After he learns his history from his mother, Daniel has "a quivering imaginative sense of close relation with his grandfather" (747); elsewhere he reflects on his "inherited yearning" for Zionism (819). Linehan notes these examples ("Mixed Politics," 335–36).

[34] Gilman, "Black Bodies, White Bodies: Toward an Iconography of Female Sexuality in Late Nineteenth-Century Art, Medicine, and Literature," *Critical Inquiry* 12 (1985): 239.

avoid preference and loses all sense of quality, for the generous reasonableness of drawing shoulder to shoulder with men of like inheritance" (814).

Deronda's identity requires a grounding in feeling and intellect as well as in physical fact, then, not only because, despite its apparent naturalization (the way, as Benedict Anderson puts it, "nation-ness is assimilated to skin-colour, gender, parentage and birth-era—all those things one cannot help"),[35] nineteenth-century nationalism increasingly required citizens to "consent to the fact," but because for Eliot sensibility transcends nationality, rewriting both nationality and "race" in the service of the bourgeois mandate to sympathize, so that what is by definition constitutive of both—a sense of difference—ceases to exist.

Deronda's discovery of and sympathy for Mirah also undercuts the argument that racial impulses underlie his attraction to Jews. Having returned from abroad yet still possessing no clear sense of vocation or duty, Deronda is a free-floating vessel of sympathy, Eliot's ethical self stripped to its essentials: a not-yet-fully formed bourgeois subjectivity awaiting, barnacle-like, the appearance of a figure to whom he may attach himself. He drifts in his boat, "forgetting everything else in a half-speculative, half-involuntary identification of himself with the objects he was looking at" (229). An image appears that appeals to his discriminating sensibility: intoning the gondolier's song from Rossini's *Otello*, he suddenly sees "a figure which might have been an impersonation of the misery he was unconsciously giving voice to." Similarly, the singing, we learn later, "entered her [Mirah's] inner world without her having taken any notice of whence it came" (227). An idea of "racial" difference gives way to a fantasy of emotional likeness expressed through the vehicle of cultural identity, of playing the same role in a cultural narrative; Mirah, with her Christian looks and her desire to be accepted as an artist expresses the same assimilationist impulse Deronda's character does. And if cultural artifacts and narratives shape and give voice to what Deronda sees, they also shape his desire to continue looking. In a version of Mordecai in the museum, the vehicle of sympathy here is the cultured eye selectively seeing and seeking its beloved; this scene at once exposes the arbitrariness of Deronda's at-

[35] Anderson, *Imagined Communities,* 143.

tachment and shows how sensibility's projections transform arbitrariness into narrative. "It was only the delicate beauty, the picturesque lines and colour of the image that were exceptional," but "there was no denying that the attractiveness of the image made it likelier to last" (228). Seeing Mirah as both image and narrative, as a "girl-tragedy" whose outline is "as clear to him as an onyx cameo," Deronda begins, "unconsciously," to find narrative form for his own life as well.

———

> "What I have been most trying to do for fifteen years is to
> have some understanding of those who differ from myself."
> (Deronda, 692)

Deronda's unconscious selection of Mirah is matched by his rejection, at the same unintentional level, of his mother. Critics tend to take Eliot at her word when she names sympathy as Deronda's chief quality. Yet in interview after interview with Gwendolen and his mother, he appears awkward, stiff, and unable to speak—unable, despite his own and Eliot's protestations to the contrary, to sympathize. Scenes of sympathy in this novel record not Deronda's emotional receptivity or effective counseling but rather Deronda as a horrified and helpless spectator to situations and individuals beyond his control, stiffly delivering moral precepts that bear more on his own situation than on anyone else's.[36]

Deronda's encounters with Gwendolen and his mother are marked by a sense of the distance between them and of Deronda's inability to bridge that distance through language. "I beseech you to tell me what moved you—when you were young, I mean—to take the course you did," he pleads. But the plea is undermined by the narrator's assertion that Deronda is "trying by this reference to the past to escape from what to him was the heart-rending piteousness of this mingled suffering and defiance." He assures his mother, "Though my own experience has been quite different, I enter into the painfulness of your struggle" (694). Differences in experi-

---

[36] One exception is R. H. Hutton, writing in the *Spectator,* 10 June 1876. See Holmstrom and Lerner, *George Eliot and Her Readers,* 131.

ence supposedly make no difference to what the novel calls an "early habit" of sympathy, and to the claim made throughout Eliot's novels for the fungibility of suffering. But *Daniel Deronda* jettisons this bourgeois ideal—the possibility that anyone can put themselves imaginatively in anyone else's place—relying instead on increasingly specific kinds of experience to justify the channeling of Deronda's sympathies in new and specific directions. "I have had experience which gives me a keen interest in the story of a spiritual destiny embraced willingly, and embraced in youth" (555), he tells Mordecai; or, "He had lately been living so keenly in an experience quite apart from Gwendolen's lot, that his present cares for her were like a revisiting of scenes familiar from the past, and there was not yet a complete revival of the inward response to them" (752).

The novel suggests that the liberation of Deronda's mother from a belief in the inevitability of identity has its cost in feeling, making her an actress in every realm of life and rendering her unable to provide the maternal feeling her son requires. The Princess doesn't just reject identity categories, that is, she rejects identities and the bonds that go with them: hers (as mother and Jew) and Deronda's (as her son). But in fact she expresses the same sympathetic principle Deronda eventually does: the belief that a specific group identification is a prerequisite for sympathy. Hence her rebuff to her son's sympathetic gestures (a rebuff that underscores the prominent position this novel holds in the history of identity politics): "You are not a woman. You may try—but you can never imagine what it is to have a man's force of genius in you, and yet to suffer the slavery of being a girl" (694). Here Eliot discloses the different effects and consequences of what might anachronistically be termed identity politics for men and women in late Victorian England. Identifying as a Jew, Deronda can overcome the effects of prejudice and escape the bitterness of his mother's rejection. But his mother is condemned for her lack of maternal feeling even as Eliot seems to sympathize with her grievances. The Princess's detachment from her son causes the emotional vacancy he seeks to fill and requires him to locate a source of deep feeling elsewhere. Jewishness, "discovered" by Deronda as the secret of his identity, provides him with the sense of authenticity and identity he has felt lacking; it arrives with the charge of feeling missing in his family, and the assertion that all Jews are family (586) justifies the substitution.

Michael Ragussis sees in Deronda a theatrical personality to match Gwendolen's:"his entire life has been a kind of disguise or performance."[37] Given the shame Deronda associates with the idea of performance, this resemblance might be said to account for his inability to sympathize with both women: their theatricality renders them threateningly similar to him, and salvation appears as authenticity in the character of Mirah and in the Jewishness that offers Deronda a chance at a true identity. But to assert that Deronda's disguise ceases when he discovers his true identity is to ignore the performative associations of Jewish identity, especially the strong Victorian association between Jewishness and theatricality—which is to say that, for Deronda, the Princess may represent the possibility that the identity he discovers is no more authentic than the one he gives up. Indeed, given her offhanded remark, "The Jews are always changing their names," it may be more accurate to locate Deronda's Jewish identity not in the fact of his birth but in his anxiety about his origins and reconstruction of his identity: not in his new name but in the changing of his name.

Not only does the novel suggest the emptiness of Deronda's sympathy in relation to Gwendolen, it also suggests that he possesses a capacity for representation similar to his mother's, though in his case that capacity is (like almost everything else about him) unintentional. While finding the Princess guilty of what the narrative calls "sincere acting," a nature in which "all feeling . . . immediately passed into drama, and she acted her own emotions" (691), Eliot also asserts that Deronda's voice, "like his eyes, had the unintentional effect of making his ready sympathy seem more personal and special than it really was" (765). What passes as sympathy for Gwendolen is the result of a "look" that, rather than substantiating his moralizing, often records simply his instantaneous response to her. Despite this, however, Gwendolen is more than ready to make him her confessor. Their initial encounter prefigures the pattern: "The inward debate which she raised in Deronda gave to his eyes a growing expression of scrutiny, tending farther and farther away from the glow of mingled undefined sensibilities forming admiration. . . . The darting sense that he was measuring her and looking down on her as an inferior, that he was of different qual-

[37] Ragussis, *Figures of Conversion*, 277.

ity than the human dross around her, that he felt himself in a region outside and above her, and was examining her as a specimen of a lower order,
roused a tingling resentment which stretched the moment with conflict"
(38). It is a measure of what is conventionally called Gwendolen's narcissism, and may also be viewed as the dynamic of the sympathetic exchange
as Eliot imagines it here, that when Gwendolen responds to Deronda's
look rather than to his words, what she responds to is her own projection:
her image reflected in his eyes. It is not that Deronda's countenance fails
to convey what he feels, for it shows his feeling all too clearly; rather,
Deronda reflects her desire to "be what you wish" (672), with a gaze
"Gwendolen chose to call 'dreadful,' though it had really a very mild sort
of scrutiny" (226). ("Often the grand meanings of faces as well as of written words may lie chiefly in the impressions of those who look on them"
[226]). And scenes of sympathy between Deronda and Gwendolen, too,
emphasize the "looks" that register his sympathy as Gwendolen's fantasy.
Though a Foucauldian reading might stress the indistinguishability of
Deronda's sympathy for Gwendolen from his power over her (indeed,
Deronda's ability to observe a face described as "unaffected by beholders"
[38] is a measure of the panoptic power the novel grants him), his power
is less a function of his own actions than of Gwendolen's eagerness to view
him as an externalized conscience.[38]

Gwendolen is no less a projective figure for Deronda than he is for her;
when, in the novel's opening scene, he feels "coerced" to look at her, the
term suggests his own conventional susceptibility to a feminine beauty he
also fears. Hence his instantaneous avowal that coercion has taken the
place of pleasure and desire: "What was the secret of form or expression
which gave the dynamic quality to her glance? Was the good or evil genius dominant in those beams? Probably the evil; else why was the effect
that of unrest rather than of undisturbed charm? Why was the wish to
look again felt as coercion and not as a longing in which the whole being
consents?" (35). Both the replacement of aesthetic terms by moral ones in
the famous opening lines of the novel (first "beautiful or not beautiful,"
then "good or evil" [35]) and the subsequent movement of Deronda's eyes

[38] For a Foucauldian reading, see Ann Cvetkovich, *Mixed Feelings: Feminism, Mass Culture, and Victorian Sensationalism* (New Brunswick, N.J.: Rutgers University Press, 1992), chap. 6.

("At one moment they followed the movements of the figure, of the arms and hands...and the next they returned to a face which, at present unaffected by beholders, was directed steadily towards the game"[38]) show Deronda working to manage his desire for what he immediately deems an unsuitable object; it is the expression of that struggle that Gwendolen interprets as disapproval. And Gwendolen helps him replace desire with moral judgment by assigning him responsibility for her shameful feeling: her conviction that he "was measuring her and looking down on her as an inferior" comes from nowhere so much as her own sense that gambling lowers her position in a moral hierarchy. Gwendolen is often accused of an overly intense attachment to her theatrical personality, but the power she bestows on Deronda suggests a desire to escape that theatricality—to replace public drama with the greater intensity of private drama, the kind of interior or "closet" drama in which she and Deronda engage.[39]

What happens in this closet drama is an exchange of subjectivities, but not in the ideal form the term "sympathy" leads some readers to expect. "What should be a moment in which identities merge"[40] is in fact a repeated opportunity for mutual projection, as Deronda and Gwendolen continually miss each other, each using the other as a screen for his or her own concerns and anxieties. Indeed, when confronted with Gwendolen's urgent need, Deronda most frequently notices, and Eliot most frequently calls attention to, the absence or insufficiency of sympathetic feeling in him—the same absence he notes in his interviews with his mother. (Deronda is acutely conscious of the gap between the sympathy Gwendolen expects and what he actually has to offer [765]). The narrator's separate observations about Gwendolen's anguish and Deronda's response to it maintain the isolation of each—something like separateness without communication.

Deronda's interest in Gwendolen, like his concern for Mirah, is manifestly a function of his interest in his own situation, especially his anxiety about the indeterminacy of his identity. (When Deronda asks Gwendolen, by way of

---

[39] On theatricality in *Daniel Deronda,* see Joseph Litvak, *Caught in the Act: Theatricality in the Nineteenth-Century English Novel* (Berkeley: University of California Press, 1992). While Daniel's and Gwendolen's misunderstandings are mutual, Eliot's tendency to let the reader know the truth behind Daniel's look suggests that Gwendolen's misinterpretations allow him to maintain his inviolability.

[40] Cvetkovich, *Mixed Feelings,* 147.

therapeutic cure, "Is there any single occupation of mind that you care about with passionate delight or even independent interest" (507), he might as well be speaking to himself; his recommendation, that "the higher life must be a region in which the affections are clad with knowledge," is exactly the cure he discovers for himself [508].) But in taking a parental, feeling role toward her and then finding himself unable, or refusing, to fulfill it, he resembles the mother who has similarly repudiated maternal feeling for him. Indeed, it would appear that Deronda's failures of sympathy have more to do with overidentification than with an inability to identify: the failure he assigns to language seems to spring instead from his own anxieties.

Deronda's inability to respond to Gwendolen increases with his interest in, and knowledge of, his own situation; the more she needs him, the less available he is. And by the time of Grandcourt's drowning it is clear that sympathy for her has become an ethical obligation he acknowledges but cannot fulfill: "he wished, yet rebuked the wish as cowardly, that she could bury her secrets in her own bosom" (754). (Seeing Gwendolen once more after meeting his mother, Deronda "seemed to himself now to be only fulfilling claims, and his more passionate sympathy was in abeyance" [752]). In the crucial scene after the drowning, he in fact hides his "look," averting his face, "with its expression of suffering which he was solemnly resolved to undergo." The scene is remarkable for its generation of false interpretations: "Their attitude," Eliot writes, "might have told half the truth of the situation to a beholder who had suddenly entered." And as Deronda grasps Gwendolen's hand, and "she interpreted its powerful effect on her into a promise of inexhaustible patience and constancy" (755), the distance between his feeling and her understanding is as great as the ostensible distance between their narratives.

The scenes of sympathy between Deronda and Gwendolen and Deronda and his mother suggest other reasons as well for Deronda's simultaneous attraction to and desire to distance himself from both, as well as for the way in which his sympathy for Gwendolen takes the form of witnessing her distress, hinting at what Leo Bersani has called a "dysfunctional" attachment to scenes of violence and suffering.[41] Deronda cannot

---

[41] Leo Bersani, "Representation and Its Discontents," in *Allegory and Representation: Essays from the English Institute,* ed. Stephen Greenblatt (Baltimore: Johns Hopkins University Press, 1981), 150.

save Gwendolen, that is—he must abandon her—because, like his mother, she exemplifies the identity he wishes to leave behind: the attraction to scenes of suffering that characterizes Deronda's relation to her recalls his vexed relationship to his own suspected origins. Eliot asserts that Deronda's activities "on behalf of others" spring from a desire to distance himself from his own rage: "In what related to himself his resentful impulses had been early checked by a mastering affectionateness. Love has a habit of saying 'Never mind' to angry self, who, sitting down for the nonce in the lower place by-and-by gets used to it" (218). In Deronda's emotional pathology, that is, sympathy is anger transformed; his sense of injury takes the form of "a hatred of all injury" and an "activity of imagination on behalf of others." But the sympathy that emerges from this process lacks passion; it is a "meditative interest in learning how human miseries are wrought" that, in Deronda's Cambridge days, "passed for comradeship" (219). Anything more, it seems, threatens to undo Deronda's "never mind" with an acknowledgment that he minds.

Deronda's response to his mother renders in psychological terms a response at the level of cultural sensibility: as the actress Alcharisi, his mother represents a degraded cultural narrative that, paradoxically, challenges Deronda's image of himself as universally sympathetic, an image he associates with a self-educated, self-originated identity: "Since I began to read and know, I have always longed for some ideal task, in which I might feel myself the heart and brain of a multitude—some social captainship, which would come to me as a duty, and not be striven for as a personal prize" (819). (It is worth noting that the novel exchanges Deronda's fantasy of illegitimacy for the "fact" of Jewish birth, and that the attempt to elevate the latter does not cancel out the equalizing effects of the exchange.) The Princess's story and profession (based on the life of the actress Rachel) locate her squarely not only in Jewish culture but in lower-class Jewish culture, but the emphasis of Eliot's retelling is on the mother's rejection of the son.[42] When Deronda responds to his mother with "impulsive opposition" (690), psychology justifies a marking of cultural boundaries: the repudiation of the Princess's cultural sensibility is recast as, and validated by,

---

[42] Welsh discusses similarities between Gwendolen's and Daniel's stories in *George Eliot and Blackmail*, 298.

the mother's abandonment of her son. It is as if "vulgar" Jewish culture rejects Deronda rather than the other way around.

Gwendolen, whose theatricality and self-absorption echo the Princess's, is similarly scapegoated throughout the novel to protect Deronda's sympathetic identity.[43] Identification with either woman would negate both his English-gentleman self and his sympathetic one, not affirming the identity he wishes to claim but rather marking its absence.[44] Indeed, Gwendolen and the Princess threaten not only the narrative of identity Deronda projects for himself but the idea of essential identity per se: the Princess rejects all given identities, especially Jewishness; Gwendolen, manifesting dissatisfaction with her own identity, seeks outward assurance and instructions to construct a new one. Both, that is, express a desire and capacity for transformation; both diplay the malleability Deronda embodies yet wishes to reject. The self-knowledge that supposedly crowns his narrative and solidifies his identity—the knowledge contained in, and produced by, the affirmation "I am a Jew"—thus effectively saves him from another kind of self-knowledge: the kind that threatens the notion that he has any essential identity to discover at all. For Deronda, sympathy as a means of defining identity enables an absolute denial of origins, a remaking of the self in ideal form; his embracing of Jewishness is thus not a discovery of what he already is but a means of escaping it. It is not so much that "Daniel's sympathy... is a function of his displaced social position,"[45] but that sympathy with Gwendolen and his mother, if he had any, would bring home to him the truths his chosen identity both expresses (in the

[43] On Gwendolen, see Litvak, *Caught in the Act,* 182 and *passim.* On the "obvious" Jewish context for the Princess and her narrative, see Carol Ockman, "When Is a Star Just a Star? Interpreting Images of Sarah Bernhardt," in *Jew in the Text,* ed. Nochlin and Garb, 121–39. For instance, Ockman writes that the theater, "hardly an elevated calling in the nineteenth century, was a logical profession for those consigned by class or race to the lower echelons of society" (123).

[44] In her book on the actress Rachel Felix, Rachel Brownstein speculates that Rahel Levin Varnhagen, introduced to George Eliot by Lewes, may have suggested to the author some ideas about Rachel: like the actress, Rahel "had espoused assimilation," and "had also believed that because she represented nothing intrinsically, she was free to stand for anything." It is this idea of representing "nothing intrinsically" that I would locate at the heart of Daniel's anxieties. Brownstein, *Tragic Muse: Rachel of the Comédie-Francaise* (New York: Knopf, 1993).

[45] Cvetkovich, *Mixed Feelings,* 153.

social displacement, the asserted nonidentity, of the Jews) and denies (in Eliot's attempt to reverse the image of Jewish degradation; in Deronda's proud acceptance of his Jewish identity). Finally, Deronda clinches the identification between Gwendolen and his own mother by abandoning her. Having supposedly transcended his anger, he symbolically repays the women whose powerful identities have wounded him by finding his identity in a religion and a nation in which women have no such power. For Deronda, assuming—better, asserting identity means affirming the exclusionary perspective on which definitions of identity depend.

And yet Deronda's spectatorship is a form of violence linked textually not only to Gwendolen's own "intentionless" violence against Grandcourt but also to the characteristic intentionlessness of sympathy and of his own sympathetic narrative. As if in bitter acknowledgment of the paralysis by which his early sympathy is defined, as well as his similarity to the woman who desperately requires his help, Deronda's confession of his inability to save Gwendolen is significantly echoed by—and significantly amplifies— her confession of her failure to save Grandcourt. The parallel suggests at least one way in which the novel's two plots, often regarded as insufficiently related, intertwine.

On two occasions, Deronda's guilt about his inability to help Gwendolen takes shape as an image of him standing by while she drowns. After she tells him of her displacement of and guilt over Lydia Glasher, "She broke off, and with agitated lips looked at Deronda, but the expression on his face pierced her with an entirely new feeling. He was under the baffling difficulty of discerning, that what he had been urging on her was thrown into the pallid distance of mere thought before the outburst of her habitual emotion. It was as if he saw her drowning while his limbs were bound" (509). In Deronda's view, the failure is not his but hers: Gwendolen's "drowning" results from her inability to move beyond her own "habitual emotion." And in the scene before Grandcourt's death, when she urgently presses upon Deronda her desire to be what he would like and he responds to her crisis with a profession of his uselessness, Deronda assigns responsibility for his inability to help her to the grander realm of language's inadequacy: "Words seemed to have no more rescue in them than if he had been beholding a vessel in peril of wreck—the poor ship with its many-lived anguish beaten by the inescapable storm" (672–73).

The literalization of these metaphors in Grandcourt's death gives meaning to them, not least by putting Gwendolen and Deronda figuratively in the same position. To stand by and watch someone drown, these parallels suggest, is to see one's wish outside oneself: to achieve one's desires without explicitly acting on them. "We cannot kill and not kill in the same moment" (72), writes Eliot early in the novel, attempting to distinguish between the multiple valences of feeling and the necessary decisiveness of action. But her novel proves her wrong. Standing by while someone drowns is an apt image for the action-in-inaction that defines both Gwendolen's murderous impulse and Deronda's sympathy: watching someone drown is an image of a necessary abandonment of responsibility, of obligatory inaction rather than clearly defined refusal. The scene captures the ambiguity of Deronda's willed-yet-unwilled identity formation, and of the disidentification his identification requires: it externalizes the emotional force of his rejection of Gwendolen and his response to his mother. As a spectator of Gwendolen's suffering—able to hear her confessions but not to save her—Deronda, like Gwendolen, remains suspended between violence and its absence even as Gwendolen does in relation to Grandcourt.[46]

If Deronda demonstrates little of his well-advertised ability to project himself into others' situations in his encounters with Gwendolen and his mother, with Mordecai and Mirah he needs no such ability but rather seems to experience an unwilled dissolution of self. Communication between Deronda and Mordecai transcends language and intention: "The more exquisite quality of Deronda's nature—that keenly perceptive sympathetic emotiveness which ran along with his speculative tendency—was never more thoroughly tested. He felt nothing that could be called belief in the validity of Mordecai's impressions concerning him or in the probability if any greatly effective issue: what he felt was a profound sensibility to a cry from the depths of another soul" (553). Deronda's encounters with

---

[46] The image of standing by watching someone drown also suggests the more generalized, cultural guilt implied by the novel's references to the Inquisition. Killing and not killing simultaneously, that is, might be taken as a description of historical guilt about the English response to the expulsion of the Jews—a guilt Daniel's representation exists partly to assuage. "The prelude to Daniel's acceptance of his inheritance as a Jew," Ragussis writes, "comes with a return to what I have contended is for Victorian England the critical moment of Jewish history." *Figures of Conversion,* 281.

Mirah and Mordecai have none of the sense of failed sympathy that characterizes the scenes with Gwendolen and the Princess; rather, they demonstrate the power of the intuitive, the nonverbal, the unspoken but commonly held sentiment. This is the fantasy of shared sensibilities that constitutes "national feeling," a feeling whose capacity to turn shared ideas into a conviction of shared genealogy Eliot suggests when she writes, of Deronda's increasing sense of commitment to Mordecai—in language that sensualizes, again through the use of visual metaphor, the idea of genealogical descent—"the lines of what may be called their emotional theory touched" (605). (In pointed contrast to Gwendolen's expansive, misguided interpretation of Deronda's grasp, Mordecai is represented as a more accurate reader of the "sympathetic hand" than its owner: "The sympathetic hand still upon him had fortified the feeling which was stronger than those words of denial" [558].)

The narrative of Deronda's discovery thus provides the justification, in sentimental, sympathetic, and romantic terms, for an identity politics that enables him to consent to what, it happily turns out, he already is. It substantiates his identity as self-inventing liberal subject, a figure whose ability "to discover purpose in apparently random details offers strongest proof of the subject's sovereignty."[47] For it transforms what he imagines Sir Hugo describing as a common "fanaticism," and a somewhat less common "monomania" (568), into a series of "plainly discernible links": "If I had not found Mirah, it is probable that I should not have begun to be specially interested in the Jews, and certainly I should not have gone on that loitering search after an Ezra Cohen" (573).

But the very "plainness" of the links betrays this identity-narrative's self-serving quality: at its end, nothing that does not fit, like the "vulgar" Jews encountered along the way, remains. The sympathetic impulse, for Deronda, is essentially a narrative one, and his tale of rational sympathy collapses the difference between finding an identity and choosing one. "And, if you like, he was romantic. That young energy and spirit of adventure which have helped to create the world-wide legends of youthful heroes going to seek the hidden tokens of their birth and its inheritance

[47] Celeste Langan, *Romantic Vagrancy: Wordsworth and the Simulation of Freedom* (Cambridge: Cambridge University Press, 1995), 232. See also Franco Moretti on the *Bildungsroman* in *Way of the World*, chap. 4.

of tasks, gave him a certain quivering interest in the bare possibility that he was entering on a like track—all the more because the track was one of thought as well as action" (574).

━━━━━

What Deronda discovers when he discovers his origins is the ratification of his feeling by fact, and what he does when he discovers the fact is to ratify it with his feeling: the nature of his identity, in a manner historically characteristic of Jewish identity, remains intimately tied to the issue of acceptance or rejection. Like his mother in being a Jew, he chooses to differ from her by consenting where she has refused. In fact, in choosing Jewish identity he replaces Judaism's matrilineal principle with a patriarchal and spiritual line of descent, embodying his grandfather's wish rather than his mother's. Replacing family with nationalist ideology, the novel replaces what it represents as an accident of birth and the emotional failure of family with what it construes as a more determined, determining emotional bond; it gives Deronda a phantasmatic, idealized family to compensate for his early disappointments. Rewriting accident as destiny, moreover, it mimics nationalism's own constructions of narrative. According to George Eliot, you *can* choose your relatives—or at least you can choose among them. The Princess highlights the invented nature of her son's identity when she disrupts his sense that "Deronda" is, as he puts it, his "real name." If, as Hobsbawm suggests, Zionism provides an "extreme" example of the constructed or artificial nature of national identity, Deronda's narrative of discovery does the same.[48]

What is revealed here is the capaciousness—the universal availability for projection—of the term "sympathy" in this novel. Deronda's affectlessness passes for sympathy until something more like the real thing comes along; it constitutes a blank the discovery of his Jewishness—his "real" identity—will fill. Sympathy in *Daniel Deronda* is the name for an attenuation of self described both as a virtue—the result of travel and a Cambridge education—and as a malaise for which a dose of strong feeling provides the cure. It attaches identity to narrative and ties passionate feeling to specific cul-

---

[48] Ironically, Daniel himself suggests that Mirah change her name from Cohen to pursue her singing career: "We could choose some other name, however—such as singers ordinarily choose—an Italian or Spanish name, which would suit your *physique*" (525).

tural ideals, embodied in an idealized self chosen to counter the degraded image Deronda has always associated fearfully with his birth; like a divining rod, strong feeling provides identity's clues. And until this feeling arrives, bourgeois subjectivity—as in Deronda's attempts to sympathize with Gwendolen—is not an identity but just a job, and an onerous one at that. But as in any attempt to resolve contradiction by division—here, the novel's split between "good" Jews and "bad"—each half retains traces of the other; *Deronda's* idealized "good" Jews reflect the pressure of feelings and qualities rigorously excluded. While the split between "good" and "bad" Jews has lately provided evidence for charges of antisemitism in *Daniel Deronda,* the division is familiar enough in discussions of transgression, in which extremes of high and low, or nobility and degradation, offer an image of resolution for unresolved social conflicts.[49] Deronda's response to the novel's "vulgar" Jews suggests the threat the unassimilated Jew represents for the assimilated one: as if granted a kind of magical, sympathetic power—the lure of authenticity—the one threatens to give the other away. But as the ideal bourgeois subject, Deronda doesn't have to sympathize with the Jews because his sympathy has become a function of his identity: simply put, he "is" one. And yet of course he is not. The character "Daniel Deronda" thus expresses both the ideality and the impossibility of Eliot's liberal ideal. For if, as I have suggested, the function of taste (or "discrimination") in the novel is to efface the difference Jewishness supposedly makes, the function of biology or heredity is finally the same.

Making Deronda born but not raised a Jew, rendering his Jewishness invisible, Eliot strategically solves the problem of sympathy with the transgressive other by eradicating otherness from the start. Deronda embodies sympathy with the Jews in the seamless boundary crossing, the transgressionless transgression, that the fact of his birth represents. For the mechanism of birth effectively renders Deronda's Jewishness intentionless: not his fault. At the same time, as the English gentleman who bears no visible traces of Jewish identity, he exemplifies Eliot's high-culture ideal. For Eliot's ideal bourgeois subject is, significantly, not the Jew who is generally

[49] On transgression, see Peter Stallybrass and Allon White, *The Politics and Poetics of Transgression* (Ithaca: Cornell University Press, 1969). For the charge of antisemitism, see Susan Meyer, "Safely to Their Own Borders: Proto-Zionism, Feminism, and Nationalism in *Daniel Deronda,*" *ELH* 60 (1993): 733–58.

discernible as one, who has no choice; he is instead the gentleman who chooses to identify as a Jew ("I will call myself a Jew" [792]), the one for whom otherness is happily assimilated through the desire and freedom the "passports" of culture and education make available. (When, early in the novel, Eliot invites her readers to envision as "the most memorable of boys" the figure whom, they will later discover, is of Jewish descent, she encourages them to envision in her novel's most significant test of sympathy's power—its ability to reach across Victorian England's least crossable of barriers—an image with which, as self-projection, they, and she, are already in sympathy. From the novel's beginning, the idea of cultural affinity serves to ward off the specter of difference.) As the Jew who is just the same as if he were not, Deronda expresses the assimilationist nature of Eliot's liberal representation: her fantasy of sympathy with the Jews.

The cure for the difficulties attendant upon nonidentity sympathy—sympathy that makes you lose your identity, in which you discover that you resemble those you don't wish to resemble—thus turns out to be identity-sympathy: sympathy that enables you to choose your identity, to identify with those who match your image of your best self. It is for this reason that sympathy in the novel takes shape as a fantasy of likeness: an identity politics in which differences between individuals are flattened out in favor of a reassuring fantasy of similitude.[50] Wonderfully realized in twin images of Cohens, one degraded and one refined, Eliot's split representation of Jews amplifies the work done by Deronda's sympathy. As an embodiment of sympathy with the Jews, Deronda incorporates the degraded origin he has always feared, while the discovery of Mirah's "refined" brother Mordecai and the transformative work of Deronda's sympathy allows him to say "never mind" to it: he may simultaneously claim and distance himself from that origin. In this way, Deronda's family drama enacts in microcosm the general European anxiety about Jewish "contagion."[51] Here again is the image: "he saw himself guided by some

---

[50] As Christina Crosby writes, "To say 'I am a Jew' is significant not as a matter of personal identity, but as an acknowledgment of the law and of mankind's necessary corporate existence" (*Ends of History*, 20).

[51] On the connection between the Jew and the city, see Gilman, *Jew's Body;* on the connection between the city and ideas of contagion and contamination, see Stallybrass and White, *Politics and Poetics of Transgression,* 135.

official scout into a dingy street; he entered through a dim doorway, and saw a hawk-eyed woman, rough headed, and unwashed, cheapening a hungry girl's last bit of finery; or in some quarter only the more hideous for being smarter, he found himself under the breath of a young Jew talkative and familiar...and so on." Describing the search for Mirah's family, Deronda cannot help but put himself in the picture. Mediated through the blended image of cultural degradation and exaltation signified by the name "Jew" (and embodied in the figure of Mordecai), Deronda's sympathy is the construction of his identity through a gradual process of refinement, enabling a phantasmatic exchange of one aspect of identity for another: good Jews for bad, that Cohen for this one.

And once this exchange has been completed, the novel's "bad" Jews disappear—demonstrating that the energy that sustained their representation was less that of antisemitism than of the exercise of sensibility as a faculty, a necessary part of the identity-shaping process I have described. For in *Daniel Deronda,* as in any identity politics, identity means knowing whom to sympathize with. Having served their function in the construction of the hero's identity, *Daniel Deronda's* less-than-perfect Jews vanish into the fictional universe whence they came.

6

Embodying Culture: Dorian's Wish

I have argued throughout this book that, in scenes of sympathy, identity takes shape as social identity: that when subjects confront each other across a social divide, the elements that define this boundary constitute—at least for a moment—their subjectivity. My discussions of *Daniel Deronda* and *The Picture of Dorian Gray* are concerned less with the attempts to sympathize across class lines that characterized earlier texts than with the way, in these late-century novels, expressions of personal affinity and desire also function as assertions of cultural identity. Because late-nineteenth-century ideologies define identity increasingly in group terms—as, for instance, membership in a nation or in a sexual category—sympathy becomes more explicitly a matter of claiming identity with, or distance from, such group identifications. Indeed, in these late-nineteenth-century texts expressions of individual identity (identity that might be defined as difference from others) become increasingly difficult to differentiate from expressions of cultural identity (identity defined as membership in a group). Thus the self Daniel Deronda develops during the course of Eliot's novel coincides neatly with his discovery of his Jewish background, while Dorian Gray's desires construct an avowedly symbolic identity, one that—for nineteenth- and twentieth-century readers—embodies both late-nineteenth-century aestheticism and modern male homosexuality. At stake in these readings is the way the scene of sympathy is also—and always—a scene of cultural identification, in which the spectator's identity is inseparable from an imagining of the other's place; at stake as well is the way in which, when individual and cultural identity collapse into one another, the other with whom one sympathizes may turn out to be—as is the case, dramatically, in *Dorian Gray*—one's self. A character who enacts the scene of sympathy within himself—indeed, of whom it might be said that he sympathizes only with himself—Dorian Gray both reinforces and extends the implications of the scene of sympathy as I have described it so far.

Dorian Gray's scene of sympathy inheres in the contrast between the hero's idealized body and his fantasy of that same body's degradation, and in the way the novel positions these as alternative images of cultural possibility. The contrast between the beautiful Dorian and his hideous picture recapitulates the scene of sympathy with which this book began: Dorian's picture is a fantasy in which moral decline rationalizes economic anxiety, marking a safe distance between the subject who might fall and the one who already has. In this case, the identity-defining other—who is, of course, Dorian himself—is manifestly both cultural fantasy and self-projection, a simultaneous internalization and anatomy of the scene Victorian fiction and Victorian culture located on the streets.

The constellation of emotions Dorian's scene evokes—the tension between fascination, repulsion, and attraction, for instance, in his relation to the picture—recalls other, earlier versions of the scene of sympathy and the recurrent questions that surround it. With whom, for example (or *as* whom) is the sympathetic spectator identified? What are the implications of self-picturing—the replacement of the self with a picture? Why is identity figured as an economic configuration, an exchange between images of degradation and ideality? Foregrounding these questions, the novels also revises them. Attributing moral significance to the blots and marks the picture accumulates, *Dorian Gray* makes of a paradigmatic aesthetic difference—the difference between beauty and ugliness—a paradigmatic cultural drama that, I wish to argue, finds its echo in contemporary formulations of cultural and political identity. The difference between Dorian's original wish and his memory of it, for instance—the difference between the impulsive expression of a desire not to age and a moral narrative about sin and retribution—encapsulates the transformation of experience into narrative that, as we have just seen in *Daniel Deronda,* characterizes the formation of cultural narratives. The drama Wilde's novel makes out of the difference between beauty and ugliness—for example, the danger of discovery, the obsessive checking and rechecking of the picture, and the adventures in "low life" whose meaning Dorian confirms on the surface of the portrait as soon as he lives them—suggests the formation of cultural identity as a moralization or rationalization of aesthetic choices whose meaning might be revealed in, or might just as well be hidden by, the face one chooses. *Dorian Gray*'s scene of sympathy suggestively figures, in several ways and with relevance to several different discourses, the aesthetic dimension of modern and contemporary identities.[1]

Neither person nor, exactly, character, Dorian is, the novel tells us, a type: the "visible symbol" of the age.[2] And, it has followed, the novel's critics have taken Dorian—and Wilde himself—to be preeminent figures for and prefigurations of aesthetic culture and modern male homosexual identity. But what happens at the intersection of character and cultural embodiment: what does it mean, as Walter Benn Michaels asks, to imagine a culture "in the form of a person"?[3]

Toward the end of the nineteenth century, historians and theorists of sexuality agree, the shaping activities of medicine and the law codified a variety of activities and modes of being into an identity.[4] In the formula-

---

[1] My sense of the way experience becomes cultural narrative, as argued here, is indebted to Walter Benn Michaels's account of cultural identities in *Our America: Nativism, Modernism, and Pluralism* (Durham: Duke University Press, 1995). I refer to the transformation of events, actions, or choices (such as, for instance, the eating of matzoh or the not-eating of pork) into identity-producing narratives. See also Foucault's narrative about the construction of homosexuality as an identity in *The History of Sexuality,* vol. 1 (New York, Vintage, 1980), 101, and Linda Dowling's discussion of the formation of a homosexual cultural tradition in *Hellenism and Homosexuality in Victorian Oxford* (Ithaca: Cornell University Press, 1994).

[2] Oscar Wilde, *The Picture of Dorian Gray* (Harmondsworth, England: Penguin, 1985), 46. Subsequent references included in text.

[3] Michaels, *Our America,* 80. Eve Sedgwick discusses "reading *Dorian Gray* from our twentieth-century vantage point where the name Oscar Wilde virtually *means* homosexual." *Epistemology of the Closet* (Berkeley: University of California Press, 1990), 165. See also Ed Cohen, "Writing Gone Wilde: Homoerotic Desire in the Closet of Representation," *PMLA* 102 (October 1987): 801–13, and Jeff Nunokawa, "Homosexual Desire and the Effacement of the Self in *The Picture of Dorian Gray,*" *American Imago* 49, no. 3 (1992): 311–21.

[4] See, for example, Foucault, *History of Sexuality.*

tions of some recent critics, what happened is that at the end of the century homosexual persons, and homosexual culture, became visible.

In the final week of April 1895 Oscar Wilde stood in the prisoner's dock of the Old Bailey, charged, in the dry words of the indictment, with "acts of gross indecency with another male person." ... The prosecutor for the Crown explained to the jury in more vivid terms what this meant: Wilde and his co-defendant had joined in an "abominable traffic" in which young men were induced to engage in "giving their bodies, or selling them, to other men...." Wilde answered these charges, as is well known, in a speech of sudden and impassioned energy. Passionately defending male love as the noblest of attachments, a love "such as Plato made the very basis of his philosophy, and such as you find in the sonnets of Michelangelo and Shakespeare," Wilde called it "pure" and "perfect" and "intellectual"...his superb self-possession and ringing peroration so electrifying that the courtroom listeners burst into spontaneous applause.... The applause of Wilde's listeners marks the sudden emergence into the public sphere of a modern discourse of male love formulated in the late Victorian period by such writers as Walter Pater and John Addington Symonds and Wilde himself, a new language of moral legitimacy pointing forward to Anglo-American decriminalization and, ultimately, a fully developed assertion of homosexual rights.[5]

Thus, although Basil's painting is entirely exterior to the text, it provides the reference point for a mode of representation that admits the visible, erotic presence of the male body.[6]

When Basil Hallward confesses his love for Dorian Gray, those who dwell under contemporary signs of Hellenism cannot help but hear the opening notes of their own song: "A while ago I went to a party...after I had been in the room about ten minutes...I suddenly became conscious that someone was looking at me.... When our eyes met, I felt that I was growing pale. A curious sensation of terror came over me, I knew that I had come face to face with someone [who]...would absorb my whole nature, my whole soul.... I have always been my own master; had at least

---

[5] Dowling, *Hellenism and Homosexuality*, 1–2.
[6] Cohen, "Writing Gone Wilde," 806.

always been so, till I met [him]. ... Something seemed to tell me that I was on the verge of a terrible crisis in my life."[7]

Offered as originary moments in the instantiation of modern male homosexual identity, these scenes (from essays by Linda Dowling, Ed Cohen, and Jeff Nunokawa) may also be regarded as illustrations from a cultural history under construction. Moments at which homosexuality is said, with some suddenness, to become visible, they manifestly demonstrate the imaginary status of cultural identity: they are opportunities for identification, places where the self may imaginatively be located. These are not just moments in the history of a cultural identity, that is, but mirror scenes for the constitution of one, delineating for reader, spectator, consumer, and critic what I wish to call the imaginary body of culture. For rather than announcing that a particular identity has currency, visibility bestows that currency; and what "currency" means, in this sense, is availability for identification ("His attraction to Dorian Gray appears as nothing other than the first act of the now well developed drama of self-realization we call coming out").[8] Registering the transformation of an image of degradation into one of ideality, of the degraded object of sympathy into a figure in whose place anyone—theoretically, everyone—may see themselves, these images exchange a scene of sympathy for one of identification, replacing one kind of sympathy (revulsion as secret sympathy; sympathy with society's "victim") with another (sympathy as identification and desire, so that the other's place becomes one a reader might wish to occupy). For to enter into visibility is to give up some degree of cultural difference at the very moment one claims it, to become part of the common realm in which cultures (or, more precisely, images of cultural identity) circulate. As theorists of the visible from Jean Baudrillard to Kaja Silverman have pointed out, rather than registering the emergence into public light of something already in existence, visibility *is* that something, signaling the inseparability of identity from its representations. Cultural identity is an identification with culture itself, both in its specific and more general forms.[9]

[7] Nunokawa, "Homosexual Desire," 312.

[8] Ibid.

[9] I am, of course, aware of the fact that same-sex desire was for the Victorians an occasion more for revulsion than for sympathy. But I am relying both on the way in which identity politics depends upon a claim for victim status and on the blend of sympathy and

Franco Moretti, Werner Sollors, and others have described a shift in constructions of identity during the eighteenth and nineteenth centuries from the (more or less) given to the invented. Invoking Benedict Anderson's idea of imagined communities, for instance, Sollors describes the way, as aristocratic power declined in the eighteenth century, "the immediate connectedness of the aristocracy was replaced by a mediated form of cohesion that depended, among other things, on literacy and 'national' (and ethnic) literatures." Literature and the circulation of printed texts in general, Anderson argues, assist in the formation of communities circumscribed less by birth or territorial boundaries than by their members' shared knowledge.[10]

And imagined communities, of course, require imagined identities— identities not limited (as the communities are not) to categories of nationality or ethnicity. Dowling's history of the Oxford Movement, for instance, which traces the homosocial codings of the Oxford Hellenistic tradition, both reveals the embedding of one culture in another and details the making of a new culture, a new group identity, out of an already existing tradition. What Dowling traces is, precisely, "the role of Victorian Hellenism in legitimating homosexuality as an identity."[11] Yet still requiring explanation is the relationship between the previously uncodified individual and the now codified group, since the formation of a new identity is the formation of new identities, and the invention of homosexuality the invention of persons deemed homosexuals. If such formations require new identities, that is, they also require the inculcation of desire for those identities—and, as a corollary, the inculcation of desire for identity itself.[12]

---

identification one might hear—and Dowling certainly hears—in the applause for Wilde's courtroom peroration.

[10] Werner Sollors, *The Invention of Ethnicity* (New York: Oxford University Press, 1989), xxi.; Franco Moretti, *The Way of the World: The Bildungsroman in European Culture* (London: Verso, 1987); Benedict Anderson, *Imagined Communities: Reflections on the Origin and Spread of Nationalism* (London: Verso, 1983).

[11] Dowling, *Hellenism and Homosexuality*, 31.

[12] Foucault's work has, of course, explored in detail the means by which subjectivity is produced through techniques such as confession and self-examination. My concern here lies closer to the problem Judith Butler explores in *The Psychic Life of Power: Theories in Subjection* (Stanford: Stanford University Press, 1997), when she asks what causes us to desire our own subjection (see 102).

In response to a literary-critical tradition oblivious to the homosexual or homosocial content of literary texts, recent readings have been devoted the act of decoding. In the case of *The Picture of Dorian Gray*, the goal has been to return the novel to its specific historical and sexual context, reading against what Eve Sedgwick calls the "alibi of abstraction": the abstract moralism, the evacuated sexuality, of its standard interpretations.[13] Yet the abstractions on which Wilde's novel relies, the empty terms of its codings, and perhaps above all its definitive binarism (beauty / ugliness) are unavoidable; it is, after all, the affiliation between the aristocratic male body and the abstraction "beauty" that allows for the text's general currency. Regarded as one of modern homosexual identity's most important icons, Dorian Gray is also a paradigmatic image of masculine beauty and desirability. In returning some degree of abstraction to the novel's interpretation, therefore—or at least returning to the abstractions on which the novel relies—I wish to locate desire for Dorian, and Dorian's desire, within a more inclusive eroticization of identity: one in which Dorian's wish to change places with his picture reveals identity itself, here allegorized as culture's visible form, to be one of the modern subject's most sought-after objects of desire. Thus the late-nineteenth-century ideology that, following Foucault's logic, is said to have redefined self in terms of sexuality—in which "who I am" becomes "what I want"—is here reimagined with ontology as desire's subject, so that what is wanted is, precisely, "who I am": identity itself.

———

Dorian's identity inheres in—is made of—the contrast and active interchange between the novel's constructions of beauty and ugliness, and interpretations tend to rest on the meanings attributed to each.[14] Yet it has

———

[13] Sedgwick, *Epistemology of the Closet,* 164.

[14] To raise the issue of the novel's aesthetic context is also to raise that of its relation to the aesthetic movement. What is important about the movement, for the purposes of this reading, is its exposure of the role played by aesthetics in Victorian structures of identity, for rather than making identity into an aesthetic issue, the aesthetic movement revealed that it already was one. Wilde's novel has always presented a signal critical problem: how can it be the case that such a resolutely antimoralistic novel is so relentlessly moralistic? Dorian's fate seems to confirm Victorian morality's counter-aesthetic position: beauty, it insists, is definable only in moral terms. And yet in playing out such a paradigmatically

never been noted that the moral weight the picture comes to bear during the course of the novel—the meaning Dorian himself comes to attribute to it—is far removed from the initial whimsy that brings it into being. Here, from the middle of the novel, is Dorian's recollection of his wish: "He had uttered a mad wish that he himself might remain young, and the face on the canvas bear the burden of his passions and sins; that the painted image might be seared with the lines of suffering and thought" (119). But what he actually says (at the novel's beginning) is this: "If it were I who was always to be young, and the picture that was to grow old!" (49). Dorian's wish for an exchange is itself exchanged, his original, impulsive desire for youth and his aversion to aging replaced by a morally charged scenario in which the picture becomes the bearer of "passions and sins." And this exchange, or false memory, is actually true to the novel's economics of degradation, since, as the picture alters, what matters is not the type of action committed—not the kind of "degradation"—but rather (as if such matters were codifiable, and self-evidently so) the amount. The picture pictures accumulation, displaying not the detail of experience but the fact of it (we can't know, from looking at it, what experience it records—as the history of the novel's reception, and the continuing need to decode the picture, suggests).

For Dorian, sin, old age, suffering, and even "thought" are rendered equivalent in a generalized picture of degradation that looks like this: "The cheeks would become hollow or flaccid, yellow crows' feet would creep round the fading eyes and make them horrible. The hair would lose its brightness, the mouth would gape or droop, would be foolish or gross, as the mouths of old men are. There would be the wrinkled throat, blue-veined hands, the twisted body, that he remembered in the grandfather who had been so stern to him in his boyhood" (153). Or maybe this: "Lying on the floor was a dead man, in evening dress, with a knife in his heart. He was withered, wrinkled, and loathsome of visage. It was not until they examined the rings that they recognized who it was" (264).

Victorian identity drama, the novel suggests the extent to which identity was, for the Victorians, an aesthetic category. For in insisting on the collapse between Dorian and his picture at its end—the novel's most quintessentially Victorian gesture—Wilde suggests that Dorian's tragedy is largely a tragedy of beauty: one that inheres in the disparity between exterior and interior values. The aesthetic movement, then, rather than being Victorian morality's opposite, develops that morality's implicit aesthetic.

The speculations of the first passage ("the mouth would gape and droop") are, for all intents and purposes, fulfilled by the second. And, in truth, as the picture reduces all degradation to a common currency, that of ugliness, it exposes the surprising presumption, given the subtleties of taste Dorian comes to embody, that when it comes to ugliness there is no question of taste (at least for Wilde's readers—in this sense both the picture and the book express a widely shared fantasy about ugliness). Age and sin, the novel's language suggests in its circulation of ugliness terms— "hideous," "horrible," "wrinkled"—are interchangeable not only with each other but also with other forms of the "loathsome," such as the figure of the "horrid old Jew" who owns the theater in which Sibyl Vane performs, or the grandfather of whom Dorian has "hateful memories."

Dorian's beauty similarly lacks specificity; like his ugliness, which attaches itself indistinguishably to the figures "old" and "Jew," it both evokes and denies specific affiliations. For despite the possibility of naming those affiliations—Sedgwick, for instance, contrasts Wilde's middle-class Irishness with Dorian's aristocratic Englishness, while for Dowling Dorian's beauty has a Hellenic textual history—within its immediate social and cultural context, the novel's ideal of beauty ("gold hair, blue eyes, rose-red lips") constitutes an evacuation of meaning: it is meant to signify nothing other than beauty itself.[15] Thus binding together its ideal of beauty with its exchangeable images of degradation, the novel forecloses its own celebration of insincerity as a multiplication of personalities into a stark division and accountability: the difference between beauty and ugliness.

Dorian's relation to his picture has, of course, been theorized in many ways, not the least powerful of which rely on the moral terms the novel itself provides. Figuring Dorian's identity in an economy of appearances, however—as the difference and exchange between beauty and ugliness— the novel allows for another kind of interpretation, one that has more to do with its role in a history of cultural identities than with the history of its literary interpretations. For the difference between beauty and ugliness per se participates in the underlying binarism of certain modern cultural narratives of identity, narratives that depend less on specific details of identity than on the positive or negative valuation of identities: the positing of

---

[15] Eve Sedgwick, *Tendencies* (Durham: Duke University Press, 1993), 151; Dowling, *Hellenism and Homosexuality,* 150.

desire or its absence. Such narratives, that is, resolve what might be a multiplicity of identities into a choice between identities, in the form of a difference between self and other. And this difference, I wish to argue, in turn reflects the condition of belonging or not belonging to a group. Embodying the imaginative possibilities of the scene of sympathy as I have described it, for instance, the contrast between beautiful and ugly images of Dorian Gray reproduces the aesthetics of contemporary identity politics, in which identity takes shape as the difference between negative and positive cultural projections. Identity politics attempts to bestow value on identities the dominant culture devalues: it attempts to transform ugliness (a particular identity as perceived by the dominant culture) into beauty (that same identity, as projected in response by the group so named), and its mechanism is the transformative power of the idea—and image—of the group. In the "identity" of identity politics, the individual and the group function as reflexes and projections of each other—mutually constitutive images—with the group functioning as the engine of the desire for identity, the body out of which individual bodies are made. Indeed, it is because of the similarity between the ideologically constructed identities of the late nineteenth century, the image making of identity politics, and *Dorian Gray*'s figuration of identity as an interplay between valued and devalued images of the self that, in Wilde's novel, "we may catch the early strains of an identity politics whose anthem will eventually become loud enough to make itself heard even on Saint Patrick's Day."[16] Even as the novel refers to a specific politics, however, the aesthetic form by means of which that politics is represented—its reliance on an idealized image of masculine identity—makes the character Dorian Gray widely available for identification: for, at the very least, "literary" sympathy.

My argument thus situates *Dorian Gray* in the context of late-nineteenth-century ideologies that may be viewed as precursors of a modern symbolic politics of identity: ideologies in which the individual is with in-

[16] Nunokawa, "Homosexual Desire," 313. Dowling recognizes, implicitly, the role of the group in the transforming of homosexuality's image: "Such writers as Symonds and Pater and Wilde...find the opening in which 'homosexuality' might begin to be understood as itself a mode of self-development and diversity, no longer a sin or crime or disastrous civic debility but a social identity functioning within a fund of shared human potentialities, now recognized *as* shared" (*Hellenism and Homosexuality,* 31).

creasing frequency imagined as a member of a group. Relevant here is the Foucauldian account of a shift from action to essence in the formulation of nineteenth-century identities. But more useful is the model of nationalism, which serves as a general model of identity from the nineteenth century onward, and which accounts for both the affective passion and the dominant trope of male bonding in *Daniel Deronda* and *Dorian Gray*. For nationalist ideology positions identity as the culmination of a narrative of desire and an effect of group membership; in it, desire for group membership is indistinguishable from desire for identity per se (thus the relevance, once more, of Julia Kristeva's description of nationalism as a condition in which "to be" is "to belong"). In this context, Dorian's wish to change places with his own idealized image may be understood not only as a desire to be an object of desire, or as a desire for a particular identity, but more fundamentally as a desire for identity itself.

Jeff Nunokawa writes that the achievement of Wilde's novel was to give modern homosexual identity a human face.[17] And indeed, the novel accomplishes this with precisely the kind of narrative sleight of hand that, belying the direction of the narrative itself, enables Nunokawa's comment to pass without eliciting the obvious questions: how, exactly, "human"? and, more compellingly, which "face"? The conversion of loss into gain the novel effects—the way the enduring image of the beautiful Dorian emerges (if one agrees that it does) from an ostensible narrative of decline—resembles what might be called the conversion narrative of identity politics: Dorian dies into representation, his beauty, prefiguring what Dowling refers to as the current wide acceptance of homosexuality by the dominant culture, functioning as a kind of projection into the future: an invitation to the transformation of the image of homosexuality itself.[18] The novel's erotics, I thus wish to suggest, is finally a cultural one, and its language of sexual desire supports a narrative of cultural desire, a desire for cultural embodiment (the same desire, expressed as both an attraction toward and revulsion against an "object" of sympathy, that, I have suggested, shapes earlier scenes of sympathy). Dorian's wish is a wish for beauty, but Dorian's beauty is a figure for the desirability of a certain modern

[17] Nunokawa, "Homosexual Desire," 313.

[18] Dowling locates Wilde at the origin of "the modern emergence of homosexuality as a positive social identity" (ibid., xvi).

configuration of identity: for the achievement of identity as a place in a cultural narrative.[19]

━━━━━

In his book on the politics of American identity, *Our America,* Walter Michaels takes aim at what he calls the essentialist bias of all accounts of cultural identity: the way in which, in his words, these accounts "understand culture as a kind of person."[20] To understand culture as a kind of person is, for Michaels, to tie actions to essence, identifying oneself with ancestors whose experiences and memories one did not share. To no good end, cultures are imagined to possess identity, argues Michaels, and inherent value is (therefore) attributed to their survival.

But how is it that a set of practices (his definition of culture) comes to be identified with personhood? How do habits acquire the nimbus of identity; why is the sum more than its parts? (Or, how is it that "modern homosexual identity" comes to acquire a "face," and what does it mean that it does?) One answer, as I have suggested, might lie in Foucault's discussion of the way late-nineteenth-century medical and juridical discourses transformed practice into identity, making "possible the formation of a 'reverse' discourse: homosexuality began to speak in its own behalf, to demand that its legitimacy or 'naturality' be acknowledged, often in the same vocabulary, using the same categories by which it was medically disqualified."[21] While this formulation begs the question, since rather than explaining personification, it personifies—"homosexuality began to speak in its own behalf"—it nevertheless suggests that desirable images of cul-

---

[19] It is, of course, important that the paradigmatic representation of this desire is figured as the difference between beautiful and ugly male bodies. As Sedgwick writes, almost everything in the late nineteenth century takes this form: "In the development toward eugenic thought around and after the turn of the century, reifications such as 'the strong,' 'the weak,' 'the nation,' 'civilization,' particular classes, 'the race,' and even 'life' itself have assumed the vitalized anthropomorphic outlines of the individual male body and object of medical expertise" (*Epistemology of the Closet,* 178). I want to emphasize both the cultural specificity of *Dorian Gray*'s images and what might be called the novel's will to abstractness: the way the opposition between beauty and ugliness encapsulates the binary construction of identity in identity politics.

[20] Michaels, *Our America,* 180.

[21] Foucault, *History of Sexuality,* 101.

tural identity emerge in response to, and are inseparable from, what Judith Butler calls the "injurious term" that gives a particular identity its name—the term that, in the Althusserian scenario of interpellation, calls it into being.[22] And it suggests, too, via the rhetoric of personification, the role group identity plays in this identity-forming narrative: that it is possible to speak on one's behalf only when identity is defined in collective terms, as something shared with others.

If we pursue the implications of Foucault's narrative, in which conflicting images of identity exist in necessary relation to one another, then Wilde's picture-painting scene—the scene in which Dorian recognizes himself "as if for the first time"—begins to resemble a positive alternative to the Althusserian scenario in which the subject is hailed as a subject of the law. Indeed, the scene provides a response, in the form of a counternarrative, to the question Butler poses about Althusser's scenario: "Why should I turn around?"[23]

> The lad started, as if awakened from some dream. "Is it really finished?" He murmured, stepping down from the platform.
>
> "Quite finished," said the painter. "And you have sat splendidly today. I am awfully obliged to you."
>
> "That is entirely due to me," broke in Lord Henry. "Isn't it, Mr. Gray?"
>
> Dorian made no answer, but passed listlessly in front of his picture, and turned towards it. When he saw it he drew back, and his cheeks flushed for a moment with pleasure. A look of joy came into his eyes, as if he had recognized himself for the first time. (48)

For Butler, such an invitation is itself compelling: the subject turns, despite his or her ostensible guilt, because identity is an offer that cannot be refused. Wilde's version, imagined as response or resistance to this scene, reproduces its form but not its content: Dorian's response to the picture enacts a fantasy of self-hailing, in which the self answers to its own desire rather than to the admonitory call of the law. What seems important, then, is not the undecidable status of the self that turns (must not that self—so the question goes—already be a subject in order to turn?) but

[22] Butler, *Psychic Life of Power,* 104.
[23] Ibid., 108.

rather the fact of the scene's replication: the way both Althusser and Wilde figure the production of identity as a turn, imagining identity as that which, in a narrative of desire, the subject moves toward. What compels and confers identity, in both these scenarios, is nothing other than desire for it.[24]

And that desire, once again, is the desire to belong. The self hailed here, as in Althusser, is not, nor can it be, wholly self-appointed: it is rather the effect of the existence of the group, of society. For if, as Butler suggests, the desire for identity is the desire to be constituted socially, then identity must take shape as the image of social life.[25] And so it does in *Dorian Gray*. In a discussion preceding Dorian's arrival, Lord Henry Wotton and Basil Hallward discuss the partial nature of their own and others' identities: one possesses intellect and talent, another beauty, another wealth ("Your rank and wealth, Harry; my brains, such as they are—my art, whatever it may be worth; Dorian Gray's good looks"). Dorian, in this conversation, is said to possess only beauty: "He is some brainless, beautiful creature, who should always be here in winter when we have no flowers to look at" (25), and when he appears he is indeed depicted as not yet in possession of an identity—as empty and available for one. Yet at the end of this scene—the scene in which Basil paints the famous portrait—Dorian possesses all the qualities Henry, Basil, and formerly Dorian himself possessed individually. Indeed, the apparent fluidity of identity boundaries in this scene is countered by the way Dorian's identity emerges as the only one that counts (there are three bodies here, but finally only one identity), and he is not only an image of the others' desire but an embodiment of their very qualities: of Basil's images and Henry's words.

---

[24] The very problem of the subject's status in Althusser's scenario suggests the answer I propose in this chapter: the subject, "already" one, locates subjecthood outside the self because cultural identity, which appears in such scenarios as identity *tout court,* is an external construct.

[25] "Called by an injurious name, I come into social being, and because I have a certain inevitable attachment to my existence, because a certain narcissism takes hold of any term that confers existence, I am led to embrace the terms that injure me because they constitute me socially" (Butler, *Psychic Life of Power,* 104). "Existence," in this formulation, is the same as being constituted socially: life is equated with cultural life, with existing within a the context of a social group.

[26] Lee Edelman, *Homographesis* (New York: Routledge, 1994), 17.

As Lee Edelman has argued, Wilde's novel inscribes identity in a narrative of desire.[26] From the novel's initial representations of Dorian as beautiful vacancy and potential, to the "look" that comes into the lad's face that Basil had never seen there before, to Dorian's "recognition" of himself in the portrait, identity is something Dorian achieves in the picture-painting scene, and it is the result not just of his own wish, but of the combined yearnings of all three. In these scenes, the group is imagined as a body, each member possessing some aspect of the whole, and Dorian is the projected image of that whole—a composite body. It is this wholeness that he recognizes as if for the first time in the portrait, this wholeness that makes the picture the place he wants to occupy. Desire for Dorian—including Dorian's desire for himself as picture—is desire for the imagined wholeness of the group. Indeed, it is the impossibility of distinguishing between desire for a particular individual and desire for cultural embodiment that Dorian's wish to change places with the picture defines, and that defines the picture of Dorian Gray.

Thus when Dorian's image appears on the canvas, the very picture of Basil's desire for him and of Henry's influence, not only does the novel dramatize what Ed Cohen has called the inscription of homoerotic desire, but it also allegorizes the emergence of cultural identity per se as an effect of triangulated desire. It is the *idea* of culture that takes shape here in, and as, an imaginary body, and the idea of the group—of the self as an idealized projection of others—that enables the replacement, or at least the overlapping, of the injurious name with the beautiful face. If the policeman's call is the call of the dominant culture, defining the respondent as guilty before the law, the alternative picture illustrates the reverse fantasy, or fantasy of reversal: it is an allegory of being interpellated as an object of desire. Collapsing the difference Freud wished to maintain, in his discussion of homosexuality, between desire for and possession of the other, it suggests a fantasy of such perfect sympathy with the other that the other turns out to be, for better or worse, the self.[27]

Producing Dorian's idealized image, the painting scene thus allegorizes the element of desire that transforms practice into personhood. For a set

---

[27] For a discussion of this issue in relation to Freud's construction of homosexuality, see Diana Fuss, *Identification Papers* (New York: Routledge, 1995), 12, 19.

of practices does not constitute a culture: only a set of practices endowed with meaning and value does. And such a set of practices, as Michaels's argument suggests, takes an embodied form: culture is always what someone else (even, as *Dorian Gray* makes clear, one's own self imagined as someone else) is doing. Culture is not a "set" of practices (Michaels's definition) but rather a reading of them: an interpretation that unifies disparate practices, attaching meaning to action and in this way individualizing it, with the idea of the individual—of actions performed by someone—giving coherence to the activity of the group. Dorian Gray thus figures in this argument as an exemplary image of a person who is also an embodiment of culture—an embodiment of a particular culture, to be sure, but also an allegory for the way culture in general takes shape "as a kind of person."

But what kind of culture, and what kind of person? The rhetoric of exchange—specifically, of changing places—that informs Dorian's wish and structures his story further reinforces the importance of the idea of culture in the imagining of modern identities. For the self, even when imagined as one's own, is constituted with reference to an external image. It is pictured elsewhere: in Dorian Gray's case, in the form of an image readily available within and appropriated from the dominant culture (an image, we might go so far as to say, of the dominant culture. For the beautiful face, making no secret of its desirability, defines the dominant culture's requirements for beauty; hence its class determination: aristocratic—and its national one: English). Dorian symbolizes his era in more ways than one: his beauty is no more idealized within the context of his coterie than in Victorian England generally, and it is the abstractness of that beauty, of course—the protean significance of his cultural ideality—that enables not only Dorian, but the novel itself, to "pass."

And here the narrative of identity politics gives way—briefly—to that of cosmetology: to the very real (no longer magical, that is) business of choosing a face.

Dorian wishes, of course, for both faces, the beautiful and the ugly— not for one or the other, but rather for the exchange between them. And his desire is fulfilled not just by the beautiful face but by the ugly one, with its marks and blotches, as well—and by the way each supplements the other, each suggests meanings the other fails to provide. For despite the exchangeability of images discussed earlier in this chapter, Wilde's novel does attribute value to ugliness. As part of the narrative culminating in

Dorian's death, the picture evinces the temporality he rejects: it ages, wrinkles, degrades. But it also reflects a process of accumulation: the portrait turns sin into gain by rendering it visible. This is, after all, where Dorian's actions appear, where his experience accumulates like capital. Like a miser visiting his wealth, Dorian obsessively checks his profits, each blotch and wrinkle challenging the novel's moralizing with an equally compelling logic of accumulation. Despite the absence of individuality the novel's general representation of ugliness suggests, then, the accumulation of marks on the picture's surface does suggest the possibility of individuality: here, at least, something is happening. Why, then, is it not a pretty picture?

In the Murad advertisement (Fig. 1), an advertisement for a wrinkle-removing cream for women and a suggestive updating and revision of Dorian Gray's picture, the lines on the woman's face are replaced by—are, indeed, only visible as—the advertiser's lines, labeled with the contents of a cultural narrative (and directed toward both the woman's image and the spectator—"the day *you* totaled the car"): the projected replacement of one face with another replaces one narrative with another. The face (and, indeed, the identity of its owner) is thus figured as a kind of map, each mark rendering experience visible, denoting a site at which something happened. But of course rather than simply making the invisible visible, the marks denote the absence of anything but cultural narrative: the map, like Dorian's hideous portrait, figures the inseparability of "real" self and cultural projection.

Since identity becomes visible only when marked as cultural narrative, both identities—the ugly (or less desirable) and the beautiful—appear as pictures (hence, as in my analysis of "A Christmas Carol," visibility itself signals and evokes desire, the distance between the self and its representations). Yet the fantasy, and the parallel in contemporary culture, is that one can participate in (embody) cultural value without giving up one's true self. In the advertisement as in Wilde's novel the "ugly" self occupies the position of the real, and is similarly imagined as detachable: that to which one necessarily refers, one's undesirable face is also—as in Victorian scenes of sympathy—that which one need not (but for the grace of God, and plastic surgery) acknowledge, or, indeed, be. And, again as in *Dorian Gray*, and *Deronda* as well, the ugly face is the particularized face, the attractive face generalized—its evacuation of experience rendering it available for a

Fig. 1. The marks of experience: *Dorian Gray* revisited.

spectator's projections.[28] (The femininity of this example is thus relevant to the novel's construction of Dorian's identity as sympathetic, for here as in *Daniel Deronda* sympathetic identity is equated with generalized and feminized identity, with the visual cues that conventionally invite a spectator's identification and fantasy.)

What happens, then, to the self one does not want to be—the self whose identifications are, or have been, refused? This advertisement's persuasiveness relies on its ability to appeal to a spectator who wants to erase, but also values, experience's marks: with its labels insisting on the very debilities the cream is to erase, the ad suggests not exactly (or not only) the effacement of experience but rather its dematerialization or internalization. Like *Dorian Gray*, it offers the spectator an opportunity to embody the cultural ideal yet preserve an alternative, "authentic" self—not exactly keeping the body that records that experience, but rather maintaining as mental picture the memory of such a body (though perhaps with less energy than one devotes to actively maintaining, or attempting to achieve, the culturally idealized one). Dorian's obsessive return to his hideous image—the way he commits his "sins" in a spirit of scientific inquiry in order to gauge their effect on the picture (124), and more tellingly the way he finds himself "enamoured" of it (135)—suggests a similar desire for a self that isn't picture perfect: a self one can call one's own. For the attraction of the ugly self, here as in the case of Hugh Boone, that hideous man with the twisted lip, is the lure of authenticity: of the cultural authority granted the idea of the true self. Read thus, as a narrative about a choice of cultural narratives, Wilde's novel may appear to be less about sin—either sin in general or any particular variety—than it is about the eroticization of particular images of cultural identity and of the idea of cultural identity itself.[29]

---

[28] Here, as in *Daniel Deronda,* it becomes evident that the generalized character—the type—is by definition a sympathetic object, the projection of a collective fantasy about the group's desires and about the way it views, or wishes to view, itself.

[29] Even as the medical / juridical establishment creates a type, Dowling's analysis suggests, a cultural tradition for that type emerges—deliberately and self-consciously, using as its framework another, previously existing tradition. The form that the "coded counterdiscourse" of homosexuality takes, in Dowling's reading (*Hellenism and Homosexuality,* xv), literalizes my claim in this chapter—the claim that culture is always someone else's—at the same time that it deconstructs the idea of an "original" tradition by suggesting that traditions always emerge in discourse with one another.

The idea of culture invests a single person's actions with the identity, or shared meaning, of the group; put another way, in cultural identity the identity of the group is discernible—made palpable—in a single person's actions. Culture, according to this logic, is always embodied, always a matter of value manifested in someone's appearance, someone's place. Indeed, as a matter of imagining the other as a person with whom one would like to change places ("I wish I could change places with you, Dorian," says Lord Henry wistfully [256]), cultural identity collapses person into place: identity becomes a cultural position, a place one can occupy. And just as culture depends on the illusion that a practice is more than a practice, so too does changing places substitute being for doing—so that culture makes itself, and reproduces itself, by substituting identity for practice, imagining practice in embodied form. The scenario of "changing places" short-circuits a scenario of imitation (I do what you do) with a scenario of replaced identity (I become you, put myself in your place) in which identity, seemingly kept intact, in fact is revealed as nothing more than a function of place. Pictured outside the self, the identity one wants—which one wants because it is pictured—appears knowable and available for occupation. (In the world according to *Dorian Gray*—the world that, the Murad ad tells us, we still inhabit—there is always a more desirable version of "you" out there.) "Changing places" replaces narrative and temporality with substitution and magic, exchanging a condition of desire in which identity is always slipping away with one in which identity is to be had for the asking—or the wishing.

Even as it is said to signal the new visibility, the emergence into public light, of late-Victorian homosexual culture, then, *The Picture of Dorian Gray* allegorizes the general desire that transforms practice into culture, that marks the difference between practice and culture. Culture appears here as a structure in which practices have meaning precisely because, and only because, someone else is performing them.[30] Why is it, I have asked of Foucault's account of nineteenth-century identities, that individuals not only accept the terms of their medicalization, but they take on those identities, begin to speak "in their own behalf"? The eroticization and idealization of group identity in the projection of an imaginary body figures culture's invitation to spectators to recognize themselves—and seek to

[30] This formulation is obviously indebted to René Girard's idea of triangular desire.

place themselves—in a symbolic structure not of their own creation. Dorian's beauty signals the (illusory) achievement of an identification with culture itself: it is the beauty of identity as wish-fulfillment, a fantasy of experience invested with value. Desire for Dorian captures the lure of cultural narrative as the context in which, at a historical moment which is ours as much as Dorian Gray's, self-recognition can and does take place. Identity as this novel figures it—and, I have suggested, in contemporary identity politics as well—is the imagined occupation of a place in a cultural narrative, a place that takes visible form as an imaginary body whose identification with the group gives new meaning to the visual fullness of the Lacanian imaginary.

Diana Fuss has defined identity politics as "the tendency to base one's politics on a sense of personal identity—as gay, as Jewish, as Black, as female."[31] But this definition classifies as personal what are obviously terms of group affiliation, terms whose appropriation guarantees visibility in the symbolic realms of culture and politics. In the model I have described here, identity politics is reconceived, following the model of late-nineteenth-century ideologies, as the creation of a desirable identity, its mechanism the projection of that identity in an imaginary body. That same desire for visibility—without, of course, the accompanying political concern—is manifest in the desire to embody a spectacularized, mass-produced version of beauty. In both cases, cultural identity takes shape as an implicit opposition between images of ideality and degradation; in both, identity is constituted as an exchange between identities—identities imagined, finally, as different versions of the self.

The body imagined as desirable, I have suggested, is the body of culture: a projection of the image of culture itself as an imaginary body. Such a formation depends not just on the desirability of particular identities but on the positing of identity itself as desirable: as that with which everyone must identify, that which everyone must desire. Thus embodied, identity presents itself as something to be desired, something to be wished for, something others could imagine being. Imagining identity as a body whose place a spectator may wish to occupy, and as a person with whom one might like to change places, Wilde's novel renders visible the element

---

[31] Diana Fuss, *Essentially Speaking* (New York: Routledge, 1994), 103.

of desire—and the transformations of sympathy—out of which cultures are made.

━━━━━━

The sympathetic spectator does not, as we have seen, sympathize with everyone—least of all when sympathy is explicitly linked to self-identification, as in identity politics. In this way, identity politics calls into question the ostensible universality, or blankness, of the ethical, liberal subject—the subject, as Eliot demonstrates in *Daniel Deronda,* whose identity is meant to transcend the logic of group identity on which it is founded. In Eliot's novel as in Wilde's, and elsewhere in this book, the rhetoric of exchangeability and impersonality on which liberal subjectivity rests—the equalizing gesture of "there but for the grace of God"—is circumscribed by the particularity of the subject's identifications. From this perspective, the illustration from Adam Smith with which I began—his contention that, try as we might to imagine ourselves in another's place, we are limited to the evidence of our own experiences—may be newly understood to suggest the way claims for the imaginative possibilities of sympathy in Western liberal thought are undermined by the very structures of group identity within which modern identities are imagined.

To return, then, to Michaels's problem with the personification of culture: the problem (if it is one) is not that we imagine culture as a person, and that we could have it some other way. The problem is that culture *is,* essentially, the imagining of the self in another's place (or, as in *Dorian Gray,* in another place): a fantasy of participating in an experience that has meaning precisely because it is embodied, because it is—at least figuratively—someone else's. And the logic of culture, at least in this account—involving as it does the externalization of identity, the nagging feeling that one's real self is really somewhere else—is sympathy's logic as well. There is no less desire in the eye that turns toward the beggar than there is in Dorian Gray's eye as it turns toward his beautiful picture, for to the extent that the beggar figures the "truth" of middle-class identity, and allows for the construction of an idealized, culturally valued alternative, his gaze will attract that of the subject who, professedly, would rather look away.

Index